Where the Grass Grows Greener

Where the Grass Grows Greener

Miklo Inaamla

2019

This book was written without the use of AI software and has not been edited by an outside party. It is the pure result of my work and imagination. The words / pictures in/on this book are mine, and mine alone. This book has not been edited to give you the rawest story with authenticity.

For information contact: mikloinaamla@gmail.com
1st Printing: November 17, 2019
2nd: June 2025
Written from April 4, 2010 – November 13, 2019, 2025

ISBN 978-0-578-62881-3

Instagram: @mikloinaamla   also on Facebook
                                                      Twitter
                                                      Tik Tok

For Myself and
For my Friends,
To all the drug takers
                    buyers
                    dealers
                    manufacturers
For the *Magical Half Dozen*
                    (Thanks, *Shura*)
And the few that know of them,
Live free or Die…

Cars are real

Cliffs are real

Cops are real

You can't fly

It's never a good time to die

And you will come out of it

Where the Grass Grows Greener

Miklo Inaamla

Miklo Inaamla

A Toke from the Bowl

There are moments in life that stand out in our memories. Some are good, some are bad. For me, these memories cause mixed emotions that must be addressed for my own sake.

Throughout the course of my life, it seems that I always find myself in a car; either waiting or driving somewhere. Once again, I was alone driving along a black highway sometime in the middle of the night en route to my other property in upstate New York. With four duffle bags in the trunk of my Jeep, I made my way through the mountains and with every turn and winding road I thought the truck was going to veer off the road and crash into a ditch somewhere if the metal road dividers didn't slow me down. I should not have been driving given my mental state, but my Darwinian survival instinct kicked in.

I was leaving one life behind and moving towards something new, but that's another story. I had packed some clothes, toiletries, drugs and personal belongings that only I would treasure. The Jeep was ready, packed and waiting on the outskirts of the property which I had just left and everything within it. There was no way I was turning back, not again. I had been driving for hours and most of the time it was silent, no radio, only listening to the sounds of the highway, the tires rotating and gliding along the smooth surface of the pavement. My heart was still racing from everything and wondered if I could survive alone.

I began to think about the drugs and what they did to me, though I should have been paying attention to the road. In and of themselves drugs are a potential source to be used positively or negatively in the hands of the user. They did not do anything to me, but in the face of political prohibition I saw an opportunity to expand my market which I seized and regretted. Some drugs gave me much pleasure while many more caused me much harm. Smoking cannabis, as a recreational drug user, already made me a criminal, so how far could I take it? How far was I going to make it?

The real answer shocks me. It had taken me far but had buried me in an emotional coffin that I had been in until I began to write these words. I have never written anything about myself, never wrote a journal entry nor a story. For some reason, I feel compelled to write my story. I guess the real reason I want to write this is because we all never asked to be born. We're born into this world unconsciously: we are the sperm that got to the egg, though we did not choose it. The problem with this is that, once we are out of the womb, we choose our own path. The path I chose was the path less traveled; yet, I sometimes think to myself that I should have gone down the other road. I should have just become a regular person, a sheep, working a nine-five job, have a wife, a house, two garbage pails, a car and two to three children. Sure, this is something my parents may have wanted for me, in particularly my mother, but it was never meant to be. It's not who I am. This is how my life turned out and not how I wanted it. Maybe I deserved everything that happened to me, maybe I didn't.

It has been at least five years since this life began, and I have thought about the past almost every day. It haunts me. When I think about certain things, I can't help but say to myself that I should have done it differently, should have handled it better but it never happens like that. You go with your gut and don't look back.

I guess the best way to start my story is from the very seed of it...

∞

I vividly remember the first time I smoked cannabis. I was eighteen years old and just out of high school; seems like yesterday, but feels like an eternity. This is one of those memories I will never forget and it's the one I think about most often.

It was one of those days where I woke up wanting to try something new. I wanted to do something that I had never done and of course, the first thing in my mind was cannabis. I had seen a few people smoke and had heard stories of it, all of which, at first, make it sound horrible. But, when you look into it, you realize that most people smoke: most of them just aren't open about it. Sometimes you'll go into people's apartments and say to yourself, *this person definitely smokes*. The real question in my head was who was I going to do this with. More importantly, who would do this with me? There were two answers: Kush and Anthony. These two dudes were my best friends. I loved them like brothers and still miss them, more than anyone else.

Kush, or so the name I chose to remember him by, was my best friend and out of all the friends I had, he was the one I knew the longest and knew more about him than anyone else. I was with him through all the good times and the bad ones, believe me there were really bad days. I had smoked with him and my other friend, Anthony, before anyone else and that pleasant memory has been with me ever since that day. When I feel sad, that is one of the memories I think about and sure for the next few moments I forget everything else and smile, but it does only last for a moment.

This is where I should explain Kush a little bit. Not only was he the best and coolest friend I had ever had, but he was also a paranoid avid drug taker and seller. There were substances he sold other than cannabis, a prescription drug was his second-best thing to sell, and those sold more than the weed. What does that tell you? There were things that I had never even heard of until I started getting into them. Whenever he would start talking about chemicals and research chemicals, I tried to pay attention. I did. But the information wasn't getting stored anywhere. I think because I wasn't really interested in it then. Everything he said about cannabis, I retained; everything else went in one ear and out of the other. Sometimes when he would talk about it, I would feel really dumb, but then I came to the point where it really didn't matter for me to care about it. He, on the other hand, was very intelligent. To say he was smart is an understatement; even though he was a little crazy. He was creative and could make anything he wanted. He even made a gun out of Legos that shot small .22 caliber rounds.

He did almost every drug under the sun. He'll take some valium and smoke weed all day. You ask him about Ecstasy and he'll tell you about MDMA, the pure form of it. He carries a leather flask around

3

with him and the only thing he puts in there is Devil Springs alcohol, hard core shit. Anthony and I were nowhere on his level at that time.

Anthony and I even gave Kush the name Kush because when we first started smoking, he would only smoke Kush strains of marijuana. Literally anything in the Kush family was better to him than anything else; every time he mentioned Kush, he would go through the list of his favorites such as Hindu Kush, Bubba Kush, Burmese Kush, Vanilla Kush, Sour Kush, Kushage, Purple Kush, Kaia Kush, Tahoe OG Kush and his personal favorite OG Kush. He saw this Indica strain as his personal medicine for his paranoia and insomnia. He had large quantities of these strains stashed away in mason jars labeled with the name of the strain and its Tetrahydrocannabinol and CBD count, THC the thing on the cannabis plant that actually gets you high. He wouldn't smoke anything else, refused to. The only thing I've ever seen him really enjoy was the sativa dominate hybrid known as Blue Dream: that is some good shit.

To the outside observer Kush could be a little bit of a sour peach but he always had a good reason for being mad at everyone. He was rough around the edges but I got to know him as the genuinely good person he was. Sometimes, he was even a better man than I was. One time we were going to see one of the Beatles at Radio City and an older couple had stop me as we were walking to take a picture of them. In true New York fashion I told them no. Kush made me seem like an asshole and he took a couple of pictures for them. After they were gone, as we were walking, he had reprimanded me about how I was wrong. Classic Kush. They were forever grateful that he took their pictures. They have a memory of a nice man and I'm their memory of a rude New Yorker.

Anthony, I had known for a good portion of my life: we met in elementary school. There's not really much to say about Anthony. For some reason, it is even hard for me to write about him because in the end there wasn't much I understood about him. He was definitely the womanizer of the group and always had women with him or ones that he could just call in the middle of the night. One thing I can say about him was that he was the best wingman; he could get you a date and drink way more than I could. I was always envious of his way with women, a part of me always kind of wanted to be him, maybe more of the idea of him.

After that first time the three of us smoked together, we became better and closer friends. We literally got high together almost every day and partied pretty hard in my parents' backyard when I used to live with them. My father had given me the backyard to use and I put a gazebo there and had some major parties there. We would smoke, drink and even get blowjobs from girls that I invited back there. We thought we were partying really hard and we tried to every chance we got. I'd get in so much trouble because we would be so loud and obnoxious that my neighbors would complain to my parents and they would yell at me for it. That's what they get for giving a boy out of high school going into college use of their backyard all the time. We also had hookahs and a radio, you know, because at that time hookahs were all the rage. We really didn't need anything else. We were living the lives we wanted to live.

So, there I was in bed wanting something else to do, something new, something exciting.

It was a craving that alcohol or cigarettes couldn't quench.

Every day we had been bombarded by it, everyone in high school smoked. I even remember a kid getting thrown out because he came in high and looked it, he was stupid. In the lunchroom they would talk about 'getting high' and I would sit there, judging them. *Look at these guys, smoking pot, doing drugs.* Now, I see all of these as missed opportunities because I would always be invited to parties but I wouldn't go because I was scared of being in the drug culture.

Boredom.

Nothing on television, nothing to listen to and sick of video games.

I actually think we were playing Tony Hawks Pro Skater 2 at Anthony's house on PlayStation 2. The three of us got sick of that real quick and we went through about five hundred cable TV channels and found nothing to watch. We finally got bored of being inside so we went on his porch and talked. I don't know how long we were out there. The sky turned grey and it started to rain: one of those freak early summer thunderstorms that forced us back inside with nothing to do.

Boredom.

The three amigos were sitting on Kush's couch staring at a television that was off (a tube television), so, we were just looking at the black reflection of ourselves)

I believe we were on the same frequency that day because Kush looked at me, at Anthony, and then back at me and asked, "Do you guys want to smoke the wah-wah?"

"Wah-Wah?" I asked.

"The mariju-wah-wah." He said smiling.

I had no idea what to say.

The idea had become a reality.

Kush got up and went over to the computer. He opened up the internet browser and there we were, looking up what cannabis does, how long it lasts, how much it takes, peoples experiences and apparently all the different kinds of strains. We were mystified by the sativas and indicas. Outraged by the laws of every state regarding cannabis made us angry because whenever we saw something about politics, it would show us something medical like how it can be used for headaches, cancer survivors and just the basic fact that we have cannabinoid receptors in our brain that activate when we smoke it. We loaded ourselves with all this information and by the end of our discussion we really wanted to smoke. It also did not help that a few days before we had gone to see the movie *Pineapple Express*. We were probably the only three people in the theater who were not high. So, I guess you can say that movie is the reason we smoked.

"I know where we can get some." Kush said with a smirk on his face.

We pooled out our money together to by a gram, which at the time was twenty dollars. Now, we get eighths for twenty.

We had a plan; I would go meet the guy, Anthony would get the cigar to roll with and Kush would grind and roll it.

I remember being on the corner of Neil and Hone waiting for some stranger to show up to sell me drugs. It felt different which made me feel cool and awesome. If I could take back all the time I spent waiting for dealers on corners, I'd have at least four of my life hours back. When the guy finally came after he said he'd be there in ten minutes, we exchanged pleasantries, swapped the money, weed and next thing I knew I was walking back to Anthony's house with a gram of cannabis in my pocket. I could smell it, which at first turned me off; but I was soon to learn that the more it smells, the better it is.

I remember Kush holding up the finished Blunt. I was nervous, who knew what could happen; I had seen *Pineapple Express* and *Reefer Madness*, we were in for a surprise.

We passed that blunt around and got high. Forever changing our lives. It's also funny to think that after you do smoke cannabis you could kind of tell who did or did not smoke. Usually, the people who don't smoke are miserable and depressed, the same people who are against cannabis for no reason and for that reason it remains illegal. Yeah, and dealers who are currently in this 'street level' also don't want it legal. It's a sad circle of truths.

One snowstorm the three of us really wanted to smoke. No one could drive anywhere. The snow was almost to our knees and there was a mandatory travel ban. What we did want to do was get high, so, I called my contact and walked to his house. He kept me waiting out there in the storm for fifteen minutes. The snow had engulfed me and it was now past my knees and had become a popsicle stick.

It was at that moment I decided to sell cannabis. I did not see it as a job but as s source of steady cash flow. It was all I knew. There was no way I could go from all of this, to a job like everyone else. I see how everyone acts when they are working people; they all get up early in the morning and run to their cars only to sit in New York City traffic for maybe an hour, sometimes more. They rush home because the parking sucks and I'm over here like *look at these suckers, taking buses and stressing out*. It really is a circus, especially Pelham Bay Station on a summer's day when everyone's waiting like sardines for the bus. Sure, I can connect with everyone. We are all living our lives and I see what's like to be a working person everyday like that, I would be content with it and do it every day, if I had to. It's a cruel world and we are only existing to make money and pay the government. What a life we live. This is how I talk myself to rationalize to myself that dealing pot is not a good way to make money but then I always talk myself into how good it is.

Kush and Anthony were very excited about this crazy idea I had. The three of us began networking and the next thing we knew we were selling it. That's how it happens, spur of the moment things that become reality.

Looking back on being that low-level drug dealer disgusts myself. Meeting people on corners, in front of people's houses. I couldn't even count the number of times I would see a police car that sent a feeling of paranoia down my spine causing my testicles to go back into my body. I would have fiends call me in the middle of the night. Non-stop text messages, non-stop calls, in the end it wasn't all worth it. Dealing on a street level is not good for the mind and soul, it could eat you up and spit you out. For me, it made me angry… There were so many I turned away because of age or attitude.

I used to even hate the people I would sell to. Most of the time I would have to say things like, "I don't care, just give me the money". People would tell me how much they liked weed and this and that and it would be enough. There was even one particular guy we used to call the Preacher. He got that name because every time he would meet one of us, he would go on and on about how cannabis is good for you and this and that, and he'd say "It'll be legal soon. You have back problems, it's good for the back". He wasn't all that bad, sometimes it would make me chuckle. I also didn't mind that he was another dealer, but he would by half pounds from me at a time, so in my mind, money is money.

I was a different person back then and will not bore you with the story of my childhood; it was normal. All you need to know is that I was from a well-off family.

It's hard to believe that I was living in my parents' house dealing drugs. It's also hard to think about my parents because the last memory I have is both of them crying and my father saying to me, "Don't come back to this house." I was not a great son at that point. I had made it clear that I was dropping out of college to 'work full time', which was not only in a retail store but dealing of cannabis on the side that made me more money than the real job.
It didn't help the situation that I built that gazebo that we dubbed, The Shanty, in the yard just so my friends and I could drink, get high and party all night. I didn't ask them, I just did it. I was young and stupid. What we did back there was horrible. There were many times the cops were called on us for being too loud and whenever we would put a firepit in there in the winters the neighbors would call the fire department. At least when the fire department got there, they thought we were cool as shit with our setup.

I guess one day my parents were just fed up with me, and rightfully so. You never think about your own actions until it's way too late. I am grateful for what they had done for me and it kills me that I haven't spoken to them in years. I often wonder what they would say to me if they knew who *I really was*. They would probably still want nothing to do with me. I'm the first child and I fucked up so I am sure that naturally, my parents blame themselves.

One day I was sitting in the kitchen eating a bagel with cream cheese: I had woken up from one of those 'weed coma's' and was still feeling high. My Mother came in with some groceries and in one of the bags was this pineapple: it was slightly misshapen and looked more like a sphere. Something clicked in my mind and it was the only time I got really creative and began drawing what I called a *Stoner Pineapple*. He's a Pineapple that smokes a lot of cannabis and his best friend is a Blunt; they would have adventures together and at the end of every story they had a *Session* together. (Session: Two or more people smoking together, usually in an outdoor environment) Eventually my Pineapple grew into a comic book with ten stories which I wrote and illustrated; I never did anything with it. I buried them somewhere and have no idea where they are. Some of them were good and a lot of them were bad. In the end, nothing ever became of it and I actually didn't think about that dude for a while.

My parents were happy when I met Sadie. They figured that she would set me straight and she kind of did. I fell in love with her the first time she spoke to me.

I met Sadie in the Shanty. Anthony had brought one of his girls and her friend back there. From the moment I spoke to her I knew that I didn't just want her physically, I wanted her. I loved how she spoke so well, she smelled so good and looked to me like a Roman goddess. We began to go out with each other long after Anthony had stopped seeing her friend. She tried to set me straight, I began to focus more on my retail job than dealing.

My parents got wind of my dealing; I still don't know how they found it.

It was a horrible night. They busted into my room and my mother said to me, "You have four hours to get the fuck out of this house."

"Where do I go?" I asked.

"I don't know and I don't care. Don't come back to this house." My father said to me.

I promised them I would stop dealing underneath my tears; but they knew all along that it would be a lie. I had disgraced them. Another part of me that says: *they wouldn't give you a chance, then fuck them. They are kicking you out. You don't need them.*

So, Sadie and I moved in together. There was no more talk of not dealing. She got a waitressing job at a restaurant and I continued to live my days. This is where my dream began: simple dream, to have enough money to buy a few houses for my friends and I and to live with Sadie until the day we die. The dream of growing older and being able to do drugs whenever and wherever I wanted, home in the middle of nowhere upstate. Sounds awesome, but too bad the American dream is littered with the bodies of people wanting more or less the same thing. The pursuit of the dream entails more than I have words to describe it.

While this is the beginning of my story it's hard for me to believe that while this was going on, other people were doing other things. That's a really crazy thought. This is what was going on before the rest of my story…

A Puff from the Joint

It was one of those gloomy early mornings in Manhattan. The sun was just about to come up and the sky was a shade of pale blue. As the sun bursts into a sliver of light from the back of the horizon the DEA clan members were barreling down a street congested with traffic. Their destination was a residential apartment building; within the confines of its walls was a man they were going to arrest/kill because he had been dealing a lot of drugs along the highways of the internet. This person had done what many could have never done. No, this is not my story. First you must know the story of the two men who created an empire and left its ruins to me.

To me, they are superheroes running around in their costumes and masks. Another group of men wear masks, but they wear them to hide the faces of cowards, the DEA scum burst open the door to the stairwell of the building and like a swarm of locusts they went blindly into whatever situation they are summoned. Blind lunatics with rifles. To me, just thinking about seeing them running up the stairs like an army is a pretty scary thought…

The mega don, our first superhero finds himself at the receiving end of this invasion of the DEA and knows his life is about to change. With a cigar in his mouth he starred out of the window. He didn't believe that he was going to die but he knew it was a real possibility. The only thing he could think of was grabbing his weapons. See, not only was our friend into collecting and selling guns but he was also well into the National Rifle Association and from what I heard was a dam good shot. The hero, whose real name I do not know, nor do I think anyone truly knows was revealed to me as Zeus, the creator of the Rainbow. He knew who was coming up the stairs, he had seen them speeding down the street toward the building. He knew they were coming for him. If it had been any other day, he would have told himself to go fuck himself but not today. They were there because of him. He grabbed the first rifle and made sure it was loaded. Then he paused for a moment glancing at the trigger of the rifle. Suddenly, a chill went down his spine, as he thought of another person: the only person that deserved to know it was time to bail on everything. His only thought was that *if there's a chance he can get out before anything happens; then why shouldn't I warn him?* Within a few seconds he grabbed his phone and sent a text to the other superhero with only one word: RUN…

With that text in the air and on its way to our other friends' phone he felt at peace and was ready. Everything was crashing down all around this man. He strapped up with his assortment of weapons and with the blaze of god and glory he held his guns highly and proudly. When the storm came, so did the knowing that he would die. He tried to figure out what to say to himself but with the cowboys running upstairs there was no time to reminisce: it all didn't matter at that point.

Taking the last few puffs of his cigar were the calmest he'd been in months. For a person on so much coke and ketamine, I don't know how he was very calm. I'm sure that would make a lot of people feel calm. On the inside, he may have been screaming and wanting to get out of there but he sure as hell didn't show it. His mind though, would not let him go… He had to stay until the Rainbow fell. It started with him and must die with him; the Alpha and the Omega. The empire had fallen and a crater was created that would not be filled for some time.

Suddenly, our hero knew he will die. Rather than speak any words to the pigs he decided to speak no words and will remain silent. He would kill anything that got in his way. He even knew when they approached the door; he could hear their boots creeping down the hallway. He heard them, I heard them, we had the same boots.

They burst through his door with a haze of smoke; because Zeus was in a drug induced state, he could only follow his instinct and no longer thought logically. For someone on that combination of drugs I'm astounded because I wouldn't have been able to figure out my name, let alone kill people. He shot six DEA agents. One thing he was certain of, in all of the thought process that was going on his brain that he really didn't want to kill anyone and he never wanted it to come to this. Killing was something he never wanted to do, but sometimes just must be done. It sucks and all but that's what happens. When a man becomes a man, it is because of decisions like that. It makes you stronger in some ways, but he wouldn't be able to feel that. After a squad of officers, Zeus couldn't kill them all. He was shot five times: twice in the torso, twice in the heart, and there was a shot in his head.

That's what I've heard and it is the legend that has floated around about this man. I know that not everything I've heard is true, but I like to think it's all true. I heard this version from the man I only knew as Panzer, our other superhero, who was a good friend of Zeus.

Together they created the Rainbow…

Together it fell upon them…

Here was Panzer, sitting on the sign of the Essex House in New York City, smoking a joint to end a good night as the sun was rising. He took a hit as he gazed out over Central Park. This was before everything, before the Rainbow. He was content with his life and was happy with his job. I don't really remember what it was, but he really enjoyed it. I had only known him as Panzer and that name suited him well, because, looking at him just reminded you of a German army tank from World War II. Sometimes it was apparent with his actions.

Panzer, known by his childhood friends as the Villager, was born to a couple who had lived in the Village in New York City. He was one of three children. From an early age, especially growing up in the nineties, he was exposed to the culture of the city, mostly the ecstasy. He had nothing to complain about: his parents loved him, had a good education and a great understanding of life. He didn't take drugs until he was eighteen for which I commend him. His first drug was the shrooms, then cannabis.

If I could help you understand who Panzer was compared to me, he preferred the first four minutes to Stairway to Heaven, I prefer the last four. I know you don't know me yet, but you will soon.

After taking the drugs, he knew he couldn't just take drugs and not have any kind of job or something to fall back on. He was determined to not end up a druggie, or a homeless person. He decided to become a lawyer and his parents helped him pay to go to Pace University where he did very well. He said a couple years in he asked himself why he was doing all this, he really didn't want to do all the legal work and felt trapped in that job. He really stopped caring halfway through. It was also halfway through that he met another student there…

I've always heard that when you're in law school it's pretty much partying all the time. Panzer told me how they met: they had had a few classes together but never spoke to each other. They both sat in the back of their room and doodled in their notebooks. He said it was actually amazing that they had these classes together because they became such great friends that it's weird that they 'ignored' each other.

They both were passing their classes with flying colors.

As I was saying, parties…

Panzer was at a frat party, one of those where they allowed other school members to join as an end of year celebration. He said they had about four fog machines, laser lights and disco balls and of course the dance music that defined the late nineties into the early double-0's. He took part in some of the drugs, smoked some weed, blew some coke, even took a half tab of acid because it was his first time. He would later say that half a tab would be stupid because there's no way to tell if you're really getting half or not. As he was walking around drinking his beer, he happened to see Zeus, and as the only person that remotely looked familiar, he gravitated over to him to start talking to someone.

Zeus was fucked up and starred at Panzer who looked frightened. Panzer asked him, "What's wrong with you? Are you ok?"

"They gave me something called a hipster flip." He said.

"A hipster flip?"

One of the other people at the party said, "MDMA and LSD."

"Yeah," Zeus said, "I'm just coming up on everything."

"That's awesome dude." Panzer said.

And for him, that night would go down in history. He joined in taking more acid and some MDMA. Their entrance into the drug world happened the same way it happened to everyone, if not everyone, kind of happened to me. They threw themselves into the psychedelic world and became the best of friends after that. They went on month long binges trying out drugs they were able to get and news ones they were just discovering. That's when they found Pihkal and with Shura's guiding voice they were introduced to the world of the phenethylamine, but getting everything wasn't easy. Zeus was the one hassling people for contacts and Panzer was selling the stuff just so they had more money to get more. They were determined to do something with all this knowledge they were gaining.

They were now fully engulfed in the drug world. Panzer was the only person I heard of taking 2c-E at school every day, which helped him study, and passed the bar while he was banging Lucy. His self-taught lesson to himself was that no matter how many drugs you're on, if you want something done, it'll help you get it done.

Zeus was like, *fuck school*. A few months before the end, he dropped out. A tune even I would soon be singing.

These two partied hard, so hard, in fact, that one night they ended up sitting by a fire in the middle of the woods in the middle of the night, smoking a fat jay of marijuana and it was there that everything was born.

Smoking the joint Zeus said, "It's really hard to find these drugs you know."

"I know," Panzer said taking the jay from him, "if only there was a better way of getting them."

"I've been thinking, "Zeus said looking at Panzer, "the internet…"

"What about it?"

"Let's use it, let's sell these drugs over it."

Panzer laughed.

"I'm serious dude. Think about it: the whole world is at our fingertips."

"You and I both know that that could never happen. We'd be caught in five minutes."

"Would we?"

Panzer started thinking as he hit the jay. All that time in school did something good to him. He was now thinking how to get around everything. He passed the jay and Zeus said to him, "Panzer, I'm not asking you to give me an answer now, think about it. Together we could do it, but I alone, no way. I need you for it."

They had a room of a few computers. They got to work creating the website. They tried to make it as impossible as they could to be able to find it and log onto it. Days they spent perfecting everything. Zeus used his abilities to get all the contacts to agree to use their site as their base of sales. He wrote out a list of 'must haves' and one by one he crossed them off when he found a secure contact. He got the 2c's, cannabis, MDMA, coke, ketamine, everything you can goddam dream of, even prescription drugs. You know, the ones they don't give out to just anyone. It took a lot of convincing from him and he even had to make journeys outside of the state and even had to travel to Oregon once. He had even traveled to Texas and met the legendary Ecstasy dealer and got him onto the site. He promised all of them it was a safe, legal bypass of the government and great alternative way of selling and buying drugs without leaving the comfort of your home. Panzer was using his skills to do other things, like setting up the website as a 'fertilizer' selling company. That's how the government would see the site before being able to log in and only if you knew where to look could you find the link to the login page. The login page would come up and it would say,

"You have stumbled onto a locked door.
In order to knock you must find the key,
It is as easy as 1, 2, 3…
This page is not real…"

This is what many people saw when they were able to get to the link. You were also prompted for a log in and password, but if you had everything, you were in and would see the page that said,

Rainbow
(Showing you everything under the sun)

Although you may remember it as its original website and most common name, *Silk Road: Anonymous Market.*

A Mecca for drugs.

Within the hours before they launched the site, Panzer was tirelessly finishing up the site, making sure everything would run well. He was doings lots of coke and drinking a lot of coffee, so much so that he never drank coffee again: the same could not be said for the cocaine.

After everything was done, they sat on the couch, launched the site, smoked a blunt of the best shit their money could buy. They each snorted a line of cocaine and Ketamine. Within an hour they watched people buy and sell with each other and watched their profit soar. Zeus poured them both a shot of Knob Creek.

"Here's for everything under the sun." Zeus said holding up his glass handing Panzer his.

Panzer took the glass and said, "to the Rainbow…"

They raised their glasses and drank.

Within a couple of years, they had expanded their market to the world. The money they were cashing in was so much, he said, that Zeus bought a three-floor penthouse in the city and together had bought a mansion in Pennsylvania. Zeus bought himself some ladies and they lived with him, cooked and cleaned. He also bought two fifty thousand-dollar watches from the Breitling family. This was the problem; both had gotten too cocky after a while. He said they paid no mind to anything else and felt invincible.

∞

For a good while, the Drug Enforcement Agency (DEA), had absolutely no idea this website even existed. Zeus and Panzer had done an excellent job disguising themselves and their business; the fertilizer cover was working. The site ran well for years; but in my opinion, it went on too long without something happening. It was around the time I started experimenting with the psychedelic world that everything happened to the Rainbow.

Tillman was new in the Texas DEA scene; he had transferred from New York. He was the only one who even had the slightest idea about anything. He had seen a rise in traffic of the drug MDMA and felt it was his duty to rid the world of these drugs and criminals who supply them. He busted little people (the ones the cops don't care about just to get enough information for the bigger guys). There were whispers of an underground drug website but they were never able to find anything. His spare time was occupied by trying to find this website; but nothing ever came up, just a lot of other things in Onionland. Until one day the 'fertilizer' site popped up and he became suspicious about it. Yet, he found nothing and wasn't able to get on the site, so, he did nothing about it. He merely threw it under the rug, for the moment, while he thought of a new way to get on it.

A dealer was arrested in Texas, selling what turned out to be molly that the Rainbow had been selling. He said not a word to any officer who spoke to him in the interrogation room. He just kept asking for his lawyer which the cops were stalling on. He sat there, hands folded and, no matter how much anyone screamed at him and told him how much he was fucked, he kept calm and had the same look on his face because it didn't faze him. He accepted whatever was going to happen to him.

At least that's how it was until this guy Tillman, came into the interrogation room. He looked behind the glass before going in and just by how the man looked, he knew he could break him. He knew he could find out whatever he wanted about him. He knocked on the door to the room and the officer inside opened the door and he said, "Leave us alone." The officer left and Tillman shut and locked the door behind him. He even turned off the camera and that's when the dealer knew he was in really deep shit. Tillman knew he was risking something but, in the moment, he did not give a fuck. Tillman sat down in front of him.

"You think you're the one we want?"

Nothing, not a word nor a said was heard.

He continued. "You think we care about a small-time drug dealer that can't even run away from the cops? We want the ones who are currently running and hiding from us. You think you're important in all of this? You're not…"

The dealer had no idea what to say, "So… Who or what do you want?"

"You give me all the information I need and I get you only a year sentence for what you're here for, that is the best I could do in this state for you. And you know I'm not lying. And I know you don't want to be in jail for the rest of your life."

The dealer weighed out his options and all he knew was that he was scared. Just staring into Tillman's eyes, you could just see the evil man on the inside just screaming to come out.

"Maybe I should just wait for my lawyer…" he said.

Tillman turned around and went for the doors. He halted before he could touch the door knob. Something in Tillman had turned sour. He knew this man knew what he wanted to know and had to get it from him. He looked up and saw the camera and he no longer cared. He clenched his fist and turned around hitting the dealer in the face.

"What the fuck you do that for!" The dealer yelled.

"Tell me everything you know, everyone you know, or you never get to feel the sun on your face ever again." Tillman said quietly but firmly.

He sat back down in front of the man and fixed up his collar and shirt.

"If you talk now, the deal still stands... What do you know?"

The dealer knew as soon as he uttered any syllable regarding anything that he would be a dead man and as of right now he is a dead man. He made the decision, so he talked...

"I get my stuff from a guy people call Don Leon. That's what I was introduced to him as. I knew him from the neighborhood and I don't remember exactly how it happened but one day we just sort of became friends. He brought me into his home, and at the time I had no idea he was a drug dealer. I just wanted to have money like him. So, I invested money with him and after some failed investments he told me he sold the drug molly and that's when I got into selling it. I became his gopher... doing what he didn't want to do."

"Who's his source?"

"That I don't know. But you get this guy, you find out the source. If I could make a guess, I'd say he buys from online, he always needs rides to the post office."

"Online? Wouldn't be the Rainbow would it?"

The dealer felt his heart skip a beat. He knew what it was and he was shocked Tillman knew about it. That's when the rat in the dealer came out and said, "You haven't been able to get on it did you?"

Tillman said, "So you do know..."

"Yeah I do, I just can't believe you knew."

"Of course, I knew. How do I get on it? How can I access it?"

"Don Leon, he's a smart guy but not all there. He leaves his computer on and he stays signed onto everything. He especially leaves his internet connected to the Rainbow so he could have constant order updates and investments. You find him, you get in his home and you'll find you pot of gold at the end of the Rainbow."

Tillman was taking everything in, thinking about it all.

"He likes to pick up his packages at the post office," the dealer said, "the post office in Carrizo Springs, that's where he likes to have everything sent and shipped from. He goes there maybe twice a week."

"What does he look like?"

"When you see him, you'll know."

Tillman got up and without saying a word went to the door. Before he could touch the door knob the dealer said, "Hey cop." Tillman turned to look at him. "Don't just think that you taking down this website and taking down whoever is responsible for creating it will destroy the drug traffic. You guys have already been fighting an already lost drug war. If you shut down the Rainbow someone else will carry on the work. People will always find the drugs they're looking for. People like you, think you believe you a doing your country a great service, are just taking the freedom away from every American you think you protect. And I hope that when that happens and someone else has taken over, that you never find that person and die before you find out."

"I'm sorry you feel that way." Tillman said opening the door, "and that's why you drug addicts and dealers are going to jail for a long time." He left the room and shut the door behind him. The dealer sat there inside the room by himself and suddenly he knew he had made a huge mistake and just wanted to die.

The trap was now set for out unsuspecting hero duo.

Tillman and his partner sat in the car staring at the post office in Carrizo Springs, Texas. They had been out there for a week and Don Leon had not shown up yet. Tillman held his sunglasses in his left hand out the window and twisted it between his fingers. He was ready to see this man, arrest him and raid his home. In the end of this that's all Tillman wanted. He wanted the login information to the Rainbow. The raid on the home was on standby until given the go ahead by Tillman.

"How long do we have to wait?" The partner asked.

"As long as it takes; eventually he has to come get his mail."

"What if he had seen us or heard about us and abandoned this post office?"

"We give it a few more days, if he doesn't come by end of the week, well call it a day."

"Maybe the dealer was lying?"

"No, he wasn't"

"How are you so sure?"

"Because I lied and told him I'd help him out for more information. I lied and he's going to jail. I haven't allowed him to have any contact with anyone either."

The Ecstasy dealer in Texas, Don Leon, was busy doing his drugs. He was all about this website and loved it. He mailed out package after package and received the number of packages back. One of his packages did get confiscated though he paid no mind to it and continued his day. The next day he went to the post office to both send and pick up a package. This man was such an idiot. He got too comfortable on the site and felt that he was untouchable and that he was eluding the system. He got cocky and deserved to die for that.

For hours Tillman and his partner were sitting in the car. They had gone through at least three cups of coffee each. The partner could not sit there anymore. For the whole week they had been there and nothing, not a sign of this man. His packages still there, left unclaimed.

"I need more coffee." he said as he was about to get out of the car. Tillman grabbed his shoulder before he could get out and they saw a white seventies Cadillac pull up in front of the post office. And the man who left the car was in a white suit, white shoes and a white cowboy hat.

Tillman got on the radio and said, "Keep positions; the bird is in the nest."

The dealer walked inside and partner asked Tillman, "How do you know that's him?"

"The dealer said I'd know when I see him. I know that's him."

Tillman made sure his gun was in his holster and he and the partner made their way inside.

Don Leon was patiently waiting on line. Package in hand and money in his pocket, he stood there, scratching his nose; most likely coming down from a serious cocaine binge. He was coming down hard and fiending with his hands, which he didn't know what to do with. All he could think about was getting his Molly and being on his way and the whole time he thought about cocaine. There he was standing online with his white suit and white everything. He was the kind of person that needed to show off everything even to people he didn't know or wanted to know.

Tillman and his partner were a couple people behind him and they were watching him like a hawk. This guy couldn't fart without them knowing. Every time he touched his nose Tillman would loath him just that much more. He was also sweating and sniffing every few seconds which made Tillman one hundred percent sure this is the man they were looking for.

Don Leon made his way to the counter, put his package on the counter and said, "I'm here to pick up a package and send this bad boy out."

That's when Tillman made his move and like vultures in the desert.

"DEA get on the ground! You're under arrest!" Tillman yelled, handcuffing him.

Don Leon knew that he had fucked up and that this was the end. He fell to his knees as they took him in custody and began to raid his home.

Tillman had sat down at the computer in the home of Don Leon and sure enough the page to the Rainbow was on the computer. He now had an account and the ability to go onto the site. He sat there and all he could say was, "Where do I begin?" Now he had all the information he needed. That's the reason Panzer and Zeus fell like dominos. The drug world suffered a huge loss. Tillman now posed as a dealer and the integrity of the site had fallen. It took the DEA almost a year to find the people who started the site. Slowly they crafted their plan and developed a way to take everyone down within the span of a few hours.

It would take them a whole day.

But first they needed proof and they needed bait...

That's when Don Leon found himself with handcuffs around his hands and shackled to the chair. He, along with Tillman and his partner, was in a motel room somewhere in Huston, Texas. Don Leon wasn't really under arrest and Tillman was acting suspiciously to the point where Don thought they weren't cops.

Tillman took off his jacket and laid it on the chair. He rolled up his sleeves and said, "You're not under arrest yet my friend."

Don was tired and really didn't want to hear these people talk. "So, what do you call this?"

"This is the discussion of how I want to help you stay out of prison. Seeing how I'm the one with the upper hand, I figured you'd be in the mood to help out."

He kept his mouth shut while Tillman stared into his eyes.

I am no snitch. I know nothing. Don't say anything. That's all he was thinking and all anyone in that situation should ever think. But like most people he was a dirty rotten cunt sucking rat. And immediately changed what he thought, *I don't want to go to prison. I gotta' look out for myself.* In the drug world, there is no room for the I, we should look out for each other, we should keep our mouths shut. But I digress...

"What do you want me to do?" Don asked and with that question I could hear the sounds of bombs and planes for it was that moment that killed the Rainbow.

"You're not asking me, right? Because I'm telling you what to do from now on." Tillman sat down in front of him and said, "You will set up a meeting with the persons responsible for the Rainbow. You have done business with them before, so it'll be easier for you to get in contact with them. You buy a good amount of whatever it is that you usually buy from them. Nothing changes… If they figure you out or find the microphone, you're on your own. We won't do a damn thing and we'll just let them, do whatever their going to do. Do you understand that?"

Don did not like a word of that. But now, he was within the control of the cops and there was really only one way this could all end without going to prison. "And if I don't?" He asked.

"You will… We have eyes and ears everywhere. I know you now, I know everything about you. If you don't do it, you'll rot in solitary confinement for ten years."

Don was fucked and he knew it.

∞

Zeus and Panzer found themselves in a hotel room waiting for a customer. A secure contact had set up a meeting between them and who they knew as the Texas ecstasy dealer.

Panzer was lying on the bed while Zeus paced back and forth in the room. He was anxious and had good reason to be. They had never met this person before and both thought it was weird that he wanted to meet them. So, naturally, Zeus had his suspicions and something was telling him that some piece wasn't right. The dealer was going to 'be in town' and wanted to discuss business on 'the big scale'. To Zeus this was all going to pay off in the end. Out of everything Panzer told me, this is the story that I love and sticks to me. My favorite story according to Panzer…

Hours they waited in the room.

They didn't speak to each other. They were silent; the only sounds to hear were the dull voices coming out from the television that only Panzer was watching.

There was a knock at the door and Panzer and Zeus sprang up like prairie dogs. Panzer turned off the television.

Zeus looked at Panzer and said, "Whatever happens, follow my lead."

Panzer nodded and felt to make sure his gun was still on his belt. Zeus opened the door to reveal the Don. There he stood, in his famous white suite and all.

"You two must be the leprechauns at the end of the Rainbow." The dealer said. He continued talking after reading Panzer and Zeus reactions which they were not amused. He continued, "Can I come in? And then we can talk business."

"Yeah there's your chair." Zeus said, pointing to the chair in the corner of the room.

Zeus gave him a cold stare and looked at Panzer, "frisk him…"

Panzer went over to the dealer to pat him down but the dealer backed away and put his hands up. "Whoa…" he said, "There's no need to be touching dicks here, I like to party just as much as you two." He then took out a vile of cocaine and did a bump off his hand.

Zeus was not amused with the dealer and shot him this question, "How can I trust you?"

"Do you not like making money?" the dealer asked.

"What can you do to prove to me that I can trust you? You already have one strike; you wouldn't let him frisk you."

Panzer was standing in the opposite corner of the room staring at the dealer as Zeus pulled up a chair in front of him. The dealer had already made himself comfortable by sitting down and relaxing.

"Do I have to do more drugs in front of you to prove it or what do I have to do?"

"Drugs aren't going to help me trust you, it's ok though," Zeus said, "we can talk about other things… How do you feel about the OPP? Do you know me?"

Don Leon was now confused, he had no idea what to say to that but, "What?"

Panzer had noticed that he swallowed and now looked nervous. Zeus looked at Panzer and Panzer drew his weapon and pointed it at the dealer. Zeus motioned with his fingers for him to keep quiet and pick up his shirt. For a moment the dealer was stuck not knowing what to do. All he knew was that he was in deep shit.

The dealer wouldn't pick up his shirt, moving his head back and forth in the 'no' position.

Zeus kept the conversation going.

"What's your favorite band?" He asked.

The dealer, contemplating if he should lift up his shirt or not, answers with "uh, um, I like the Doors."

He lifted his shirt and Zeus quickly processed the fact that he had a microphone taped to his chest. The next thing he was processing was how they were going to get out of this situation. Now that he knew the cops were outside listening.

"The Doors..." He said, "I'm a Floyd man myself..."

Zeus got up and asked him, "Want something to drink?"

The dealer didn't want to answer but his mouth was faster than his mind, "No".

"You sure? The tap water in New York is the best in the world."

"Don't need it."

Zeus grabbed the bucket of ice and poured water into it. He walked over to the dealer and put the bucket in front of him as he sat back down. Panzer still had his gun pointed to him.

"Do you like music? What kind of music?" Zeus asked. He motioned for him to slowly rip off the microphone. The dealer knew he had to, or else he would die. He knew it and Zeus was already thinking about killing him. Slowly the dealer ripped off the tape, he hated that both pairs of eyes were on him and that the jig is up. Zeus must have known the dealer was thinking something because he motioned for him to keep quiet.

"Yeah, I enjoy music." The dealer said as he took off the microphone.

With the microphone off, Zeus signaled the dealer to drop the microphone and its amplifier into the bucket of water. The dealer thinks twice about yelling for help. But he remembered in that moment who he really was, he was really a dealer, just like these two. He knew that they had done what no one before them could have. Bottom line was he had respect for them and in his ashamed state he dropped the microphone into the bucket.

Meanwhile...

Agent Tillman and his partner were in the car listening to everything that was said, even though Panzer and Zeus said not a word of anything that could incriminate him. They even heard the last few seconds before the microphone and transmitter hit the water in the bucket. They knew they would find the wire and that's all Tillman wanted, to shake the Rainbow to its core.

The microphone had been off for maybe five minutes. They heard nothing, not even any interfaces on the frequency

"What should we do?" The partner asked.

"We do nothing." Tillman said, "The bait is inside, they know were watching so it's their move. We wait now…"

"What if something happens to him?"

"Who cares, one less drug dealer off the street."

"You're just trying to piss them off, aren't you?"

"I'm trying to get to the source. We scare them, they get stuck like a deer in the headlights and they crumble like the twin towers." And with that said Tillman did what he wanted and at the moment was satisfied. He had no plan to get Don Leon back nor would he waste his time on that. So, he drove off without a care of what would happen to him. He drove around the block for ten minutes and then pulled onto the corner which was a block behind the hotel; there was a method to his madness. He made sure he was far enough for no one to see but close enough for them to see everything and it worked…

With the microphone gone, Panzer and Zeus just gave him a cold stare as they figured out what to do with him.

"Any other surprises?" Zeus asked.

The dealer shook his head no and Zeus said, "So we should kill you now, we should just beat the fuck out of you."

An eerie silence overcame them.

Panzer still had the gun to him. Zeus swept the room to make sure nothing would be left behind. They had to figure out what to do with him and neither knew where to begin.

"What do they want?"

The dealer put some words together and said, "I don't know. They just want to know; they want to see what happens who's at the other end of the line."

"What happens if we leave?" Panzer asked.

"We can't trust him anyway." Zeus said.

For a few minutes no one said a thing. Zeus knew everything was fucked. It was a thick silence one could feel and touch.

Panzer still had the gun to him, there was no longer any trust left in his bod; a firm grasp of the gun and desperately wanted to pull the trigger. As he was telling me all of this, he paused and stopped the story. I can see him now sitting on the couch in my old apartment smoking a cigarette. I listened intently when he was telling me this story. He said he had known Zeus for a long time and until that day had never seen him act like this, he said, "I had known Zeus for long time before all this. It wasn't until that day that I saw the Walter White in him come out. We all have some Walter in us, but it doesn't show. At least the good ones have some White in them. Like all good things, it passes and ends. Rainbow was at its peak. I don't think anything like that will ever happen again."

Zeus was now weighing out some options, not knowing which the best one was.

"How much do they know?" He asked the dealer who was very scared at the moment. He was silent but not only his face but his silence spoke volumes.

Zeus knew what Panzer was going to say, "They know everything." He said in fear, not really fear but a deep saddening of disappointment. He sat down on the bed with the gun between his knees. Zeus was feeling the same way and he could almost cry but showing emotion other than anger wasn't an option. With every second he grew angrier. He went from green Hulk to red Hulk in a nanosecond.

"Everything!" Zeus yelled, "Everything!" From his pocket he reveals a pair of handcuffs. Before he could do anything else he had to cause this man some physical pain so he punched him in the gut. "Everything we worked so hard for you just took it all away." He said almost quietly but with the rage of a rabid dog. The package was yours wasn't it?"

"Package?" Don asked, catching his breath still from having the wind knocked out of him.

"One of our shipments got confiscated." Panzer said.

Don Leon now knew lying would get him nowhere and had actually forgotten about that package. Once they said that, the DEA scum finding him made a lot of sense. He didn't tell them that, he wouldn't have the nerve to tell. He didn't have to say it, because they already knew. That's why Zeus handcuffed him to the radiator. For the second time in his life, this man felt how it was to be a kidnapped soul.

"I don't know what I'm going to do with you," Zeus said, "but from now on, you're my fucking hostage."

They both huddled together on the other side of the room to speak quietly. They wanted Don to hear nothing but also wanted him to worry, he could only hear them as if they were mice.

"I'm worried." Zeus said to Panzer, something he had never heard him say.

"What should we do?"

"I don't know, whatever we do we better get outta' here alive and not in cuffs."

"I say we find out whatever he knows."

"He doesn't know much, because they would have arrested us already. Which means they're just fucking with us."

Zeus went over to Don and asked, "Are they outside?"

"Yes."

"Car?"

"Unmarked black Lincoln."

"Where?"

"At the corner across the street."

"Doesn't mean they'll still be there." Zeus went over to the window, opened the curtain and looked outside. There it was, the unmarked looking as if it were looking dead at them. To his surprise they were pulling away as he was looking at it.

"We have five minutes to get him outta' here."

Franticly they packed up whatever stuff they had.

Zeus took off the cuffs from Don off the radiator but cuffed his hands. "You move, you die." He said taking the gun away from Panzer. "You'll go in the back of the car. You make any sound and I'll slit your throat and burry you next to Jimmy Hoffa."

With the gun to his back they left the hotel room, Panzer, holding the duffle bag, was trailing behind. When they got to the car, Zeus knocked out Don by a pistol whip and fell down like a flock of seagulls. Quickly, they threw him in the back of the car and were off into the sun riding nowhere.

Tillman and his Partner had seen them leave from a far, they had seen them walking down the steps of the hotel and getting into their car. Calmly, they began to follow the duo.

Zeus and Panzer were too worried to look at everything; too scared to think anything would happen to them. Their plan had changed drastically within the past two hours and now were on their way to the mansion in Pennsylvania which was the last safe place that could be thought of. Hours they had driven, the day turned to night and Tillman was still a decent way away from them but he had another trick up his sleeve, it was then that they pulled over to have a rest for the night.

"Think they know he has a tracker in his shoe?" The partner asked Tillman.

"Not a chance in hell." He said as they stared into the night.

Zeus and Panzer were full speed into their plan. Zeus drove like a mad man without a head. When they finally got to the mansion sometime in the middle of the night they still had no idea what to do with him.

He must die. Zeus thought for a second.

Don had no idea how long he was out for. He awoke in the back of their car in complete blackness. All he saw was the opening to what he thought was a garage and when he tried to get out, it triggered a noise. He was caught and they dragged him out of the car.

Panzer had come to a realization also, they could not keep this man and thought for the first time, *this man has to die.* Both Zeus and Panzer nodded to each other. An unspoken decision. He was dragged on his feet to the woods and not a single word was spoken. *This is what has to happen.*

After about five hundred yards walking, they threw Don on the floor and walked a few feet away from him.

"You're going to kill me aren't you guys?" Don asked.

"Yes." Zeus said.

"I deserve it, I guess." He said.

"Yes. You do." Panzer said.

"We're all going to die, people like us, we die every day. You guys are going to die the same way I am. Fuck you both…"

Zeus shot him in the head. It rang and echoed through the valley and was carried with the wind into the trees, dissipating into the night.

It wasn't over, this was just the beginning of the next stage.

∞

"It is the dawn of a new era." This stocky DEA agent was saying in front of a crowd of his superiors and inferiors. "The internet has brought a new wave of crime, the selling of illegal and illicit drugs. In our ongoing effort in the ridding of the streets of these said substances and the people who make and traffic it, one of our men have been able to tap into one of the online stores known in the Silk Road as the Rainbow. Agent Tillman will be leading a special unit; you men have been handpicked from your qualifications. This task force I am dubbing the IDTF, The Internet Drug Task Force. He will now inform you of everything you need to know, please welcome Agent Tillman."

Tillman walked up to the stage and shook hands with this man who had given him a hell of an introduction. After the man had left the stage, it was only then Tillman thought of what to say.

"Gentleman, a new day had risen. This will not be easy and some of us may die but most of us will live. We will break laws, though not intentionally. We need to stop the distribution of these drugs. Here is everything you need to know. I had stumbled across a website known as the Rainbow, for months I tried to get access to it, it wasn't until we caught a dealer who had been buying drugs from the site and picking them up from the post office. We arrested him and made him give us access to the website where we had set up a meeting between him and the men who run Rainbow. These men kidnapped him and killed him; we know this because we followed the signal and found the grave. We had put a tracker in the shoe of the dealer and were able to track them to a location in Pennsylvania. Having this information, we were also able to find a second location associated with these men, a penthouse in Manhattan. We will be split into two teams, Alpha and Omega. We will be joined by the local swat team who will meet us at our starting points. Alpha is my team, we will raid the mansion, but only after Omega has given us word that they have entered and secured the apartment building in the city. I want as little time between as possible, so no one on the inside can communicate with each other. I want to catch these fuckers. Once Omega has given us word, we will raid the mansion. To both teams, whoever is in there, everyone gets arrested. No one leaves there and if they do, shoot on sight. Men, be careful out there. Operation Pot of Gold will commence in two days, before dawn on Friday, before the glimmer of sun hits the land. Until then we prepare..."

The men didn't move nor say a word. They all nodded and, in their minds, they were screaming with Tillman.

Nothing lasts forever and like I said before, you can't go too long without something happening. The partnership of Zeus and Panzer was on rocky ground at this point. Neither liked how the other was acting. Panzer said it must have been all the drugs they were on and killing Don. Now that they knew a package has been confiscated and that the DEA had it. There was nothing more they can do. When a second package got confiscated, they turned on each other like dogs. They beat each other up and cursed each out for the rest of the day. When the day was over, they were both bloody and bruised, blaming each other for destroying everything they built even though nothing had happened yet. They could not be in the same room with together. It was over. They sent out an email saying to pack everything that was packable and ship everything they had in stock. They had gotten wind that the DEA was going to make a move. Panzer tried to get Zeus to try other ways, but he wasn't ready for any type of logical conversation and in a fit of rage drove to Manhattan, where he would live out his last two days in his penthouse while Panzer stayed at the mansion to rush some big orders, so if anything did happen he would have something to fall back on.

Zeus knew this was the end and knew this day was coming. Within the two days he had stockpiled weapons and ammunition at his penthouse. He loaded all of them as he smoked his cigar and looked out the window to the cold New York City early morning and by the time he saw the police lights for him it was too late to do anything. In the distance he saw the blue and red lights and knew it was for him. Loading up his guns he felt at peace and was calm. He sent out his text to Panzer and made himself a line of his own 'fuck my face' some 2c-E, Cocaine and Ketamine. He snorted that line like a champ and was fucked up, mosy likey he felt the effects in a few moments. By the time the DEA busted though his door he must been in a different galaxy.

He took out as many of them as he could. He got a few headshots and was shot in the left arm twice. He did not use most of the weapons he had, except for the handguns and the AK-47 he grabbed from under his desk. After a few minutes of bullets flying, Zeus was hit so hard that no amount of drugs could keep him fighting and went down. Zeus was dead and with him sank the Rainbow.

Meanwhile, Panzer was taking care of large orders of Lysergic Acid Diethylamide. Putting a few ounces of it into different bottles, labeling them as the ever-impressive fertilizer. He was content to where he was at the moment. He felt nothing could happen and that what he and Zeus started was at the peak and one of the safest and best things ever. He sat there doing his work. All around the mansion everyone was doing what they needed to do. Meth cooking in the basement, phenethyamines cooking elsewhere, Panzer filling the LSD, orders being boxed and labeled ready to be shipped out. There was a pep in everyone's step though, there was this looming feeling of a raid.

The mansion was supposed to be fortified. The perimeter fence surrounded the building and cameras were set up all around the property, but at the moment no one was watching the cameras and the DEA snipped the wires for all the cameras. The fuckers were waiting outside until they got the signal from Omega to go in. They were now the prey for the dreaded pigs. The fucking pigs. If it wasn't for this moment, I would have been doing nothing but still selling cannabis and the feud with my nemesis would have never escalated. How's that for some perspective?

Panzer said the air had gotten thicker. The room he was in suddenly darkened and felt as if he had just taken a bad batch of LSD. What he realized a little after was that he was getting some of it on his finger which was being absorbed into his hand and effectively into the bloodstream through his sweat. So, yes, he was tripping. When explained all this to me I actually doubted if anything at all had even happened, but I knew it happened. I remember hearing about it on the news; remember seeing the people taken out of the mansion in handcuffs. He was then calm and totally feeling the LSD. It engulfed him and enjoyed being on something he was packing up, especially when it didn't cost him any money to do. His phone recived a text message, from Zeus and all it said was: RUN.

At that moment the cops busted through the gates of the mansion and cop cars barreled into the drive way with a swarm of police officers following. They busted through the front door and for a moment Panzer had no idea what to do. He grabbed a vile of LSD, put it in his pocket and started running. First out of the room and into the hallway. There, he heard the screams and gunshot of the police. He was freaking out. Not sure if it was real or not. He ran down the hallway and into an intersection of hallways and that's when he saw the cops barreling towards him. Little did he know it was Tillman who had seen him and yelled at him to, "Stop right there!" He ran the opposite way and remembers there is a room with a couple guns in the drawers. He smacked into the door breaking it and frantically tried to find the guns, looking through every draw. He found it and quickly made sure it was loaded. He shot a couple officers and made a run for it. Every hallway he turned down he was blocked by a cop running towards him, Tillman. Finally, he broke into a room that had a couple windows facing the back of the property. He jumped out the closed window and shattered the glass. Running as fast as he could he jumped on the gate and climbed. Tillman shot at him from the window as he climbed out of it. Panzer ran to the gate and climbed up it, jumped from the top of the gate and fell, got up and started running. He said he never ran that fast before and never since. He ran into the woods where he surely thought he was either going to die or be arrested but he didn't. The morning darkness was now being broken by the rising sun. It turned out to be a really beautiful day.

Tillman's plan had worked.

Panzer said he was in the woods for a day and a night and by the middle of the next day had crossed into the State of New York. He said he was so happy to stare at the sign that says 'Welcome to the Empire State'. He knew I lived there and now his mission was to find me. He had found a new empire and I was part of it. He thought I could carry on the legacy...

Where the Grass Grows Greener

34

A Rip from the Bong

"I have to tell you something." The Bodybuilder said.

L Señor was sitting at a desk with stacks of cash around him as he was in the middle of counting one. Now he had lost count and didn't know what to think, anything could have come out of this guy's mouth, and no matter how ludicrous it would sound, it would always be true. "What?" He asked.

The Bodybuilder, or so the name that he had only been referred to as, looked at him and around the apartment. He didn't want to tell L Señor what he had done but now sort of had to. "I had relations with someone's sister."

L Señor was taken aback by what he said. He already knew there was more to the story. "If they have siblings, they're all sisters. Do I want to know *whose* sister?"

"Someone not good to have done it to."

"So, were these relations forced? If that wasn't the case, you wouldn't be this nervous."

The Bodybuilder was sweating and wiped his head with his hand, took a breath and said, "I was on all the HGH and GHB. I was horny, really horny, met this woman and I slipped a little GHB in her drink. She was all over me and one thing led to another she was touching me; I was touching her. Went to her apartment and all of a sudden, she says something wasn't right and kind of started to fall asleep so I just fucked her... I couldn't control myself."

L Señor was ready to kill him. He even started to think how he would get rid of the body. He leans back and put his head in his hands, "Dude, I don't want to hear you speak again for a very long time." He got so upset that he got up and screamed at the top of his lungs, "*his* sister"! He punched the wall, which was made of concrete; his hand was not broken and covered with blood. "You fucked us. They're going to kill you; they're going to kill me… You're a stupid motherfucker… Do you understand what happens when you do things? You're just sitting there and you came and now what happened because of that."

The Bodybuilder was silent and rightfully so. There's not much you can say to that after a friend of yours for more than four years suddenly yells at you for something you did like one of your parents. There was nothing he could say to make the situation better, instead he wanted to try an overused apology, "I'm sorry dude, I fucked up."

L Señor took a deep breath and with a look of disgust as he gazed over to the now upset Bodybuilder, "Grasp the situation like your dick and familiarize yourself with the plot of the story!"

The Bodybuilder had nothing to say.

"I don't get it. When we got out here, you promised me it wouldn't be like it was in New York. We left everything. We didn't just leave the business there; we left our lives. You fucked me and you're fucking me, again." He sits and applies pressure to his hand, catching his breath. Still quietly raging on the inside.

There is a tension in the air, but each interprets it differently.

They're going to kill me. These are my last hours. L Señor thought to himself.

The Bodybuilder hadn't moved but needed to speak. Some weird mental insurance, or assurance of his own thoughts. "*He's* going to kill me."

"Yeah, and I'm not protecting you this time. I'm looking out only for myself and the guys. I'll feed you to them if I have to."

For a moment neither said a thing and the only sound to be heard was that of breathing.

"You need help," L Señor said, leaning back into the chair, "all those drugs… You fucked up your brain." He got up and stood, "I'm not protecting you. I'll be by your side in this, but I'm not with you. Not like Pablo ever helped anything."

The Bodybuilder was filled with regret. He admitted to himself that he was a drug addict. He now knew he had fucked up everything. *L Señor is going to die because of me. He shouldn't.* "Pablo is gonna' come after me. You guys shouldn't die because of my actions. Leave, don't stay around me."

L Señor was very mad because he still thought of this man as a friend and as a friend he would be there to fight. Inside his heart he knew that was a terrible decision, but, his mind told him that this is a friend and that's what a real friend does. He questions what a good *friend* is. "No, I'm staying." He says in an unsure tone.

The Bodybuilder knew that in order for him to leave he had to say something really hurtful and outrages to L Señor. The words he needed weren't in his everyday vocabulary and had to search deep down for them. He could feel himself mustering up the courage that was slowly building inside him. He stood in front of L Señor and said, "I hate you. You yell at me, but you followed me out here. I didn't force a gun to you; you pulled a knife. You thought you were always better than me. Maybe you are, but you shouldn't say it. You're not a real friend to me, you never were."

That's all he needed to hear.

L Señor was stunned, not sure if what he had said was true. For a moment he didn't know what to do. He took a breath and opened his mouth to say something but there was nothing that could be said. He turned around, walked to the door, opened it and slammed the door shut behind him as he furiously left the apartment. He knew and let him believe.

The Bodybuilder was fixed in his position for a minute. Slowly he was breathing in silence, he wasn't at peace with what he had just done. He had to leave something to let him know why he did what he did. The Bodybuilder wrote a letter to L Señor that was three pages in length. He put a lot of thought into what he wrote and wished he could talk to L Señor about it after.

He would be dead a few hours later and L Señor would never get this letter because when they killed him, blood splattered all over the table. Then the police took it as evidence and that's where it sat for the remainder of its years, maybe even still today.

∞

I can't believe they really killed him.
Didn't think they'd really do it.

L Señor thought this to himself repeatedly as he contemplated his revenge for him. Deep down inside he knew that what he said to him was not the truth and had only realized it after that the Bodybuilder was really protecting him. Sometimes it's only after someone dies do you really appreciate them more.

L Señor, who had half a bottle of Knob Creek inside him, calmly and aggressively walked to the front door of a house with his flunkies not far behind him. His flunkies were crouched down and their shadows from the sun followed them all the way up the path to the door. There was good reason and somewhat good intentions for what he was going to do. It would change everything… He stood there for a moment and signaled to his flunkies to pause where they were. Like the blind mice they were, they stopped dead in their tracks. He was soaking everything in, it was a warm day, looked around at the blue sky and breathed in the fresh air. The right moment had to overcome him to bust down the door, I do have to give him credit, it was his first time. It's not every day you bust open someone's door and kill them.

I guess this takes some practice.

With a gust of sudden energy, he took his foot and with all his might and strength he kicked open the door and it flew open. Another thing that flew was the body of a live man that had been sitting in his chair and when the door busted open his natural reflexes were to get up and run out of the room; but he did not run, instead, when he got up he had to turn around and look at who was doing this. He saw L Señor and his flunkies; no sense in running, he's going to get you anyway.

L Señor took the gun that was strapped in the holster on his chest and pointed it at the man whom he had known for a good amount of time. He no longer saw this man as an equal nor did he give any slack even if he had known him for a while. Firmly, he held the gun to the face of this man and the man thought of things to say. He took a breath of air and yelled, "What the fuck! What do you want?"

L Señor didn't want to speak, so they stared at each other and the man again asked him, "What the fuck do you want?"

"I know you know why I'm here, I just want to know, and you already know what I want to know." L Señor said adjusting the grip of his gun.

The man knew there was nothing he could do nor say to L Señor to make him leave, the most he could do was tell him the truth, the truth was the only way of being able to live past this moment.

"L Señor," he said, "you had to have known this was going to happen." That made L Señor think and lowered the gun. The flunkies made a circle around the man. He continued, "You guys came out here from New York and you thought you were the shit. The Bodybuilder was an asshole and he did really bad things, it all caught up with him in the end. I don't know why you're now so upset about it all, especially after what he did to you and everything I've heard about him. You're in the clear, no one's after you, why are you making these problems for yourself?"

"Don't make me reflect on what happened, the point is that it happened and people have to pay for it. My business partner is dead..."

"So, what dude!" The man yelled.

L Señor took a deep breath, looking at one of his flunkies, Rico. He turned back to the man and hit him in the head with the gun. The man fell to the floor screaming, "You're a crazy motherfucker! What the fuck is wrong with you?"

L Señor took the man's head and grabbed him by the hair and asked, "How long did you know?"

The man was silent.

"How long did you know? How much other stuff did you know?"

The man knew it was the end of the line, "months."

"You knew for months didn't say a word?"

"I said nothing to anybody. I was worried. Could you imagine if I told the Bodybuilder that 'oh hey, *he's* going to kill you. Just a heads up.' He would have killed me just for that. You would have killed me too." L Señor didn't show it, but he agreed with what he said.

"Well I'm going to kill you now, so good job on prolonging your life a couple months, what was it all for?"

"You know me... Do you think I wanted any of this to happen? Do you think him raping Pablo's sister did that much, I mean he was really *really* mad about that, but, I knew this all before that. He stole the money from him; he stole the cars that day. You guys both killed those two guys that night in the desert. What you should be doing now is getting the fuck out of town because no one wants you here."

"We trusted you. You should have warned us." L Señor said cocking the revolver and pointing it to the man's head.

"Are you on drugs like he was? Are you ok in the head? Go ahead and kill me. Think about this, you came here for answers but you already know the answers to who killed him, you know it was Pablo, so why did you come here? Go back to where you once belonged. You knew what he did didn't do a thing about it either and let it happen…"

L Señor cut him off mid-sentence and said, "Stand up."

The man stood up and L Señor shot him in the foot and fell to the floor in pain, screaming. L Señor looked around for the keys to the man's car and when he found them on the table, threw them at him and said, "Don't tell me where I belong. Now drive yourself to the hospital."

L Señor and the flunkies quietly and calmly walked out of the man's house, got into their truck and drove into the sunset.

They were all silent in the truck as L Señor drove. It was so quiet that L Señor could count how long he was breathing and how many times he breathed in a minute. The four flunkies, as I liked to call them, were four of the closest things L Señor had to real friends. They weren't really his friends, nor were they his enemies. Everything had balanced out for them and they were being paid very well by L Señor up until this day. By now the four of them were having their own doubts about continuing with L Señor and was up in the air what was going to happen to them.

L Señor took out a cigarette and opened the window as he puffed on it.

"Rico." L Señor said.

"Yeah boss." Rico answered from behind the driver's seat.

"Should Pablo get a visit from us?"

"No."

For a moment L Señor couldn't think of anything to say.

"That's a pretty strong *No*."

"Whatever you're thinking," Rico said, "please don't think about it any longer. The Bodybuilder deserved everything. You know it. I know it. If no one is after us, why should we go find them?"

"I've accepted all of this; I don't want to go for revenge. I don't want to go back to New York, that place seems black and white to me now. Maybe we can work for him? Not like we…" L Señor stopped himself and in his mind, he rephrased everything. "I've never done him wrong and I am the connection."

"Why don't you want to go back to New York?" Rico asked.

"I just don't, life is out here now."

40

Rico thought about it and said, "Maybe we should see Pablo boss." If Rico had said no, L Señor would had changed his mind and went back to New York but since he said no, they would stick to his plan. What the flunkies didn't know was that his plan was to get him as a friend and then to kill him at the peak of his trust, though this is not what happened.

Pablo was the drug lord that was run out of Mexico by his own people. The Bodybuilder and L Señor had made many deals with him that kept them all in business and had given them 'permission' to stay in California. He was also the man that could sent them away and of course the Bodybuilder had done him dirty. As L Señor was thinking about all of this, finally understood why he killed the Bodybuilder. He accepted it now, though I have no idea why he cared so much for him. That's something even I don't know about. There's something missing from the stories he told me.

They drove out of Los Angeles for about three hours and around dusk had arrived at the compound that Pablo called 'Fort Mercer'. Out of the shadows of the desert they saw in the distance a huge fortified wall with two gunmen on the sides with automatic weapons looking at them as they slowly approached the gate.

Pablo was watching them come closer from his office in the building; he knew they were coming, but L Señor thought he was going to surprise him. It's amazing that everyone always thinks thy have advantages over people.

They pulled up to the gate.

L Señor lowered his window and extended his arm to press the bell.

"State your business." A voice said from the speaker.

"L Señor for Pablo." He said in a confident voice.

Silence.

"Pablo does not want to meet with you."

"Tell him L Señor does not miss the Bodybuilder and that I would like to continue in our business partnership."

The gate in front of the car opened and slowly L Señor drove into the compound. The five of them were nervous as they entered because they were greeted into the courtyard with the two men with assault rifles that were watching them from the roof.

They were in the belly of the beast.

They got out of the car, the flunkies following behind L Señor as he took charge and stood in front of them.

Pablo came out from the house within the compound. As he walked to them L Señor contemplated what he was going to say, or what he was going to do.

"L Señor, I thought taking care of the Bodybuilder would send you away."

"Why should I go away? My life and money is here."

"Sure, your life is here." Pablo said. After a moment of silence, he followed up with the question, "What the fuck do you want?"

"My team and I are now guns for hire. We've been doing dirty work for a couple years, so why stop now?"

"You," Pablo said pointing at him, "want to work for me?"

"Yeah."

"Go back to the Yankees."

"We could keep the money flowing."

"You think I need your shitty money? Look around you, this is all mine and I need your extra money? Sounds more like you need the money. I spent two hundred thousand dollars making sure no one heard from the Bodybuilder and I need your help?" Pablo said as he turned away, but he stopped, he had something extra to say, so he yelled this at the top of his lungs, "You and the Bodybuilder are a disease!"

L Señor was silent.

He continued, "You two came out here and thought you were god's gift to us. He had promised me what you promised me and after all that you both had done You have the balls to come here and ask me for a job? Did you forget what you did?"

"I didn't do anything and you know that."

"You are guilty by association and what he did to me I hold you accounted for as well. Now leave before I kill you."

"I apologize for what he did to you, now that's he's gone our partnership should start over."

"He raped my sister and impregnated her. Then proceeded to call her a whore and went around town saying that." Pablo was now very upset and angry. He pulled out a handgun from his back and pointed it to L Señor. "I was going to be a big man and let you live. I wasn't going to do anything to you because I know it wasn't you. But you keep beating a dead horse!"

L Señor had dug his grave and now he had to lie in it. He knew what Pablo was going to say next. "I was going to let you stay here… Pack your shit and leave. I'm putting out an order to my men; they see you or any of your bodyguard fuckers and they'll kill you on sight and bring your head back to me on a platter. You have twenty-four hours, after that, I find you and kill you myself." Pablo lifted his gun to the air and let off three shots. "You motherfuckers should leave now."

L Señor stood there for a moment while his flunkies got in the car. Pablo was still in his stance with the gun held up in the air and the two of them were having a staring contest. L Señor was angry; his plan had not gone how he wanted it to. He knew that Pablo wasn't kidding and that he should have listened to Rico. L Señor accepted his defeat and made his way back to the driver's seat of the car, as he opened the door Pablo touched his shoulder and said, "I'm sending you home because you don't belong here. We're still good and I want you to keep the business flowing. Honestly, I can't see you because when I see you it makes me think of *him*."

L Señor got in the car and Pablo said to him, "The two we dealt with have been having problems, make sure everything is good with them and keep 'em in check."

L Señor nodded and backed up the car. They were off to their domical to pack some of their things and before they knew it, they were off on their road trip back to New York. L Señor's plan had worked and over and over again he thought, *nothing changes, keep the business running*.

They had made their way back to New York where they went to the old self storage place that was owned by the Bodybuilder, the place where they'd stay whenever they had to come back for pickups. You could spot this building right off of the Bruckner Expressway just before you get to the FDR and Willis Ave Bridge. After unloading the truck, they found themselves sitting around in the warehouse; this property now belonged to L Señor. They were now at the bottom and needed to do something to make their livings, even though they really weren't living. The group was exhausted considering they had driven from California. None of them were in any clear state to be thinking and were all thinking about themselves. For the moment they weren't a whole, just in the hole together and not as one.

L Señor was thinking about many things, mainly he was thinking about why he had left New York in the first place. He and the Bodybuilder were getting by, selling drugs like low level drug dealers, he did not want to be like that again but it seemed that he had no choice. Inside he was angry, inside he was screaming at himself, inside he was thinking of why they had to leave the city in the first place. What he was really mad about was how Pablo had made him feel like a pussy. He was mad that he didn't hurt him and that he let him talk to him like that. Deep down he felt he was scared but the other part of him grew up and from that day on the man that I knew as L Señor was born. He would never let anyone do that to him again; no one would ever make him do anything he didn't want to do. Never again.

Rico was sitting on a chair in the corner with his head in his hands. This was the good flunky, he had a conscience, something was eating him up inside. All of this bothered him and he didn't know how much longer he could go on with this charade he was putting on. He wasn't who he presented himself to be. He was good. He was bringing up the courage within himself to say to L Señor that he had had enough of this. He wanted out, but this was his only income, this was what he was already used to doing, there was nothing else. This was the life he was having.

"What now boss?" Carlos, the third flunky, said.

"*He* said keep the business running. Over here nothing changes, we know what to do, we keep the supply coming and going, collect the money and do the deeds, the same way we always did." L Señor said.

"So, we work for Pablo now?" Rico asked.

"We always worked for Pablo, come to think of it, the Bodybuilder didn't do a damn thing."

Rico took a deep breath and said, "I think we should lay low for a couple of days, we went through a lot, we need time away from all this."

L Señor got up and said to them, "I'm going away for a couple days. Come back here in a couple days, I have to think. I need time alone. Settle in, find places to stay, if you can't this place will always be here." He walked out of the warehouse and one by one the flunkies left.

Rico had enough of this shit.

Rico was still sitting there, now his head was up and he was upright in the chair just staring into the empty space of the warehouse.

After a couple minutes he said to himself, *so this is what my life is now. This is what I made it. It is what it is.* He got up and left the place, had no intention of returning to it. He was sorry but it was time to move away, though inside his heart he really wanted to stay.

∞

L Señor and the remaining three flunkies met again two days later at the self-storage warehouse. Rico was noticeably absent. L Señor had known for a while that Rico wanted to leave this life behind and was disappointed and angered by his decision to not come back. There was a feeling of lose and sense of having to move on.

Rico is not coming back. He thought to himself.

Carlos, one of the other flunkies, asked the question L Señor did not want to hear, "Do you think Rico is coming?"

L Señor knew the answer but did not really know how to answer and admit it. Unfortunately, whenever he was in the presence of a flunky his ego would get fatter and would portray himself to be the boss. He was honest with them and they with him. If he had lied to them and said that Rico would come back, they would know he was lying and the trust would go out of the window.

Carlos was now thinking more than ever about his role in all of this. The three blind mice were now opening their minds to the true nature of L Señor.

L Señor knew this.

He said to Carlos, "I want to say yes, but I think not... If you guys want to leave it's ok. Even I don't want any of this anymore."

This is why we should end it. He thought.

For a moment there was silence but the third flunky spoke, "What else is there for us? Well for me? I know nothing but what we have been doing. With everything we have gone though, I see no reason to leave it all behind now. It is what it is..." This flunkeys' name was Jose, a fat Hispanic man whose physical appearance was like that of Marlin Brando crossed with Big Pun.

Neither of the latter two were ranked as high in the mind of L Señor as the fourth and final flunky. This was only because Rico was not there, of course; who otherwise would have been number two.

Miguel sat in the back and for the most part didn't say a word, nothing that could have been added to the conversation.

L Señor was going through a lot of emotions and was going to let his own guard down which was something he had never done before. Instead of telling them what the plan would be and what they are going to do, he opened up a discussion about it. This was because he himself had no idea what to do. "What should we do about Pablo?" He asked.

There was an awkward silence. No one quite knew what to say.

"Okay." L Señor said, "Do we continue in our business with him?"

Miguel came out of his coma, fearing that maybe he had died because he heard L Señor ask for someone's opinion. Something that has never been done before. He had to speak, "if we're voting on it, I vote no."

"No." Jose said.

"No." Carlos said.

"We've already been at the bottom and made our way halfway up to the surface, now we're at the bottom again, but we could be at the top breathing in the fresh air." Miguel said.

"Seems that my vote doesn't matter anyway," L Señor said, "breaking away from Pablo isn't going to be as easy as 'oh hey Pablo, we're not doing this anymore'. We're going to have to have to take him out. We have to kill him."

"Go back to Cali'? Nah, I'm good." Jose said.

"We'll just have to make him come here." L Señor said.

Carlos was now visibly worried. "How do we just get him to come here?"

"Have any ideas?" Jose asked.

L Señor took a breath and said, "Stop sending the money. We'll kill *the middlemen*, and after a couple of weeks without getting any money, Pablo will waste no time coming here."

"He'll kill us." Carlos said.

"Not if we make it look like we didn't do it." Miguel said.

For a moment L Señor thought and finally asked...

"Miguel, do you remember where *those two* lived?"

Miguel, who had his head buried in his hands, raised his head and asked, "The ones we had to straighten out that time?"

"Yeah."

"Of course, I do."

The two they were referring two were the two men whose main purpose in life was to send the money from New York to Pablo. They had messed up once before and L Señor had done something that shall not be spoken about especially by someone who was there. Anyway, these two were going about their lives; one was in the middle of eating a tuna sandwich on white bread when there was a knock at the door. He got up and without any care walked to the door, it opened to reveal L Señor and the remaining three flunkies.

His heart dropped.

"L Señor… Pretty sure we sent out the last payment." He said.

The other one had heard this, dropped his magazine and got up from the couch, not before grabbing a gun and putting it in his pants. He thought he was slick but in fact, they had seen him take the gun.

L Señor held up his hands, spread them out and said, "All I did was come here to talk some new business. Can we come in?"

From inside the room the other one said, "Only you."

"One other, Miguel, comes in with me. You can drop the gun to; I have more ammo then both of you combined."

The other one took out the gun and dropped it on the floor. L Señor and Miguel walked into the room; L Señor took the gun from the floor as Miguel was pointing his own to them.

"So, you didn't just come here to talk, did you?" The first one asked.

L Señor took the chair where he was eating his sandwich, turned it around and sat on it. He thought about his next words. "I did come here to talk."

"About what?" The other asked.

"Well I came to talk… You," He said pointing at the first one, "are going to shoot him. Then you're going to kill yourself."

Neither knew what to say.

"Why?" The first one asked.

"Either you do it or we do it and still make it look like how we wanted."

"What did we do?"

"Nothing… It's what your job is that killed you. We're going to kill Pablo; the only way to get him here is to stop sending him money. How do we stop sending him money? We kill you two, who supply the money to him and he'll come here and I'll kill him off."

"I don't want to die." The other said.

"It's not about wanting. I want this shit over but I have to do things to do it."

"You want him that bad," the first one said, "I'll get him here, I can get him to come here."

"There's no negotiation."

"You want him, I get him..."

"You have a minute to tell me how."

The man could feel his heart beat faster and faster. To him it wouldn't matter, he was dead either way. There was nothing he could think of.

"You've wasted ten seconds..."

"I could tell him there's a problem with the buyer. He would come here for that."

"Won't be enough, trust me."

At that moment L Señor had a great idea, *he could tell him there was a problem with the buyer. Then we could kill these two; then Pablo would come here. Complaining about the buyers, and then your funds turn up dead.* "You're going to have to kill him."

The other one was shaking as he was standing and started crying, tears running down his face as he began to plead, "No, I don't want to die. We didn't do anything!"

L Señor pointed to their phone, looked at them and said "Call Pablo and tell him about the problem."

He was hesitant to pick up the phone. Having L Señor and his flunkies there made the decision easier and thought if he did it, they would leave them alone. He walked over to the phone, picked it up and dialed the number. For the moments of him dialing and waiting for the ringing to stop no one said a word. He looked at L Señors' eyes and when one of his men answered the phone all the man could say to him was, "I need to speak to Pablo please." He said physically shaking, "Tell him it's an emergency... Pablo... There's a problem with the money this week... The buyer is a problem... No... No... I understand... Okay..." That's when he hung up the phone.

L Señor took out the gun from his back and handed it to the man.

"But... we don't need that anymore... I got him coming here..." The man said.

"I never said this wasn't going to happen. You assumed it wasn't and now it still is."

"That is not what you wanted?"

"Either you die by your friends' hands or by mine, make peace with yourselves because either way you're dead in five minutes." L Señor stamped his foot on the ground and the other two flunkies came in and surrounded them. The three flunkies had their weapons pointed to the two. "I was told to kill you guys the first time. I got in a lot of shit because I didn't and you know what? Not killing you wasn't worth it. It's time to bring order to the universe and do what should have been done that last time. It's not my fault that didn't change your life around and you haven't done anything but sit here and act like tuff drug dealers when you're only the shit stains of a real operation." L Señor got up and handed the gun to the first one and said, "Three men have their weapons at your head, if this gun goes anywhere other than pointing at that man's head," he said pointing to the other one, still standing and shaking and still crying, "your dead before you can fire a shot… Make your peace with each other and do it."

"Don't take the gun." The other one said.

L Señor gave him the gun forcefully putting it in his hand. "Don't act like this wasn't what was going to happen. You both knew what you did and I know what I did." L Señor walked away.

The first one pointed the gun at his friend, "I don't want to kill him…" His friend was shaking even more now screaming and begging him not to kill him. The first one shot him in the head and the screaming was over. Within a millisecond he realized what he had done and immediately put the gun into his own mouth and pulled the trigger.

L Señor and the three flunkies knew it was done and they all calmly left the apartment. They left and shut the door and with two dead men in the apartment the plan can now begin.

L Señor was leaning against a building in the early morning hours of the day dressed in a black hoodie with black pants and stared at the pay phone, most defiantly looked like a mad man. He was waiting to make a phone call, more like waiting for the phone to ring. Pablo had sent him a message to contact him. Not a message you can read, Pablo had sent L Señor a gift of two men who beat him up and told him Pablo would call him and when. There he stood in the blue morning darkness, cold and nervous. For at least twenty minutes he stood in the cool breeze waiting for the phone to ring.

You never pick it up on the first two.

Let him wait.

Not the third time either.

At the fourth ring L Señor aggressively went to the phone and answered it, "What do you want?"

"Is that any way to talk to your friend?" Pablo asked.

"That's cool that you thought I was your friend."

"Yeah, you're right; you're not my friend... I know I don't have to ask you what's going on because I know you know what's going on."

"It's not like Cali'. It's tough here. *Those two* were in their own problems, we found them like that."

L Señor was then drawn away from the conversation by the dawn of the sun as he watched the street brighten up and for a second, he wasn't listening to what Pablo was saying. L Señor wished everything to be as it did before all of this. Nothing could be taken back. His own silence was drowned away by Pablo saying, "I know this was you, it has your name written all over."

L Señor didn't want to believe that it had not worked.

"Pablo, I did not do a damn thing. You sent me here to make sure the money flows. I'm going to make sure it flows again."

"We'll see." Pablo said as he hung up the receiver on his side.

L Señor was still holding the phone to his ear when Pablo hung up. He was frozen in his pose; it had happened so fast and not really the way he wanted it to. He put the phone back on the receiver and he knew he had done it.

So, it begins.

L Señor thought this because he thought Pablo would not have anything to do to them; let alone find them.

L Señor has never been more wrong.

Pablo was now being driven across the country with his posse. They drove across the desert and watched as the sun rise in the east and set behind them in the west. He was making the mistake of not understanding history because he was repeating it. In his mind, he had planned everything out, made his contacts and was being protected by the people he knew and the people he chose to surround himself with.

He was now going into uncharted territory and New York is a whole lot different than the west. He was coming to the city not knowing the city, if you are not used to it, the city will take everything from you and destroy you.

The advantage goes to L Señor.

It is true, New York City can kill you, it can bring you down if you're not strong enough.

L Señor and his flunkies were busy. The three remaining flunkies were collecting the rest of the money so they could send it to Pablo. This was part of the plan. Tell Pablo there's a problem, show the problem and here comes L Señor to save the day. The flunkies were moving boxes containing the shipment of the drugs they were selling into the vehicle of the buyer, who was giving L Señor the briefcase of the money. With the money in his hand L Señor got a little too full of himself, *now I'm in control*. They buyer shook his hand and asked, "Same time next week?"

"Of course." L Señor said.

"Whatever happened to the other two that would make the drop?" The buyer asked.

L Señor did not want to say anything but he had to, "They wanted out. So, I let them go."

"Oh," the buyer said, "they had been saying for a while that they didn't want to be part of this anymore. It is getting dangerous. I heard about a DEA agent by the name of Tillman, he's the plague and wants to bring what we're doing to an end. They had heard that to."

"What do you think of that?" L Señor asked.

"Many rumors over the years I've heard, but nothing ever seems to happen. It's all paranoid talk, drug addicts telling me so I really don't listen to it all. Time is better spent doing other things or making money." The buyer had something else on his mind, "Any chance of getting marijuana? All the dealers of that here aren't around anymore." The buyer asked.

L Señor was very mad that he asked him that. Was he not happy with what he is getting now? Instead of flipping out, L Señor thought about it and didn't want to shut the door on that completely. He felt that selling or getting cannabis was below him and that that's only for low level drug dealers which he no longer considered himself.

"I'll look into it." L Señor said, it could be something more he could make money on without Pablo knowing or getting involved.

Suddenly, he had the thought that cannabis could be a real option of making money in New York.

The buyer walked to the driver's side of his truck. When the flunkies were done, put it the door of the truck he waved to them, got in the car and drive away.

"Do you think this is going to work?" Miguel asked.

L Señor was still not going to lie to them, "I hope so."

The flunkies got into the truck while L Señor watched the buyer drive into the distance and out of sight. For a minute, he thought about getting in the truck and following him to take back the products so they could have both. He felt his keys in his pocket and thought to himself; *no, that was me once. I wouldn't want anyone to do that to me. He doesn't deserve that.*

L Señor and his flunkies were sitting around in the warehouse unaware that Pablo was on his way there, they all kind of knew he was coming but no idea when or for sure. That's when there was a knock on the door of what they thought was their hiding place. The knocks echoed through the empty warehouse and like statues they were fixed to their chairs and positions. The four of them were silent as if they didn't want to move to make any noise or give any sign that anyone was there. The sound of a gate opening was a clear indication of hazardous weather ahead.

L Señor and the flunkies stood on their feet.

In walked Pablo.

Everything they were thinking flew out of the window.

"So, this is where you boys reside. No one was going to answer the door?" He said with his posse of two armed guards beside him. This is when L Señor knew he was in deep shit.

"What are you doing here?" L Señor asked.

"Protecting my business."

"Why? Are we not good enough to do this on our own?"

"I've decided that the west was boring for me, I needed some new scenery. I knew my friends would be here."

No one in the room was a friend.

"We're still not friends." L Señor said.

Pablo laughed, "You're funny. It seems that you guys need baby sitters."

"Fuck you Pablo... We don't need you watching us." Miguel said.

"L Señor you should keep your mutt on a short leash."

"My men can say and do whatever they want."

"Don't forget you all work for me!" Pablo screamed at the top of his lungs taking out a bowie knife from his belt and waving it around. "I'll kill all of you and not even care. Things will be different now. You fuckers thought you could come to my side and do what you did; now I shall control your side. I know you guys are responsible for the two."

"Is this how you treat friends?" L Señor asked.

"Are you deflecting from the two?" Pablo said.

"No sir..." L Señor said.

"No sir? Do you think this is a fucking game?" Pablo yelled as he put the knife to L Señor's' throat. "You and that mother fucker always thought everything was a game! I'd slice your throat open and pop out your eyes! You guys fuck up anything and I'll kill you all before the day's over...God as my witness I will kill you. Your jobs are to be here every morning and do as I say... The five of you are now my dirty workers. Be here in the morning..." With that said, the knife found its way back into the belt holster and Pablo and his posse left, not before one of his men destroyed the wooden table they had.

It was in the silence between after the door had shut that Miguel said, "We should have killed him right there."

"No," L Señor said, "We got him where we want him. He's not gonna' die easy, were gonna' jerk him off a lil bit and then take him out..."

"You see the guns they had? Our handguns wouldn't do anything to those shotguns and assault rifles." Jose said.

"Let's get here before he gets here tomorrow." L Señor said. "Miguel," he continued, "take the guys and stock up on some protection. I don't know how any of this is going to go."

∞

L Señor found himself being driven by Pablo outside the city somewhere between Buffalo and Kingston. He was very nervous, for the past month L Señor and his flunkies have gone through a lot. Pablo has used them for everything big and small; used them to send a message to someone, meaning that they either killed or almost killed someone just to prove a point. They found themselves robbing people because that's what Pablo wanted and they all finally couldn't take it anymore. The flunkies had reached their boiling point and had been pressuring L Señor to take him out sooner.

Pablo was getting too comfortable. Instead of being a boss, he become a dictator.

This piece of shit is too comfortable here.

That's all L Señor thought as he was in the passenger seat being driven by him. He was not really sure where they were going or why they were; he made sure there was an easy way to grab his gun and, in his mind, kept picturing havening to grab it from the holster on his hip. L Señor had the feeling of death, seriously thinking Pablo was going to kill him upstate and burry him.

There was a house in the distance. L Señor was now even more worried by the sight of it. The house was getting closer and closer. What he didn't know was that Pablo himself was nervous too, although he did notice his mannerisms change. They drove out of a clearing to a road that stretched to the front of the home. Looking around the area made L Señor scared, a house in the middle of nowhere surrounded by nothing but forests.

When they go to the front of the house Pablo said to L Señor, "Stay here, I don't know how long I'll be." L Señor stayed and Pablo got out and knocked on the door of the home, after a couple of minutes was let in. L Señor was worried so he drew his weapon and kept it down and out of sight. The wait for him to return felt like hours. He felt that he was going to be killed and wondered if it would be a good time to kill Pablo but he didn't know who was in the house and why they were there. Something was very off. It made no sense,

A half hour later Pablo exited the home and got into the car with a briefcase which L Señor saw. He was intrigued so he holstered his gun.

"L Señor this is our vacation money."

Vacation money?

"I've already taken mine, go on vacation for a week or two. I'll be spending time with my new girlfriend." Pablo said.

"Don't talk to me like were friends." L Señor said.

"If I really wanted you dead and didn't like you, you should know that people like that don't last and you would've been dead already. Now shut the fuck up about this whole friend thing. You've been very angry lately, maybe you need this time off."

"Whatever you say, sir."

"Get out and walk back now."

He certainly did not need to be told that twice.

L Señor got out of the car. Pablo backed up, turned around and drove away.

I'll get you, you motherfucker.

L Señor stood there and watched him as he drove away. After he was out of his view, took out his phone and called Miguel, "The son of a bitch left me here."

That's when L Señor heard the click of a gun and realized someone was holding one to his head…

As he was watching Pablo drive away men came out of the trees and stormed the car, taking Pablo out and beat the shit out of him. L Señor slowly dropped to the ground. The man pistol whipped him and L Señor was out like a light.

Miguel had heard something but he had no idea what it was nor where L Señor was.

L Señor woke up tied to a chair. He was freezing and couldn't help but shiver. His hands were tied behind his back and each foot to a leg of the chair. Whoever put him there did not want him to get out. Looking to his right, an empty chair with cut rope around it, like someone took someone out of it. Everything was hazy to him; also had a vague idea why he was here and what was actually going on. He started to yell but the sound of him yelling was muffled by the cloth that was around his head and in his mouth. He was getting claustrophobic and had to urge to get out of the rope. Franticly, he started moving but soon realized that he couldn't get out of the rope. It was too tight and without independent movement of his legs he really could not do much. What really scared him the most was not knowing how long he had been there or what was done to him.

He was hearing a lot of footsteps from outside the door of the room; also, a lot of commotion. *Whatever is out there should stay out there, don't come inside.* He heard yelling and a gunshot followed by a big thud. Someone had just died.

The door opened and a man came in.

The man stared at him.

L Señor was squirming a lot, trying to get out, and was also yelling through the cloth. Shutting the door behind him, the man squatted down in front of L Señor and took out the cloth from his mouth.

"Where am I?" L Señor asked.

"Where is it?" The man asked.

"Where's what?"

The man slapped L Señor. "Where is it?"

L Señor yelled, "Where the fuck is what?"

"Pablo took the money and where is it?"

Of course, Pablo took that money, vacation money my ass.

"The briefcase?"

"Yes."

"Last I saw it; it was in the car with us."

"Where is it now?"

"I don't know. He kicked me out of the car before he drove off."

The man was very angry now. He wiped his face with his hand and looked at L Señor in his eyes. "You don't know where it is?"

"No."

"We searched the car… It wasn't in there."

"I don't know where else it could be. It was in the car, he kicked me out and I watched him drive away…"

The man had made a decision already, "Pablo just killed one of my men and he escaped with the briefcase. Fucking bastard."

"So, it's Pablo you want, just let me go?"

"You have ID on you?"

L Señor hesitated to answer.

"Do you have ID on you?"

"Yeah in my wallet, in my pocket."

The man felt around his pockets and took out his wallet and the ID. "I know who you are now and where you live, or where you lived by the looks of it. I have your name and I'll find you."

"Find me, about what?"

"You're going to kill Pablo and bring his body back to me, with or without the cash."

"You want me to kill Pablo?"

"You have to."

"Bring his body back here?"

"Yes."

"It wouldn't help if I said I wanted him dead to and that I was only with him to kill him."

"No, because I don't believe you." He untied L Señor and told him, "Don't fuck me, because I won't hesitate to kill you."

"I'm not lying; I want to kill him for myself."

"Then why were you with him?"

"To keep him closer…"

The man took out the bowie knife the Pablo had from his pocket and showed it to L Señor. "His body is to be brought here… If I don't get it within the week, I'll come for you, your family; and your friends, and those Spanish guys you keep as your bodyguards."

L Señor sat in the warehouse with the three remaining flunkies. This time L Señor was the one with his head buried in his hands. The silence was getting annoying and became too much to bear.

Miguel was tired of not talking, he thought someone needed to say something, "How are we supposed to find him if we don't know where he is?"

L Señor did not answer.

"How do we find him?" Miguel asked.

Jose and Carlos were sitting next to each other just staring at L Señor. No one knew it, but those two made an agreement with each other that after the killing of Pablo they would disband from the group.

L Señor should have had an answer by now.

"L Señor… We need some words from you. You can't be silent, were going to die." Miguel said.

"Then leave." L Señor said still buried in his hands.

Miguel stood up and said, "I'll leave after we kill Pablo."

"Us too." Carlos said.

L Señor lifted his head and leaned back into the chair. "After we do this, you guys are leaving?"

"Yes," Miguel said, "we can't go on like this. There's nothing left for us and I refuse to go back to being a stupid drug dealer."

"It's over." Jose said.

"We've gone through too much shit… What we've seen, no one should see." Carlos said.

"I don't know where he is." L Señor said, "I haven't heard from him since being thrown out of his car yesterday."

"So, the question is how do we find him?" Miguel asked.

"The real question is how do we rob him of all his money and then kill him?"

The three flunkies were confused by that.

Carlos opened his mouth and asked, "Were going to rob him?"

"We find him, make him give us his money and then I kill him." L Señor said.

The flunkies were silent.

"This isn't over yet. You guys should know the deal by now."

Miguel was weary of this, "How much money does he actually have that you want to rob him?"

"I know many things about Pablo you guys don't. He's a multi-millionaire."

"I don't believe you."

"Why don't you believe me?"

"Why does he live like shit if he's a millionaire? Why does he pay us in shit if he's a millionaire?"

"He doesn't want anyone to know that. I only found out recently. I'll make him hand everything over to me and ill split it with you guys, I'll even save a piece for Rico."

"How are we going to do this?"

L Señor got up from his seat and started walking back and forth within the same six feet. "How many men did he bring with him?"

"I've only seen two." Carlos said.

"Two and their never far from him; good reasons why they're not." Miguel said.

"I know where the two are." Carlos said and the other three looked at him almost in awe.

L Señor looked at him wondering how, "How do you know?"

"I drove them once."

∞

Once again L Señor and his flunkies were making their way down a yard and to the front door of a quiet home. When L Señor got to the door he signaled for his flunkies to hold in their places and they did, frozen as statues. L Señor was again taking in the moment; slowly he breathed in and out. Signaling again for Miguel to bust down the door and L Señor moved out of the way as Miguel with all his might busted down the door and they all flew in like flies to meat. One of the men inside heard the commotion and grabbed his gun but when he exited his room and was in the line of sight of Miguel, he then had a bullet between his eyes. The other one was nowhere in sight but L Señor knew he was in there.

"Come out, come out, wherever you are." L Señor said loudly enough for the whole house to hear.

The other one was in a fetal position in his room holding a handgun to his face; he was scared out of his mind.

"I know you're in here, just come out and face the music… Don't make us come find you either because I'll just kill you then."

The man was breathing very hard and now had broken a sweat. "You'll kill me anyway!" He screamed.

"Yes, I will. Just come out slowly, you don't want to die like this."

"I don't want to die!" The man made his decision, stood up with his gun pointed out. Making his way out of the room, into the living room where L Señor and his flunkies stood in position with their guns pointed at him. He was clearly out numbered.

"L Señor, what do you want?" The man asked.

"Where is Pablo?"

"I don't know."

"You can't lie to me."

"I don't want to tell you."

"Fine, don't tell me."

The man breathed a sigh of relief, a little too soon.

"You know what I'll do," L Señor said, "I'll just visit *her*."

"L Señor, this has nothing to do with Sheila."

"You tell me where Pablo is and she won't die."

"Why? What did she do? What does she mean to any of this?"

"She means nothing, she's part of nothing and I don't give a fuck about her. You and Pablo are going to die. If you choose otherwise, then you'll live but she won't."

"Why?"

"You know what, you bring us to Pablo and the two of you can live happily ever after."

"Really?"

"Yes."

"Are you just saying that?"

"No, for one thing, I want you to drop the gun. The other thing, I really just want Pablo. You show us where to go and where he is... We don't ever bother you again."

He dropped the gun on the floor.

"Please, don't tie me up; I'll do whatever you say."

"I wasn't going to, we have a lot more ammo than you do, you would just die then."

"Please stop saying I'm going to die."

"Where are we going?"

"Albany County."

"Is he alone?"

"He's with some girl."

"When I asked if he was alone, I meant did he bring anybody to protect him?"

The man looked at the body of the other man, back at L Señor and said, "we were the bodyguards. He told us to take a vacation."

L Señor knew this was the end.

For three hours they drove upstate. The five of them in a pickup truck on the highway, L Señor was driving with Miguel in the passenger's seat while the other two flunkies were in the bed of the truck making sure the man didn't jump out of the moving car. They both had their guns to him. The man was trying to figure a way out of this.

"L Señor, he pays you good?" He asked them.

They were both silent, didn't even give him the light of day.

"He'd kill both of you if he had the chance." He said.

Carlos and Jose still didn't move, if anything, all they could give in an answer was a smirk.

"Don't you guys want something better than all of this?"

"Yes." Carlos said.

"So, let me go and come with me."

Jose couldn't hold his tongue anymore, "killing Pablo is our way out of all this."

"Will that really make you happier?"

They both looked at each other and then back to the man.

"You protect Pablo, but talk shit about L Señor when in fact you have no idea what Pablo has done to us and what L Señor has saved us from. You see one half of the puzzle and can't figure it out. We're the other half and we have the answers." Carlos said.

"If you keep talking, we'll kill you against L Señor's wishes." Jose said, "He won't yell at me for it if you're already dead."

"You're going to die anyway." Carlos said, "So, you should enjoy the rest of the ride."

The man fell silent and reflected on his life. Was this all worth everything? For him the answer came slowly, but the answer was a simple *no*.

They followed his exact directions to the place. When they got closer L Señor started to debate what to do with him after this was done. About a half hour into his contemplation they pulled up just down the road from a house that was in the middle of a clearing; there was no other house in sight.

L Señor and Miguel got out of the car and walked to the back of the pickup truck.

"Did he give you any trouble?" L Señor asked.

"No." Carlos said.

"Is this where he is?" L Señor asked the man.

The man hesitated but ultimately said, "Yes."

"Good... Miguel please take care of him."

Without any sort of hesitation Miguel took out a knife from his belt and sliced the man's throat cleanly from left to right. The man fell to the floor and now for L Señor the plan was coming together. He gazed off to the house and in the middle of his own thought he said to the flunkies, "After this we'll bury him and the girlfriend here. Pablo well take back to the city."

It was the first time all three flunkies had looked at each other, giving the look like maybe we shouldn't be doing this. They all had minds of their own, L Señor was not forcing them to do anything, as a matter of fact, he gave them a choice and they made it. This was their problem. They made their choice but were now thinking maybe this wasn't the best idea. L Señor on the other hand was thinking very highly of himself because the flunkies had decided to be behind him and in that moment, his ego was so large that he even thought *to hell*

61

with Rico. The flunkies were going to pick up the man's body but L Señor told them, "Leave him; we'll take care of these fuckers first."

L Señor began walking to the front door of the house.

The flunkies looked at each other, dropped the body and followed him.

L Señor got to the front door and touched it ever so softly. He did not want anyone to know he was here just yet.

Miguel was wielding a shotgun with a door buster attached to the front, L Señor knew this and signaled for him to bust down the door. Miguel did not want to, but he also wanted this to be over. *Maybe the man was right*. With all his might, Miguel held out the shotgun in front of him and ran to the door, but had a sudden change of mind. L Señor for a moment thought, *I don't want to have to kill Miguel*. Instead, Miguel knocked on the door. L Señor was intrigued by this.

The door opened to reveal a woman but there was no time to see who she was. Miguel, L Señor, Carlos and Jose flew into the house checking every nook and cranny. Jose tied up the girl and L Señor found Pablo in the bedroom.

Pablo was caught very off guard. When he looked up and saw it was L Señor & Company that had come into his home, the was nothing left in his CPU and could not process that. He also was not good at controlling his own emotions.

"L Señor… What are you doing here?" He asked, very nervously.

"Getting you back for everything you've done."

"I'm sorry, are you delusional? What I've done?"

L Señor was silent.

"What have I done to you? I think the question you should be asking yourself is what have you done?"

"I think the question you should be asking yourself is 'How did you find me?'" L Señor said.

"Why now?" Pablo asked as Miguel tied him up.

"You took the money from those people. They said I have to bring you dead to them or else I die… Survival of the fittest." L Señor said as he punched him in the face so hard that he passed out.

Pablo woke up tied to a chair and his mouth shut with duct tape.

What goes around… comes around.

Slowly, he began to realize that he had no idea where he was. It was a green room where the color green looked more like a rusted version of itself with one door, the only door in or out.

L Señor came into the room, dragging a metal chair behind him as he went to sit in front of Pablo. He picked up the chair and slammed into the position, right in front Pablo and he sat down on it.

For a moment he stared into Pablo's face and watched as Pablo was gasping for air; sweating more than he ever did before and shaking. Pablo was infuriated and if he could have, he would have killed L Señor right there. He was also saying his last prayers to himself.

"I don't speak of things that were done before I got back here to New York." L Señor said. "Memories are like people and you don't speak ill of them. You are a memory that won't stop. A memory that I wish I could forget. Sure, the Bodybuilder and I did some things to you, but you hung me out to dry the other day and the way I see it, that outweighs everything else."

A moment of silence.

"You and Martha Stewart have a lot in common. You never took care of the little guys, and the little guys are what did you in. Ironic, huh?"

Pablo's eyes were bulging out of his head, not physically, but because he was so worried that his eyes could not get any wider. He was breathing very heavily; accepting would be the hardest part for someone in this situation.

No one knows how long L Señor tortured him for. Some say days, some say weeks but he only had a week to bring Pablo's lifeless body back to the men who wanted it more than L Señor. L Señor had to save himself and his crew.

L Señor had killed Pablo.

L Señor and the flunkies disbanded and went their separate ways.

Where the Grass Grows Greener

A Hit from the Blunt

For a good while, the Drug Enforcement Agency, or DEA, had absolutely no idea this website even existed. There were whispers of it through the hallways but no one was able to find it. That's probably what they want us to think, but we'll never know. Tillman and the Partner had been traveling between Texas, California and New York for about five months investigating any leads they may had gotten. They busted the little dealers for information, most of the time they never got anything. There was also developing a certain reputation among the Onionland because of their tactics. The Partner would silently refer to it as reckless.

It was luck that when they returned to Austin that a man had gotten arrested with some of the same substances the Rainbow had been selling. A report had come over Tillman's desk about a surge in traffic on a site claiming to sell fertilizer. It had been dismissed it as much. In the back of his mind he knew that there had to be at least a handful of different drug sites on the dark web and even began to think of everything else there is in Onionland. None of that was his problem, the task was to find the source of the drugs.

Zeus and Panzer had done an excellent job disguising themselves and their business. The site ran well for years but, in my opinion, had gone on too long without something happening. In my experience, nothing is all just rainbows and unicorns. There were multiple sites and some of those had different products; also sold them in different ways. It was a transfer of power that should not have happened. Too many hands in the pot becomes a terrible stew. The fertilizer front did not go away either, one of their problems was the marking of everything, every product they shipped out had a unique stamp somewhere on it. This was also mentioned on a lot of the forums within the sites, but no one ever seemed to listen.

A dealer was arrested in Texas, selling what turned out to be MDMA that the Rainbow had been selling, a clear connection. This man they had caught said not a word to any officer who spoke to him in the interrogation room. He just kept asking for his lawyer which the cops were stalling on. He sat there, hands folded, no matter how much anyone screamed at him, told him how much he was fucked, kept calm and the same face. It didn't faze him. He accepted whatever was going to happen to him.

At least that's how it was until they got Tillman to come into the interrogation room. He observing the man behind the glass before going in, just by how the man looked, he knew he could break him. Tillman had heard it all and knew he could break him, he would be leaving with all of the information he wanted. He knocked on the door to the room, the officer inside opened the door to let Tillman, who said to the officer, "Leave us alone." The officer left and Tillman shut and locked the door behind him. He even turned off the camera. That's when the dealer knew he was in really deep shit. Tillman knew he was risking something. In the moment, he did not give a fuck.

Tillman sat down in front of him.

"You think you're the one we want?"

Nothing, not a word nor a sound was heard.

Tillman knew he was nervous and that there had to be a secret inside this man.

He continued. "You think we care about a small-time drug dealer that can't even run away from the cops? We want the ones who are currently running and hiding from us. You think you're important in all of this? You're not…"

The dealer had no idea what to say, "So… Who or what do you want?"

"You give me all the information I need and I get you only a year sentence for what you're here for, that is the best I could do in this state for you. You know I'm not lying. I know you don't want to be in jail for the rest of your life."

The dealer weighed out his options. All he knew was that he was scared. Just staring into Tillman's eyes, you could just see the evil man on the inside just screaming to come out.

"Maybe I should just wait for my lawyer…" He Said.

Tillman got up and acted as if he was going to walk out of the room, halting before he could touch the knob. Something in Tillman had turned sour. He knew this man knew what he wanted to know and had to get it from him. He looked up, made eye contact with the camera lens and realized that he no longer cared. He clenched his fist, turned around and hit the dealer right in the face.

"What the fuck you do that for!" The dealer yelled.

Tillman got in his face and quietly said to him, "Tell me everything you know, everyone you know, or you never get to feel the sun on your face ever again."

He sat back down in front of the man and fixed his collar, shirt and tie.

"If you talk now, the deal still stands… What do you know?"

The dealer knew as soon as any syllable was uttered regarding anything that he would be a dead man.

He talked…

"I get my stuff from a guy people call Don Leon. That's what I was introduced to him as. I knew him from the neighborhood and I don't remember exactly how it happened but one day we just sort of became friends. He brought me into his home, and at the time I had no idea he was a drug dealer. I just wanted to have money like him. So, I invested money with him and after some failed investments he told me he sold the drug Molly and that's when I got into selling it. I became his gopher… doing what he didn't want to do."

"Who's his source?"

"That I don't know. But you get this guy, you find out the source. If I could make a guess, I'd say he buys from online, he always needs rides to the post office."

"Online? Wouldn't be the Rainbow would it?"

The dealer felt his heart skip a beat. He knew what it was and was shocked Tillman knew about it. That's when the rat in the dealer came out and said, "That's only one of the sites. You haven't been able to get on it did you?"

Tillman said, "So, you do know…"

"Yeah I do, I just can't believe you knew."

"Of course, I know. How do I get on it? How can I access it?"

"Don Leon, he's a smart guy but not all there. He leaves his computer on. Stays signed onto everything. He especially leaves his internet connected to the Rainbow so he could have constant order updates and investments. You find him, you get in his home and you'll find you pot of gold at the end of the Rainbow, you may also find the Silk Road."

Tillman was taking everything in, thinking about it all.

"He likes to pick up his packages at the post office," the dealer said, "the post office in Carrizo Springs, that's where he likes to have everything sent and shipped from. He goes there maybe twice a week."

"What does he look like?"

"When you see him, you'll know. Keep an eye for a white Cadillac."

Tillman got up, without saying a word, went to the door and again before he could touch the door knob the dealer said, "Hey cop." Tillman turned to look at him, "don't just think that you taking down this website and taking down whoever is responsible for creating it will destroy the drug traffic. You guys have already been fighting an already lost drug war. If you shut down the Rainbow. Someone else will carry on the work. People will always find the drugs they're looking for. People like you, think you believe you a doing your country a great service, are just taking the freedom away from every American you think you protect. And I hope that when that happens and someone else has taken over, that you never find that person and die before you find out."

"I'm sorry you feel that way." Tillman said opening the door, "and that's why you drug addicts and dealers are going to jail for a long time." He left the room and shut the door behind him. The dealer sat there inside the room by himself. Suddenly, after he was able to process this, knew he had made a huge mistake and just wanted to die.

In the other room the Partner was waiting for Tillman to return.

The air was tense in the room when Tillman walked in.

The Partner said to him, "Carrizo Springs is only three and a half hours away. Think this Don guy shows up?"

"I think this guy has no idea about anything."

"Are we going to just stake out a post office?"

"Never been on a stake out before?"

"I have, just not in the mood to sit in a car for maybe a week."

"Hopefully, he comes in two days, Rookie."

Unfortunately, two days into their stake out, nothing had happed.

They were both bored of staring into the post office.

"This place looks like a jail." The partner said.

"Fitting for our friend to be caught in such a place." Tillman said, taking his sunglasses off and twisting them between his fingers. He was ready to see this man, arrest him and raid his home. In the end of this that's all Tillman wanted. The login information to the Rainbow. The raid on the home was on standby until given the go ahead by Tillman.

"How long do we have to wait?" The partner asked.

"As long as it takes, eventually he has to come get his mail."

"What if he had seen us or heard about us and abandoned this post office?"

"We give it a few more days, if he doesn't come by end of the week, we'll call it a day."

"Maybe the dealer was lying?"

"No, he wasn't"

"How are you so sure?"

"Because I lied and told him I'd help him out for more information, I lied and he's going to jail. I haven't allowed him to have any contact with anyone either."

"Fuck." The partner said in a tone that Tillman picked up on.

"What? Does this offend you in some way?"

"You are a very stern name with the law and it shocks me when I hear you say things like that."

"This is what we do. If we followed the book, we would never get anywhere. Everything we saw with Pablo and L Señor, and you still see like that?"

"Is that why you still call me Rookie after two years?"

"Yup."

Day Three. They had gone inside and paid off an employee that informed them the package had arrived and that no one had picked it up yet.

For hours Tillman and his partner were sitting in the car, from the very moment the post office opened, each had gone through at least three cups of coffee, black, no sugar. The Partner could not sit there anymore, for three days they had been there and nothing, not a sign of this man.

"I need more coffee." He said as he was about to get out of the car. Tillman grabbed his shoulder before he could and they saw a white seventies Cadillac pull up in front of the post office. A man got out of the car wearing a completely white suit, complete with both cowboy shoes and a hat.

Tillman got on the radio and said, "Keep positions; the bird is in the nest."

The dealer walked inside.

The Partner asked Tillman, "How do you know that's him?"

"The dealer said I'd know when I see him. I know that's him."

Tillman made sure his gun was in his holster, looked at the Partner, "Time to go meet this guy."

Tillman and the Partner were standing a couple people behind him, watching him like a hawk. This guy couldn't fart without them knowing. Every time he touched his nose Tillman would loath him just that much more. He was also sweating and sniffing every couple seconds which made Tillman one hundred percent sure this is the man they were looking for.

Don Leon made his way to the counter, put his package on the counter and said, "I'm here to pick up a package and send this bad boy out."

That's when Tillman made his move. Like vultures in the desert, they had taken him into custody. Tillman gave the signal to raid his home and were already finding out just a lot of new information, even from the car. Never drive your personal vehicle to buy or sell drugs.

"DEA, get on the ground! You're under arrest!" Tillman yelled, putting the handcuffs on him. Don Leon knew that he had fucked up and that this was the end. He fell to his knees as they took him in custody.

Tillman had sat down at the computer in the home of Don Leon and sure enough the page to the Rainbow was on the computer. Unbelievable, he now had an account and the ability to go onto the site.

"Where do I begin?" He said.

Now he had all the information he needed. There's the reason Panzer and Zeus fell like dominos. The drug world, lowkey, suffered a huge loss that day. Tillman now posed as a dealer and the integrity of the site had fallen. It took the DEA pigs almost a year to find the people who started the site. They crafted their plan in secret and developed a way to take everyone down within the span of a few hours. It would take them about another six months to actually carry the plans out.

But first they needed proof, bait they already had…

That's when Don Leon found himself with handcuffs around his hands, shackled to a chair. He, along with Tillman and the Partner, were in a motel room somewhere in Huston, Texas. Don Leon wasn't really under arrest and Tillman was acting weird to the point where Don thought they weren't cops.

Tillman took off his jacket and laid it on the chair. He rolled up his sleeves and said, "You're not under arrest yet my friend."

"Do I owe you money?"

Tillman chuckled and said, "No, but I am going to cost you a lot of money."

Don was tired and really didn't want to hear these people talk. "So, what do you call this?"

"This is the talk of how I want to help you stay out of prison. Seeing how I'm the one with the upper hand, I figured you'd be in the mood to help out."

He kept his mouth shut while Tillman stared into his eyes. *'I am no snitch. I know nothing. Don't say anything'.* That's all he was thinking and all anyone in that situation should ever think. It did not take long for him to squeal. This is because like most people, he was a dirty rotten cunt sucking rat and probably went from saying he wasn't a snitch to changing his mind within a few seconds. *'I don't want to go to prison. I gotta' look out for myself'.* In the drug world, there is no room for the I, we should look out for each other, we should keep our mouths shut, but I digress…

"What do you want me to do?" Don asked.

With that question I could hear all the chaos of all the raids that would eventually take down the Rainbow and all of these other sites.

"You're not asking me, right? Because I'm telling you what to do from now on." Tillman sat down in front of him and said, "You will set up a meeting with the persons responsible for the Rainbow. You have done business with them before so it'll be easier for you to get in contact with them. You will buy a good amount of whatever it is that you usually buy from it. Nothing changes… If they make you or find the microphone, you're on your own. We won't do a damn thing and we'll just let them… do whatever their going to do. Do you understand that?"

Don did not like a word of that. But now he was within the control of the cops and there was really only one way this would all end without going to prison. "And if I don't?" He asked.

"You will… We have eyes and ears everywhere. I know you now, I know everything about you. If you don't do it, you'll rot in solitary confinement for ten years."

In a very subtle and low tone the Partner finally spoke. "Tillman." He said in anger with a hint of frustration.

Tillman knew what he meant by the tone and he became mad at him.

"Shut up Rookie, if you don't want me to call you that anymore, you might want to start shutting the fuck up or start acting like me. I need you with me. Are you with me?"

"Yes."

Don was now more fucked and he knew it. Chained to the chair he sat silently. Tillman said he may have been making peace with himself. There was a certain part of me that felt for Don Leon.

A couple of days later, it was time for the show. The Partner was taping the microphone onto Don Leon's' chest; he wanted to say something to Tillman but also did not want him to say anything about being a Rookie again, so he decided to just do his job. The stage was set and they were to meet Zeus and Panzer in a couple hours. The script was simple, meet them at the Hotel of their choosing in a place of their choosing, send Don Leon in and wait to see what happens. Tillman knew what was going to happen, it was all part of the movie, just something to make the chain of events begin.

"When you get in there, I want you to act comfortable," Tillman said to Don Leon while reaching into his pocket, "Take this and do some in front of them." He handed Don a vile of white powder.

"What is this?"

"Cocaine… Don't act like how you're acting now, act like you're in a good mood."

Don took the vile from him and looked confused. I would have been too.

Tillman looked at his watch and said, "It's about that time. My friend."

"Don't call me a friend asshole."

"You're right, get the fuck out of here and don't die crossing the street. That's the last thing we need."

Even though he did not die crossing the street, a lot of cocaine was put up his nose which dulled his faculties and had forgotten why he was actually there.

Don Leon stood in front of a door at this motel and casually knocked on it. He could hear mumbling from the other side but could not make out any words, especially in his state.

The door opened to reveal the surprised faces of Zeus and Panzer; they were surprised by the blinding white suit our friend here was wearing.

"You must be the leprechauns at the end of the rainbow." Don's demeaner changed when he read the body language reactions. They were not amused. He continued, "Can I come in? Then we can talk about business."

Zeus pointed to the chair in the corner of the room and said, "Yeah, that's your chair."

Tillman and the partner were both listening to them through their headphones. The windows were closed and the air became humid and stifling. It was just the two of them breathing in each other's air. The partner was already nervous and when they heard Zeus say:

Zeus: Frisk him.

The partner knew this was not going to be good. All bets are off.

Don Leon: Whoa, there's no need to be
touching dicks here, I like to
party just as much as you guys
do.

There was then a sniff, as in, Don doing more cocaine.

Zeus: How can I trust you?

Don Leon: Do you not like making
money?

Zeus: What can you do to prove to me
that I can trust you? You already
have one strike; you wouldn't
let him frisk you.

"This is no good," The Partner said shaking his head in disapproval.

Tillman looked at him with the corner of his eye, also in disapproval said to him, "necessary evil."

Don Leon: Do I have to do more drugs
in front of you to prove it or
what do I have to do?

Zeus: Drugs aren't going to help me trust
you, it's okay though, we can
talk about other things... How
do you feel about OPP? Do you
know me?

Tillman was focused on the conversation and had no idea of the popular culture reference, but the partner did and said, "What the fuck are they doing?"

Don Leon: What?

There was a moment of silence and the two of them became worried. They heard breathing and after a few seconds there was some loud rustling.

"Their going to find it." The partner said.

Zeus: What's your favorite band?

Don Leon: uh, um, I like the doors.

There was more rustling, then they both looked at each other and knew the microphone was found.

Zeus: The Doors... I'm a Floyd man
       myself... You can never trust a
       band that doesn't have a bass
       guitar... Want something to
       drink?

Don Leon: No.

Zeus: You sure? The tap water in New
       York is the best in the world.

Don Leon: Don't need it.

Zeus: Do you like music? What kind of
       music?

A louder rustling was heard and the partner said, "fuck they found it.
"Just as I wanted them to." Tillman said.

Don: Yeah, I enjoy music.

The signal went dead, the microphone itself was in the toilet by this time and Tillman had already switched off the receiver.
"You're not going to wait?"
"Wait for what?"
"The possibility of it working again."
Tillman got a little agitated and said, "where did *they* get you from?"
"What should we do?"
"We do nothing, the bait is inside, they now know we're watching. It's their move."

75

"What if something happens to him?"

"Who cares, one less drug dealer off the street."

There was an awkward moment of silence between the two. The mood was actually tense. The Partner lowered his window and with that burst of fresh air circulating the mood improved.

The Partner took a deep breath and said, "You haven't told me anything, all you do is call me a rookie. I'm not trying to be you. You are the complete opposite of what I want to do here."

"Why don't you be someone else's partner?"

"In the end, you and I are here to serve the law, you have different methods and get shit done… You're just trying to piss them off, aren't you?"

"I'm trying to get to the source. We scare them, they get stuck like a deer in the headlights and crumble like the Twin Towers." He was satisfied with that statement. Never did he have a plan to get Don Leon back nor would he waste any amount of time thinking about it.

He was really thinking about the next series of events and was uncertain if they would exit the motel through the front door. The thought of confusing his partner made him chuckle and proceeded to drive around the building for ten minutes before acting on a hunch of intuition that they would in fact exit through one of the back doors. Tillman made sure they were far enough for no one to see, but close enough to see everything. The method to his madness always paid off for him.

After a few grueling hours of sitting in the car they finally were able to observe the three of them leaving the motel, they had waited for the cover of night. Tillman and the Partner were looking right at them and followed them for a long time on the road.

"Think they know he has a tracker in his shoe?" The partner asked Tillman.

"I forgot about that. There's not a chance in hell, especially if I forgot." He said as they stared into the night.

Eventually, they came to the famous mansion in Pennsylvania where they only observed Zeus and Panzer leaving the car. They had no idea what had happened to Don Leon, nor did Tillman care at all. Tillman had come to the conclusion that they may had found the tracker.

The signal could not be found.

For the next three days Tillman and the Partner sat in the car observing the mansion from a far with the camouflage of the woods. It is from this stake out that they learned everything they needed to know, particularly who was there and who to follow.

Just like the big bang, everything was over in a second. Tillman and the Partner found themselves in a place where nothing more could be done. Tillman was growing frustrated in the car. This was clearly visible to the Partner who had not said a word for at least a whole day, nothing he could have said would have helped their situation.

"Three days." The Partner finally said.

Tillman was silent, thinking... Then he spoke, "We come back in six days with a warrant."

"How do we get one without saying anything about what we did?"

"We were observing a suspect who was kidnapped... We have to know what's going on with him in order to properly continue our investigation."

The Partner was stunned, "Does anybody actually buy that garbage from a guy like you?"

"All the time."

∞

Not only was Tillman on the scent of the Rainbow, but he had Pablo and L Señor by the balls. They had no idea. The radar did not go out too far from them but they were definitely watching L Señor more than Pablo. Which, in hindsight, is a really strange thing.

Tillman and the Partner found themselves back in Texas following dead leads of L Señor and Pablo. It's a long story but they were never able to find them. The ironic part is that they probably never knew the DEA was watching. There is good reason to believe that Pablo had something to do with that, most likely paid off a lot of people and had a handful of informants.

Tillman was drinking his morning coffee while reading the newspaper at his desk, not really reading, but skimming over everything and listening to the ambient sounds of an office; the low rumble of voices, phones ringing and the hum of the air conditioner.

The need for nicotine caused him to crave a cigarette, something he was trying to quit. Through the window he saw that the sun was rising in the sky which made it a beautiful shade of blue with hints of pink and dark purple. He needed some outside air so the cigarette was the perfect excuse to go down thirty flights of stairs to be outside. One last swig of his coffee and the caffeine chorused through his veins causing him to get up from his chair and walk down the hallway. He could not wait to be outside so he took out the pack from his pocket and put a cigarette in his mouth, probably a bad time to do this especially when you are about to pass the office of your supervisor. Tillman was noticed.

The man in the office had in fact seen him walk by and had something important to say.

"Tillman." The stocky man said hoping he had heard.

Tillman heard but did not want to stop. He took the cigarette out of his mouth and turned around going into the office.

"Yes Sir." He said.

The man waved for him to sit down and said, "I was just reading the report you wrote on the progress of the Rainbow…"

Tillman sat down in the chair in front of the man's desk with the intention of caring what this man had to say, he wanted the cigarette more. This man was his superior and of he had something to say, you had to listen.

"Do you think Pablo has some connection to the websites?"

"Hard to say really… We aren't too sure what Pablo does. We know he brings in tons of cannabis and people seem to die around him. We have not observed any instances of them going to post offices or receiving packages in a regular form. It's L Señor and his guys who we should be watching more. We have less of an idea who they are.

"Our agent working on them says that Pablo is dead."

"Pablo is dead?"

"Yes, and your friends have popped up in New York."

"When did this come in?"

"I just got off the phone from confirming if the intel was trustable, it is… Apparently, Pablo has been dead for six months."

It was even more evident to Tillman that one of L Señor's gang was in fact an informant. This was something that was never specifically brought up; but in recent months had been getting the treatment of it being very nonchalant within the higher ups of his department, skeptical of everything he heard. "We just got back from New York. They don't need us there."

"I don't want to send you back there, you're doing bigger stuff here... They want someone whose already familiar with the operation."

Tillman wasted no time, if they needed him that bad, he was going to take charge of everything. It's about that time in another story where two young wolves would be set free from captivity and seek revenge... The partner was sleeping at his desk outside of Tillman's office. A deep, well needed sleep. So, Tillman smashed a rolled-up newspaper on the desk and he woke up startled with the sight of Tillman saying to him, "Get ready, in two hours we're going to the city..."

Half asleep the Partner asked, "Austin?"

"New York," Tillman said walking away.

Confused, the Partner asked, "New York? We just got back from there." He got up to follow Tillman and yelled, "What's in New York?"

He and the Partner, whose name I was never told, were frantically walking down the hallway to the elevator. This was a newer partner for Tillman, maybe a year or two, so he felt that a lecture for the rookie was appropriate. With a deep breath he said, "We are able to do our job because we haven't always done everything right, we do what needs to be done."

"We sent a man to his death. What can we do that's worse than that?"

Tillman stopped walking, which caused the partner to stop. He looked into his eyes and said, "We have to follow L Señor."

"He's in New York? What about Pablo?"

"He's dead." Tillman said walking away.

The Partner for a moment was frozen, confused and worried for what that meant for them.

New York City had been good to Tillman, not only did he get his start in the DEA there but he was also born within it. The Partner was from Texas and hated every minute of being in the Big Apple.

The first thing they were informed of was an arrest of someone dealing cannabis in the Bronx who was carrying products with the same quality and branded with the logo of the Rainbow, however small or un-noticeable it was. They followed the dealer and eventually saw him meet with me. It would have been nice to have some sort of spidey-sense. I, in turn, went to go meet L Señor, because that's what I used to do. That's how they found him again, through me. After a while, they saw me leave and they stayed to follow L Señor. Apparently, L Señor was up to a whole lot more than I knew.

They followed him for days and the craziest part was how L Señor always gave off the authoritative vibe that made you feel that he was always one step ahead, turns out he was as clueless as the rest of us. Not one of his flunkies noticed, never did he even think to notice.

One day I went to meet L Señor and it was not good. Tillman and the Partner had seen me going into the building. Then, a while later, they observed Rico going into it also. A handful of moments after that and we were all getting into the truck, leaving together as one, and of course, I was in the front passengers' seat.

"That's not good." The Partner said as they were looking at us through their windshield.

"No, it's not."

"Why do you think Rico is back?"

"I don't see that as a problem… Who the guy is in the front seat is what I want to know?"

"He seems out of place, doesn't he?"

"Yeah, it's just never good when the whole gang goes out together."

The whole time these guys were following us. I had so much on my mind that I had never thought of any repercussions.

They saw us when we got to the to this dead-end block where it looked like they were about to post up. They were half a block away and had to make it look like they hadn't noticed them, to act casual.

Tillman knew something was up and as he was driving, he said to the partner, "This is no good."

"No, this is excellent, we got them now…" The partner said believing his words.

The partner didn't see what Tillman saw; this dead-end block was just off of Interstate 95 which has a huge wall separating the highway from the service road. There would not be anywhere for them to sit and watch; you know, the sneaky things they have been doing and only thing they seem to know. They always watch from the shadows.

∞

"It is the dawn of a new era." This stocky DEA agent was saying in front of a crowd of his superiors and inferiors. "The internet has brought a new wave of crime, the selling of illegal and illicit drugs. In our ongoing effort in the ridding of the streets of these said substances and the people who make and traffic it, one of our men have been able to tap into one of the online stores known in the Silk Road as the Rainbow. Agent Tillman will be leading a special unit; you men have been handpicked from your qualifications. This task force I am dubbing the IDTF, The Internet Drug Task Force. He will now inform you of everything you need to know, please welcome Agent Tillman."

Tillman walked up to the stage and shook hands with this man who had given him a hell of an introduction. After the man had left the stage, it was only then Tillman thought of what to say.

"Gentleman, a new day had risen. This will not be easy and some of us may die but most of us will live. We will break laws, though not intentionally. We need to stop the distribution of these drugs. Here is everything you need to know. I had stumbled across a website known as the Rainbow, for months I tried to get access to it, it wasn't until we caught a dealer who had been buying drugs from the site and picking them up from the post office. We arrested him and made him give us access to the website where we had set up a meeting between him and the men who run Rainbow. These men kidnapped him and killed him; we know this because we followed the signal and found the grave. We had put a tracker in the shoe of the dealer and were able to track them to a location in Pennsylvania. Having this information, we were also able to find a second location associated with these men, a penthouse in Manhattan. We will be split into two teams, Alpha and Omega. We will be joined by the local swat team who will meet us at our starting points. Alpha is my team, we will raid the mansion, but only after Omega has given us word that they have entered and secured the apartment building in the city. I want as little time between as possible, so no one on the inside can communicate with each other. I want to catch these fuckers. Once Omega has given us word, we will raid the mansion. To both teams, whoever is in there, everyone gets arrested. No one leaves there and if they do, shoot on sight. Men, be careful out there. Operation Pot of Gold will commence in two days, before dawn on Friday, before the glimmer of sun hits the land. Until then we prepare…"

The men didn't move nor say a word. They all nodded and, in their minds, they were screaming with Tillman.

That gloomy morning in Manhattan must have felt very different for Panzer and Tillman. As the former was smoking his cigar watching the lights of a cop van barrel down a street, Tillman was also feeling the gloom of that morning in Pennsylvania.

Tillman was on foot with a few agents walking towards the mansion through the woods. The trucks were waiting about a half mile down the road waiting for the signal. Once they got to the fence it was decided to keep positions there.

"Omega." Tillman said into his radio, "Status?"

Through the air waves and frequencies of static, a voice came through and said, "Approaching the building now, should be secure within the next twenty minutes."

He was mad, in his head he said *twenty minutes* sarcastically. "Into the radio he said, "It better be exactly twenty."

Again, through the static the voice said, "…inside the building. ETA ten minutes."

"Alpha, stand buy, we have an ETA of ten minutes. Ground team, turn off the cameras."

Three agents with semi-automatic weapons found the electrical box inside the compound of the mansion. They were the ones who turned off the cameras.

If you were there with Tillman and listened closely, once he said that, you could have heard the faint sounds of those trucks starting up in the cold. It radiated through the woods and it must have scared the wildlife with all those diesel engines.

Through the static the voice over the radio said, "Building is secure, target is down."

Tillman hesitated for a moment before saying into the radio, "Alpha team, Go!"

There was a handful of trucks that suddenly sped through the woods on this small dirt road. The ground had to have been rumbling.

By this time, the sun had risen and its beams had illuminated the area.

The trucks had sped past Tillman and the ground team as they were running to the gate. The trucks did not stop and the first one in line burst through the gate and the it went flying in two big pieces.

Shots were ringing out all over the place as they entered the mansion.

Tillman was staying behind his team observing everything until he decided to go do some investigating as they were clearing the house.

He found himself in an intersection of hallways.

That's when he saw Panzer, although he didn't know who that was and screamed, "Stop right there!" Panzer ran the opposite way and into another room. Tillman followed, but when he got to the closed door, he stopped and tried to listen for any sounds coming from the room. Sure enough, he heard drawers opening and rustling. There was only one thing that could be going on, a search for a weapon.

Panzer had found a gun and made sure it was loaded. He had the advantage of knowing what doors to go through and where they would lead. The DEA had no idea what to expect on the inside. This was one of the things I had heard was that there was a lot of confusion amongst them. This place was huge.

Tillman heard the sound of another door and went into the room, following Panzer who had just shot a couple officers outside of the other door and made a run for it. Every hallway he went down he saw an officer and began to backtrack but was blocked by Tillman with whom had made eye contact. Finally, he broke into a room that had a couple windows facing the back of the property, jumping out of the closed window shattering the glass. The adrenaline kicked in and he couldn't think about if he was hurt or not, he forced himself to get up and start running. Tillman had taken a few shots at him from the window. Panzer ran to the gate, climbed and jumped from the top. No time to stop, another dose of adrenaline and he was gone. Tillman's plan had worked. Unsatisfied by this man who had just escaped him, Tillman vowed that he would find him again, and that for now he had let him go.

The DEA went through every nook and crevasse of that place. For two weeks they found everything they couldn't have imagined in there. Who would have thought that in the middle of nowhere, literally nowhere because no one knows where this place is, this mansion would have been making drugs in an unbelievable laboratory? A treasure trove of information, one of which was the infamous book that was in a vast majority of labs at the time, and most likely still today, was *Pihkal*.

I also thought it was weird that the media solely focused on the *Silk Road*. There was no mention of the Rainbow. It was soon after that I, along with maybe a handful of others, realized that the *Silk Road* and *Rainbow* were two separate entities. A lot of things could have been avoided if I had known that. There were two different investigations happening simultaneously within the DEA. Both had gone down at the same time. Red flags for the drug world, looking at it now, they didn't want anyone to know the Rainbow was down. We had all fallen into their pockets, which will soon become more apparent.

This may have been a gross exaggeration but they claimed the *Silk Road* was worth between one and four billion dollars and had confiscated twenty-six thousand Bitcoins which at the time was worth four million. It so happens that it went down the same way the Silk Road did, just with a hint of international spice. A drug dealer had been arrested in Australia in 2013, same way Don Leon did; there is a lesson here, it's not the Cannabis that gets you detected, it's MDMA and Cocaine. As you can imagine, the domino effect happened and identities were compromised. Eventually they got the creator of it, Ross Ulbricht who was arrested in October of that year on the charges of computer hacking, conspiracy to traffic narcotics, money laundering and attempted murder. This guy was crazy. He paid seven hundred thousand dollars for three murders that never actually happened.

A Hit from the Vape

In this time in my life I had been having these weird dreams. I'm not saying that I never dreamt at all but that dreams were not a recurring thing for me. I had them once in a while but never every night. There were mornings I would wake up thinking about them and would spend a good number of hours remembering and debating what they all meant. Dreams were always something interesting to me since most of them were really elaborate and would resonate with me. One particular dream always seemed to happen at weird times and would cause me confusion when I woke up. A white room, a foggy white room where the only thing I could see were my hands. Nothing was in the room and there was absolute silence. Other than white, the only other two colors that were flashing by in small hazes of vapor were orange and green. In the distance a blob of those colors I could see but not touch, nor could I really make out what the shape was.

I woke up in the middle of the dream to find myself sleeping on the floor of my bedroom rather than being comfortable in my bed. There are only two reasons why I would be on the floor, one is the fact that I either decided to be on the floor or two, that I was so inebriated with alcohol that I physically couldn't make it to my bed. I was up but I couldn't move at all. So, this was the result of alcohol, that's why I hate it, you don't care what you do or where you sleep, wherever you drop is good enough. I was wearing the same clothes from the night before and the wood floor around me was still cold so I knew I was there for a while. Looking around the room I noticed I felt funny. Things were moving and everything was grooving; one of the legs of my desk moved and pointed at me. So many thoughts ensued my mind as I was stuck on the floor. I could have moved but my mind would not let me. For some strange reason I was enjoying every minute of it. At the time, I had only recently found out is that there is conclusive evidence that the human body produces DMT, Dimethyltryamine, though it is unknown how or where it's produced. From what I knew about DMT at the time I just thought *oh it's that hallucinogenic drug.* I now believe that I was in the middle of tripping and when I woke up, I was still well into feeling it; because I was woken out of REM sleep, I think this is what causes us all to dream. I'm not going to lie and say that I was in pain, because I was enjoying every minute of it. It was more of a placebo effect; I was so fixated on it that my mind may have been making me believe what I was feeling.

Thinking about the dream made me feel content inside, made me feel happy. For a long time, I thought about this and wanted to understand it all; but it's just a dream. *So, what's to think about?* It's not a substance, just echoes of a conscience mind. The first real thought in my head was about how I shouldn't be on the floor and that I had to go into the bed. Slowly, I got up and made my way in between the sheets of the bed.

In the bed already was Sadie. I hugged her as she slept and smelled her hair. I was home; there was nowhere I would have rather been then there. She turned to me with her eyes open and we locked our gaze with each other.

"I've been thinking about things." She said half asleep.

"What have you been thinking about?"

"Where did the Five Thousand Dollars come from?"

I had forgotten that I left the money on the table. It should not have shocked her that I would have left that kind of money on the table, that was a regular thing. What she really should have been concerned about was the amount, usually it was double. We were making more money than that.

Still, it was kind of weird that she had asked me particularly about this money, there must have been a feeling.

"Kush and I had to take care of something last night… It didn't go well."

Her face went from this half-asleep person to someone deeply concerned.

She sat up in bed, crossed bother her legs and arms. "Miklo, I don't want you selling anymore."

To me, this was a bombshell.

"Sadie, it's ok, what happened last night won't happen again."

"Yes, it will… From here on it will only get worse."

"No, it won't"

"I don't want to go back and forth saying yes and no. This isn't a good life for us. What happened last night? I had a feeling something was going on."

"Something happened but it's over now and it won't happen again."

"Stop selling drugs."

"What am I going to do then? This is all I know."

"All you know? What are you a moron? Find something else…"

"What am I going to do? Work retail and make shitty money in a shitty job?" I felt bad because I couldn't get those words out without having an attitude and she definitely did not deserve that. For those few moments after I said that, I thought about my life and how it would be being one of those people working a real job. To me, it was not what I wanted to do. *Maybe there's a way you can make a lot of money now so you don't ever have to work again.* That idea, at the time was far-fetched, but in reality, it made somewhat enough sense for me to want to be over it.

She laid back down, turning away from me, covering herself with the covers.

"Maybe I can get out of this."

She did not want to hear the maybe and did not say a word to me for the rest of the night.

∞

Kush and I were in his apartment smoking a joint, watching *Seinfeld* on TBS. That was sort of a ritual for us. Almost every day at six in the evening we would get together and do this and called it a smoking session. We were sitting there, passing this joint back and forth. He had got some killer Durban Poison from this new connect he found and it was getting us insanely high.

His cell phone rang and he was shocked by that, frankly so was I.

"You don't turn your phone off anymore when your home?" I asked.

"I do, must have forgotten."

He looked on the front screen of his Motorola Razor to see who was calling him.

"I gotta' take this." He said, walking out of the living room.

I was still smoking the joint but I could hear him faintly from the other room. I could not make out what he was saying but it seemed like kind of an agitated tone.

I took another puff and when Kramer burst through the door of Jerrys' apartment, I could not contain my laughter which was cut short by Kush asking, "Do you want to come with me to meet this guy?"

"Now?"

"Yeah, it's a big order or else I wouldn't be doing this."

"How much is it?"

"He wants 'a pound of Kush's finest Shiva'."

"A pound, even that would get me off my ass."

He seemed worried about it though. He stood in the doorway of the living room for a moment and didn't move until I asked, "Is there a problem?"

He looked at me with a weird face.

The next thing I remember, we were both in my truck, in the backseat rested this pound of Durban Poison Cannabis, it was vacuum sealed but still had a faint smell to it because we had no time to wash it with Everclear.

We had gotten to the location he was going to meet this guy, somewhere under the El, elevated train, on Westchester avenue. It was no longer the early evening hours; it was around ten o'clock at night and the streets were dark and desolate only being illuminated by the glow of the orange-ish street lights.

We were parked and the trucks lights were off.

I could tell something was up with Kush. He reached in his pocket and took out a .38 Special revolver, handed it to me and said, "Take this."

No one has ever handed me a gun before and I was of course nervous. "Do you think I need it?" I was holding it and was afraid to even put my finger on the trigger. I then realized he hadn't even given me the gun yet, that's how scared I was. I felt cold and worried I had made a terrible decision and that this was not my life. This was not who

I am. *Sadie is right.* As I'm thinking this I can see Kush's lips move as he's speaking to me.

"You might," He said, and in true Kush fashion gave me a quick rundown of the weapon, "it's a .38 caliber revolver with six shots in it, currently loaded. No safety on it so be very careful."

For a minute I wouldn't take it.

We had been selling drugs for years and I never needed a gun.

"Take it Miklo, you never know. I got one too."

I took it from him, put it on my back between the belt and my pants, never had done anything like this before. I remember my heart pounding. At this point I wasn't sure if the drug dealing life was for me.

Kush prepared and put the pound in the backpack. He received a phone call telling him to exchange bags with the man walking up the block who had the money in it.

Kush got out and started walking up the block toward the man.

I was sitting in my car watching everything. I got even more nervous that I took the gun out and held it in my hand. I was so nervous I thought I was going to accidently shoot off the gun but I did not.

Everything seemed that it was going well until I noticed another man walking across the street towards Kush in a violent way. It was night time so I couldn't really see anything nor could I hear anything because the train was passing by overhead. That's when everything went to shit. They pulled a gun on Kush and took the bag. I didn't even think, I started the car and sped down the block, jumping out of the car and pointing the gun at the men. They wouldn't stop so I fired a shot at them. It was the first time I had shot a gun in the air; I wasn't physically affected but my ears rang like they never did before. They wouldn't stop. So, I shot the one with both the bags in the foot and he fell, dropping both of the bags.

The other one, who was coming from across the street, just ran away.

The one I shot was crying, screaming bloody murder, Kush and I grabbed the bags and we got in the car and sped off.

Kush knew that he didn't open his bag but he opened the man's bag he saw the five thousand dollars in it. He looked at me and said, "Dude, we have both the bud and the money."

I could not believe it.

"Take this." He said to me handing me the bag with the money.

So, not only did I not believe this but now I sure as hell did not believe that he was giving me the five thousand dollars cash. "Why?" I asked him.

"You just stopped something from happening to me and we got everything without anything happening to us." He nudged the bag to me and said, "take it."

I took the bag from him and threw it in the back seat.

I had a bit of a mental crisis that night when I was driving home from Kush's place. I shot someone. There were so many ways I was justifying it in my mind but the cold hard truth was the I was wrong. Maybe no one had to get shot. Maybe they would have come to a reasonable outcome.

The gun did not shoot him, you shot him.

This did not make me feel good.

∞

Now, here I was lying in bed next to the love of my life. It's strange how life is. You think something and the next day someone is telling you the same thing you were telling yourself because of what they said.

"How did you get the money?" She still had not turned around to look at me.

I decided that I would not lie to her. I love her so deeply that to lie to her would in fact be lying to myself. I told her the story and when she turned around to look at me, I almost started crying. She knows I'm a sensitive man and she cried for me while giving me a hug.

"That… I never want to happen again." I said to her as she was hugging me.

"I still want you to stop." She said.

"I know."

I gave her the impression that I really wanted to stop.

I was lying and it killed me inside.

I did not sleep at all that night. It was hard forcing myself not to think about what had happened. The memories wouldn't stop and my mind put that on repeat. *What should I have done? What should I have done differently?* If only there was a way to explain the repercussions of my decision to sell drugs and to keep selling drugs in under a page. From that day on, my life changed and the things that happened as a result of that I can never forget.

It's all tied in.

My mind kept replaying the moment the bullet went into the guy's foot. I can still remember seeing the blood coming out and hearing the shot. Numerous times I got up in the middle of the night to vomit, literally sick to my stomach for this for a couple of weeks until I had repressed it so much that there was no more thinking about it.

After the third time vomiting, I decided that I couldn't stay in bed and smoked a joint on my porch at three in the morning.

I could not listen to music nor watch television. I didn't want to talk to anyone and I didn't want anyone to call me. Flashes of guns and blood. Smoking cannabis didn't help either, it just enhanced my feelings and I felt like shit.

Be a man.

Be a man.

Men have shot men before; he did not die.

I was right, it was either shoot him or something would have happened to Kush and you know what, I rather have that guy dead than Kush. With that statement the event no longer bothered me.

I hadn't thought about it until this moment of writing it.

At least I didn't wake up Sadie all those nights.

The next day I had to go to work and by work, I mean Kush, Anthony and I had to keep doing what we had been, dealing Cannabis. We each had specific jobs in this. I was one of the sellers, meaning I would drive around and meet people with bigger orders. Anthony was the small-time dealer, that meaning that he sold Dubs (one gram for $20), Eighths (3.5 grams for $50 each) and Quarters (about 7 grams at $100 each). Kush's job was to keep getting the cannabis, he I felt, had the worst job of going to meet the contact every few days to get more product. Between the three of us we would bring in enough money in one day to pay all three of our rents, for two months.

Why would I leave this?

Sadie was on my mind that day though. She told me not to do this anymore and I expressed my feelings of that to Kush and Anthony.

We were counting the day's money when I said, "Sadie doesn't want me to do this anymore."

They both looked at me, each giving opposite reactions.

"Good, we shouldn't be doing this anymore." Kush said.

I was shocked. "How long have you been feeling like that?"

"Months."

"What about you?"

Anthony looked at me and said, "This is the only job I know, not going to leave it now. More people smoke weed every day. Why have someone else reap the benefits of this market?"

A statement I can agree with.

I looked at Kush and asked, "Why should we stop?"

"Paranoia," he said, saying it like the word itself was causing him pain, "once it sets in, it's on. I feel like we're being watched all of the time. When I call the contact to go get the supply I wonder if it'll be the last time I see the sun. Every time I leave that building I think I'm going to be arrested. Every time I see a cop car I shake and hope they don't stop me." He took out a flask from his pocket and took a long swig of it. "There's a big part of me that does not want to sell anymore." From his pocket he took out what looked like two Vicodin pills which he shoved in his mouth.

Many things I had to think about. "So, do we shut this down?"

We looked at each other and after a moment of staring at each other, we kept counting the money.

That was a NO.

We are not shutting down.

"Too bad there isn't a better way of selling this. Maybe off the streets."

That's when Kush said something that I wish he never said, "I've heard of a website where you can buy and sell every drug known to man."

"A website?" I asked.

"I've never been on it nor have I seen it but I have heard of it, I'm surprised you haven't heard of it."

"Wouldn't something like that get shut down in a minute?" Anthony asked.

"It's on the dark web."

"What's it called?" I asked.

"There are a few of them. One of them is called the Rainbow."

"Rainbow?" Anthony said, "that does not sound like a drug website. Sounds like something out of Resident Evil."

"Do you think that would be better?" I asked.

"I don't think you'll be able to find it." Kush said.

I sat down at my laptop. Taking that as a personal challenge I spent a good part of the day trying to find this elusive website. *An internet website that sells drugs?* I had to get on this.

I downloaded Tor, the application for getting on the dark web, routed my computer with a VPN and I was in business.

The best way to find something that couldn't be found was to go on drug forum sites and eventually I saw someone refer to the Rainbow, so I knew it was at least real. Also, I had the thought that I found it so easily. There always one chicken that clucks where it can be heard.

Then I stumbled onto a website that had a weird address but in the address bar was the word rainbow. When I clicked on it the page loaded and said:

"You have stumbled onto a locked door.

In order to knock you must find the key,

It is as easy as 1, 2, 3…

This page is not real…"

For a minute I could not find any other link on the page; but in the bottom right corner the mouse turned to the hand and was able to click on it. The next page loaded. It was a login page. I had no login and didn't know how to get one. I decided to highlight the page seeing if I was missing anything and when I did I saw the message that said:

"If you want to come in,

Knock on our IRC door,

Be prepared to know and answer…"

I was confused by this but on that page was another link and when I clicked it, it was a forum in some weird address. I found out that IRC is an internet chat program that encrypts its messages so that they cannot be seen; pretty much a way to communicate without the authorities knowing.

I called Kush in excitement and told him I had stumbled upon the website.

He was silent after I said it but then he said, "You actually found the site?"

"Yeah."

"Are you on it?"

"No, I need to 'be prepared to know and answer' and need to get IRC chat program."

"You need to get on that." He said.

"If I get on it, what am I going to do?"

"Miklo, if you get on, I'll supply the initial product to get you started."

"Get me started? You don't want in on this?"

"I'm not sure yet. If you want to try it, the offer is there."

Kush just said to me that he would invest in me joining this website and going on with this. This was an opportunity I was not going to miss.

"If you're in," I said, "then I'm in."

"Ok." Kush said.

I had to set up an 'interview' with the Rainbow for the next morning.

When the next morning came, I signed onto the chat room and waited. I then got a message saying that the interview had begun and it was questions I sort of knew the answer to and things about drugs I sort of knew. The questions I don't remember but I remember thinking *how are they going to know that I'm not a cop*? I guess it was all about the answers I gave, I gave them answers I thought they would want hear.

I was interrupted by Sadie asking me, "What are you doing?"

I was startled and had forgotten she was even home. "Nothing, just talking to someone I haven't seen in a while."

"Oh." She said, "Who?"

I quickly looked at the name of the person on the chat room and I said to her, "My friend Panzer, haven't seen him since St. Clare's."

"Oh." She said again walking out of the room.

The first conversation I had with Panzer was on the encrypted chat client on the internet. I didn't hear his voice and had no idea what he looked like. We were conversing but weren't speaking in the general sense. The first real step into the site was acting normal and really showing that you weren't an authority figure that was going to bring it all down. This conversation was very formal; honestly, I don't know why Panzer trusted me, I don't know how I was able to get onto that site. I wound up having a great conversation with Panzer about things and found out that he was actually one of the creators of the Rainbow and I established with him that I have a cannabis connection in New York City which they did not have connected to the site. I don't think any of the dealers in the city would have trusted this website like I did. I spent an hour talking to Panzer and after that we became pen pals through the computer.

Panzer: Who are you?

Miklo: Miklo.

Panzer: Who are you?

Miklo: I am a man who lives in The Bronx and 23 years old.

Panzer: Why do you want to be on this site?

Miklo: I want to be on this site because the world is huge and I'm only in the center of mine. I want to broaden my market.

Panzer: What products do you have?

Miklo: Cannabis is the only thing I can get. I've been selling a long time and tired of this street dealing.

Panzer: How did you hear about this?

Miklo: A friend had heard about it and I spent a few hours tracking down IP addresses.

Panzer: How can you prove we can trust you?

Miklo: I don't know. How do you guys do that?

Panzer: Do you have a driver's license?

Miklo: Yes.

Panzer: Provide your number.

Miklo: I'm trusting you with my identity. Here is my number, *******

Panzer: I will contact you here when I find out.

Panzer has left chat. 8:54

Panzer has entered chat. 9:25

Panzer: We now know who you are. You will be granted permission to our website on a trial basis. Please, refer to the sites Rules & Regulations and continue to the home page.

Miklo: Thank you.

Panzer has left chat. 9:25

Panzer has entered chat. 10:43

Panzer: How much cannabis can you get every few days?

Miklo: How much?

Panzer: Pounds.

Miklo: How does this work though?

Panzer: Refer to site Rules & Regulations on setting up

banking/payment information. For payment, you are going to need to familiarize yourself with Bitcoin and download the Coinbase app. Everything you need to know will be there. When that is done, get five pounds of cannabis in the next three days. Send to **** ******* ***, *****, *** ****, *****. Once we receive the package and it is quality checked, payment will be sent to you.

Miklo: What does the payment look like?

Panzer: This is your first transaction; this is a special one. We pay twenty-five hundred for the first few pounds of product you sell on the market. Think of it as an investment to you and you are on probation. After that, you are free to sell on the marketplace and make the prices and quantity that you want to sell.

Miklo: Is all of this worth it?

> Panzer: We connect with people all
>
>   around the world and substances
>
>   are sent within it on a constant
>
>   basis.
>
> Miklo: Sounds good.
>
> *Panzer has left chat. 10:46*

After spending about an hour on reading the rules and regulations I knew this was something I could get on board with.

The major problem I had was that I had no idea if Kush would even let me meet the guy. I knew he had to meet him tomorrow.

Again, I was at Kush's apartment smoking a joint with him. Really, I was there for his contact but he was reluctant to tell me about the man whom he gets his supply of cannabis from. He knew I was now part of this site and that I was putting the wheels in motion for a new business. He knew money was involved but wouldn't say anything to me. It almost came down to me interrogating him but that was something I wasn't ready to do, especially to Kush. I did not understand why Kush was acting like this. Sometimes, when he did something like this, I wouldn't think about it because that's how Kush was, if he knew something was wrong, he wouldn't go on with it. He definitely had a deeper understanding of people. What I also did not understand was that he had never said anything bad about his contact, he had known and done business with him for almost a year and everything seemed like it was peaches. I kept reminding him that important things were going to happen to the both of us through our deals. That did not seem to work in getting him to talk to me. Even bringing up the amount of money we could make did nothing. Sometimes, he was just really stubborn. Selfishly I decided to go hang out with Kush, purely for the reason of talking to him about this.

I felt bad about this. I had never used someone like that.

"I'm on the site." I said.

"Wow, I can't believe you did it and that quickly."

"I don't want you to invest in me, let's do this together and split the profits."

"I don't want to be doing this in my life much longer."

"This is a lot of money we can make. We can do it a few times and see how it goes."

I could see in his face that he really didn't want to do it. But he knew I was right; more money could be made there then here physically.

"Miklo, I'll do it a couple times."

"Nice, that's what I'm talking about… Actually no, a couple of times isn't good enough."

He was silent.

"Do you really want out of this?" I asked him.

"Yes."

"Bring me to your contact so I can meet him and I'll leave you alone about it."

"No."

"No?"

"That's right."

"Why won't you let me meet your contact?"

We had been smoking a joint and when I asked him that he took a long puff, exhaled and said, "This is no good for us. Dealing is not good for the mind, body or soul."

"This is it man. What else are we going to do? You have a Bachler's in Psychology, do you want to be a psychiatrist?"

"No."

"No, exactly.

Later that day, more in the evening hours, we were sitting in his car smoking a joint watching the water over the rail of the street on Bay View Avenue in the back corner of Pelham Bay Park. I took a hit and passed it to him and then him back to me for a few tokes. When he gave me the joint halfway through, I said to him, "Why don't you want me to meet the guy?"

He took a hit, looked me and said, "There's something bad I feel from him."

"Something bad?"

"It's his name that scares me, or what he says his name is."

"What's his name?"

"He calls himself L Señor."

"L Señor? Like what Pablo Escobar called himself?"

"No, like the L is something else, probably his first name. He is not someone I trust."

"Did something happen to make you think that?"

"No."

"What's his deal?"

"All I know about him is that he had some problems in the west and now he's here."

"Problems."

"Yes Miklo, you know, problems only us drug dealers have." He said that in a really angry tone. I had struck a nerve.

"You know that I'm going to find out who this guy is and I'll just do business without you."

"You'll do it without me?"

"Yeah."

"Sure, coming from the guy who wouldn't take a gun from me the other night... I'll bring you with me next time, only because I know deep down inside, you're just a pussy."

"Fuck you!" I yelled.

"Yeah too bad I know you. Did you even tell Sadie?"

"Of course not." I wasn't going to tell him that I did tell her, even though it wasn't everything.

"Yeah, exactly... Do you still have that gun, or did you throw it in the garbage?"

"I still got it."

"Good, bring it but keep it hidden."

He took another hit and said to me, "I'm meeting him tomorrow afternoon, meet me at my apartment at one."

Kush may have been right but he seems to forget what happened in the past. At that moment I wasn't sure if I wanted to continue in this life, not that I was anywhere close to where I got.

"What is your plan anyway?" He asked me and I had to scramble my thoughts together to make it sound worth it.

"I was talking to one of the creators of the Rainbow yesterday for an hour. He expressed that they did not have a solid Marijuana contact in New York so I said I would be able to supply the website."

He became serious, what I was saying was making sense to him, "What are you going to tell L Señor?"

"That I can keep buying massive amounts of marijuana from him and possibly more soon."

"Are you going to tell him about Rainbow?"

"No, why should he know. I'm sure if he knew he would cut the middle man, which would be us, out of it and wouldn't need us."

"I hope you know what you're doing."

"If it makes you feel any better, no I don't…"

I got home to find Sadie sleeping on the couch with the television on. I shut the door and quietly walked over to the couch. The first things to come off of my body were my shoes and socks. Slowly I sat down on the couch not to startle her and when I did sit, I pulled her closer to me. Feeling her warmth, I knew I could never lose her.

"I missed you." She said.

"I missed you to."

I can tell she was waking up. With her groggy voice she said, "We can always borrow money from my parents if you want to stop dealing."

"No way."

"And drugs are the way?"

"No… But asking your parents for money is not what I want to do. We make it ourselves or fail together."

The contact asked to meet him at night instead of the afternoon. Kush thought it was weird.

I didn't think anything of it and when I said that to him, he replied, "Of course you don't."

I was in the passenger seat of Kush's car wondering where we were going and if any of this was a good idea. I kept saying to myself that *this is a mistake, this is not good*. There was another part of me that kept saying to go on with it, that I had already gone too far. I didn't like where the road was going, the neighborhood. We were on the Buckner expressway heading into the South Bronx in the middle of the night. On either side you could see the factories and a McDonald's sign a few blocks away. Some factories had lights but most did not, they never seemed to have any life inside and with that thought I felt weird. I suddenly began to feel the night time and somehow made myself more nervous than I had been.

In the distance I could see the sign on one of the buildings, a self-storage place, which is not weird for the area, but I got the feeling that that was where we were going.

I had to calm myself down. I opened the window and leaned against the door so I could be like a dog with my head semi out of the window. The road was smooth and the sound of the tires against the asphalt was relaxing and cool spring nights breeze engulfed my head with each breath becoming better, cleaner than before.

We were getting closer to the self-storage place. A white building with orange windows and a huge orange loading dock gate. The only way you could tell it was being used was the fact that it had a generic self-storage sign with one light on it to illuminate it in the night. You could tell this was a front. I was surprised no one else did sooner. It was like they didn't even care that they were doing an illegal operation out of a place like this.

"I assume were going to the self-storage building?" I asked Kush.

I could tell he was mad and definitely wanted to say something aggressive but chose to say to me, "There is no turning back now, you bothered me for days to meet this guy."

Awkward silence filled the car.

I decided not to talk to Kush for the rest of the ride. Instead I would focus on the passing streetlights.

"You better be care what you agree to, if you get to agree on something."

"With the Rainbow, all is possible Kush."

"What the fuck does that even mean?"

"No."

"No?"

"Yes… No."

"I really hope you know what you are doing because now you're just trying to piss me off."

"All I know is, I don't want to be dealing drugs for the rest of my life… I just want to be rich and live with Sadie for the rest of my life. If this is what brings me to that moment, I have to seize it."

"I do agree that we're not the kind of people to have regular jobs."

"Exactly, this is it. This is how we get out of the struggle."

It is from this point that I do not remember going into the warehouse.

My next memory is being in front of L Señor up close and personal studying his face. This particular memory for me always felt

102

overpowering. Whenever I even glanced over the file in my brain I would immediately think of a dark force. Everything about it just did not sit well with me, I was so nervous that I thought *when I think back on this all I'm going to remember being uncomfortable and scared.* I also felt that I was shaking the entire time, Kush later told me I was fine.

So... Here I am with Kush, inside the lair of L Señor with these guys. In fact, maybe these three weird bodyguards of L Señor made me feel like I did. They were all unique but indistinguishable. They were spread out across four tables within a rectangular area and in the middle came out L Señor, the chief among the Algonquins. They each were spread out evenly through-ought the room and had their own desk, although they each had their own way of sitting at their desks. They looked like scary guys, like they had done shit and were not afraid to let you know about it. I remember looking at them, making eye contact and immediately looking away as not to offend them. That's how nervous I was the first time in there. In my head I called them 'The Flunkies'.

The huge room we were in was very unsettling; the vast majority of which was shades of grey and green with long tube lights around the ceiling. It smelled like plaster and you could feel the damp, dirty air. Or it could have been the asbestos.

"What do you have for me?" L Señor asked. He said it so forcefully that it sounded like a command. He was dressed in a black button-down shirt with a black tie, black dress pants with Bates tactical boots and had one and a half inch tunnels in both of his ears. He was semi built with muscle and had this huge presence that you could feel. Whenever he was in a room with you in there, you knew he was in there, and would feel the dark force engulf you like flames. He wore black Dickies with what I realized only by the tag on the shirt was that he was also wearing a black Dickies button-down short sleeve shirt with a black tie. Upon further study of his face, you would go back to looking at the one and a quarter inch tunnels he had in his ears and tattoos you could not really make out on his arm, all I ever saw was black with touches of dark green.

I was frozen for what seemed like a few minutes but was really only a few seconds, "I would like to know how much you charge per pound and how many you can get in a week?"

L Señor gave me this face of confusion. "How many are you talking about?"

"Anywhere from five to ten pounds, depending weekly on the market."

It seemed like L Señor was thinking.

"You guys were coming to me for a couple years already for two or three pounds a week, and now you need five to ten?"

"Yeah, nothing less than five."

"Two thousand a pound." L Señor said in a firm voice.

"Seventeen hundred, I will be buying five or more a week."

L Señor looked around to his flunkies. They were still sitting at their own tables, looking at Kush and I like we were in the den of the lions.

It was at this moment I said to myself; *You fucked up.*

"What changed?"

I knew there was going to be a question about this sudden spike. "The market is good; we've broadened out and expanded."

I felt that he got jealous and had the feeling he looked down at us, you know, because he's this big-time middle man. I stood my ground and I could feel that he did not like that.

"The market... Seriously, we can talk about weight and prices, but I just wanna' know what made you come to the point of getting more. That seems like that's something good for people like us to know. Maybe a mutual opportunity of some sort."

Don't say something stupid, figure out something good to say, think quick...

"I've been doing this for years. I'm tired of meeting stoners on street corners, sketchy blocks and shitty buildings. I've had enough, if I could open a dispensary I would. Sure, I could just go to California to do that but fuck that. I hear that cannabis will be legal in Colorado within the next couple years, but I can't wait. I want to do other things but I still want the income from cannabis. Maybe one day, you and I can get into business together when cannabis becomes legal here in New York but until them I am done with the small stuff. So, I made arrangements and here we are..."

"That really didn't answer the question."

"I sell to people that buy weight. I sell nothing less than eight ounces."

"Eight ounces, huh? Eighteen hundred." L Señor said in an optimistic voice.

It was a weird switch of tone in his voice but I said, "Seventeen hundred."

"Eighteen hundred, and you have any problems you come to us. Can I trust your team?"

"We don't need protection... I stand at seventeen hundred. You'll be seeing us a lot more and I'm sure making some more money on the side. I don't really see a downside of this for you. How's Kush? He would be a pretty good indicator of the sort of people I would associate myself into business with. I'm sure you wouldn't be doing business with him if you didn't trust him. You worry and control your team and I will worry and control my own. We won't interfere. The less you know about my people, the less I know about your people, the better off we will all be."

I guess he liked that, I could tell he appreciated the honesty.

"When you do you need the first five?" He asked.

"Today is Wednesday, Friday latest."

"Okay..." L Señor said in this happy-optimistic tone, "Tomorrow night between six and nine be here, we'll have it."

"Let's start with seven."

"Okay, seven it is."

"Seventeen hundred?"

"You have a deal Miklo..." He said. I thought it was over but he had more to say. "There is something about you that I both like and dislike. I'm not sure if you're nervous or this is just how you always look... But you should loosen up and smile a little."

"Smile." I said.

"Yeah. Smile because if you fuck me, you'll never be able to smile again." He said pointing his finger at me. Kush and I walked out of the room and down the hallways with two of the flunkies following to make sure we left the building.

Kush was not happy about what went on in there. His paranoia was at an all-time high and there was really no way to talk to him in that state. Anything I said just bounced off of him.

"What are you trying to do? He knew there was something you weren't telling him." Kush said to me in this authoritative way; like an older brother telling his younger sibling how to act.

"That was kind of the point, we did broaden and expand our market, he doesn't need to know how. Unless he winds up being the guy I was talking to on the website, then I think we're okay."

"You have twelve thousand dollars?"

"Yeah, of course I do…" I got mad at him for even asking, "how do you not think I have money for that, you should know that I wouldn't do this if I didn't have money. Come on bro, keep your paranoia out of it."

"It's not that, asshole. I just hope you know what you're doing because this guy does not fuck around. That man cannot be trusted."

After this, Kush would not go pick up the *ish* without me. Shit like that always made me mad with him, *of course I was going to fucking go with him*. At least he came with me, he could have just told me to fuck off and get it myself.

This time, there was a definite feeling that this was different. It was not repealing and drew me in as a new life. The warehouse room felt a lot brighter to me and the flunkies did not look as scary. It was like working in retail and being in the breakroom with people you barely know that have to just get along with each other to sustain everyone's each individual life.

That's some sick shit, right?

This time the flunkies were doing things. When they aren't staring at you, they look less intimidating. It's funny because after this, Kush told me that he felt worse the second time and every time after that he felt worse and worse to the point of, he eventually not coming with me. That is way too far from here. It is crazy to think of him there because it became so out of place.

When we entered the room, I saw the seven pounds on the table in front of L Señor, who did not say a word first; one of his flunkies came over to me and said, "I'll take the money."

So, I took my twelve stack and handed it to him. He counted it in front of me. Every dollar he touched and made sure it was real, I guess. I thought he was going to take out one of those counterfeit pens and start marking them.

"It's all here." He said to L Señor as he turned around and walked away.

"That's a lot of cannabis, my friend." L Señor said to me.

"Yeah it is." I said, picking up the bag and throwing it on my shoulder.

"Since our last visit I've wondered how you were able to expand your market so much for the amount of product you are buying. Wouldn't you like to share the information with people and maybe make a little bit more money?"

"It's the maybe thing that gets me. Like I said, people buy weight. If it's not worth it I don't sell it."

"I like your attitude. You should come work for me."

"No thanks, I like working for myself. I don't have to pay myself for protection."

L Señor laughed. It was not natural, it was forced.

"We offer more than protection…" He said menacingly.

"Nope, all good. Don't go selling me any vacuums."

The three of us tirelessly sealed and cleaned all the shipments and put them into USPS boxes. There were fifteen boxes in all and had decided that one person could bring all of these to the post office. We would each go to different post offices and send out five.

Kush had the bright idea to make a fake company logo and slap it on the box. He designed some weird brown monkey.

Standing in the post office was a weird feeling. I was waiting online and watching everyone interact with the workers there. These government workers at this location couldn't give a shit what I was sending out.

When I handed the boxes to the uptight black lady behind the bullet proof glass in the window she commented on the box, "What are you in business or something?"

What a weird thing to ask.

"Yeah," I said pulling shit out of my ass, "I'm a carpenter and sell things online."

"Better get a better logo."

When I got home, I made sure to send Panzer a message. I felt that I was letting him know too much by telling him everything I did and that he probably viewed me as an idiot.

Miklo: Seven Pounds incoming.

Seen

Panzer has entered chat.

Panzer has left chat.

That did not make me feel any better.
He totally thinks you're an idiot.
I knew it would be a couple days before there would be a response.
Sure enough, a day and a half later, I checked my Coinbase account and I had received seventeen thousand five hundred dollars.
Not bad.
L Señor has no idea what I'm doing. I kept telling myself, *smarten up, don't be stupid.*
That day I also received another message from Panzer.

Panzer: Fifteen pounds?

Miklo: Fifteen, sure. Should I just go for

an even twenty?

Panzer: If you get twenty, there will be a

much bigger payout for you. If

we can do this once a week, on

a routine schedule this will work

out just fine. You won't have to

sell to buyers, you'll just deal

with me.

Miklo: Deal

Panzer has left chat.

Twenty pounds was going to be a tall order.
I was dreading having to deal with L Señor.
That was the choice I made.

A couple of hours later I was again with Sadie and we were spending much needed time together. We had drifted apart and there was a sense of silent separation. We both had the same feelings but would not verbalize them, more of less afraid to. We were out having dinner somewhere on the avenue, killed a bottle of wine, stuffed our faces with food and then decided to go to New Rochelle to play pool. We had so much fun that night. I got the sense that we were both on a natural high with each other. Mutual love was shared and we each cared deeply about the other. I could go on about Sadie but it hurts, it's also extremely hard to write about it. This night was special to me, it was the last one that I remember fully spending it with her. It was also the beginning of the end for us. The problem with us was that once we got to this particular point in our lives we were on different planets and dimensions. We loved each other but it felt like a hollow kind of love.

In bed with her that night was incredible. We did not have sex but we were just in each other's arms.

That was it.

She had something to say, but once again could not verbalize it.

I debated asking what was on her mind, I couldn't ask, nor did I really want to hear what she was going to say. I was tired of having the same conversation.

"You don't plan on stopping selling drugs, do you?" She asked.

Although I had prepared for that it still became a mood killer.

"I do plan on stopping, but right now. I got something really good going. More money, less time dealing."

"What does that mean?"

"It means that I'm trying to make a large amount of money in a short amount of time, so I'll be comfortable enough to stop dealing, to get something better."

"Truth?"

"Always truth."

"What are you doing that's different?"

"I'd say I'm the middle man."

"Of what?"

"I got some new contacts that deal in big orders, we get the product, deliver them and that's it. It's not on street corners or shady areas. I'd say it's better."

Definitely do not tell her about the Rainbow and mailing out drugs.

Don't be a fool.

The next thought in my head was not to lie to her, but I really did not want to deal with the argument after.

We didn't look at each other as we were both staring at the television. I don't even remember what was on. I was just lost in my own thoughts. When Sadie and I first started going out together I used to write things like this:

A flower blossoming,
A beautiful rose,
Glistening in the sunlight.

Now, those feelings I used to have weren't there anymore.

The next morning, I woke up in bed to find that Sadie had already left for work and was feeling very upset about the current state of the relationship. She had told me before that if things got really bad with the dealing that she would leave me. I don't know why I tried to push the limits but at the time I felt I had to. Lying in bed I did not want to even get up. There was no reason to get up. I picked up my cell phone to call Sadie but at the last moment I decided not to. No sense in talking on the phone.

I had to get up though.

I had to go meet L Señor.

∞

I must have met L Señor two dozen times in the span of two months and each time it progressively got weirder.

He got weirder.

It had even gotten to the point that Kush would no longer go with me. It gave him too many bad vibes that he claimed would follow him home.

So, I went to meet the guy alone. Always carrying my huge red Marlboro luggage bag which L Señor would always comment on, "Miklo, again with this bag? Do you just want to be a beacon to the police?"

My answer was, "It's bright and inconspicuous. They would never have any idea what was right in front of their face."

I became nervous when it was the time to ask for twenty pounds, it is quite a big jump from seven to twenty.

"Today, I'm going to need twenty pounds."

L Señor stopped whatever he was doing and looked at me. The flunkies were even looking at me like I was crazy. How dare I ask Mr. Señor to buy twenty pounds.

"Twenty?" L Señor asked.

"Yes."

"A week ago, you came in here asking for seven pounds and now you want twenty? Do you see how that would make me want to ask you how you are selling so much?"

"Yeah I can see that."

"How far have you broadened and expanded?"

"Pretty far. Most of my clients buy nothing less than a quarter pound, my stuff goes quick."

"How many people do you have working for you?"

"I think this falls under our original agreement which was, you worry and control your team, and I'll worry and control my team."

"I did not agree to that, but I also did not disagree with that. I like your style and attitude."

I didn't want to acknowledge that so I said, "I'm going to need twenty pounds a week from now on."

L Señor waved a finger in the air and the flunkies started to gather the twenty pounds which they were stuffing into my Marlboro bag. I gave him the stack of thirty-six thousand dollars. He looked at me funny when I did hand it to him.

The twenty pounds barley fit into that bag.

"Maybe bring a different less conspicuous bag next time." L Señor said.

"Nah, I'll bring this one."

The next time I went to meet L Señor was even weirder.

This time, while the flunkies were filling up the Marlboro bag with the cannabis, he called me into a smaller room where he was counting money and told me to sit in the chair across from him.

He sat down and put onto the table a bag of money that had blood on it and began to count the money. Blood was getting all over his hands. The blood was still semi fresh and that sent alarm bells in my head. The smell of the drying blood stayed with me for a while after and I couldn't eat for at least a day.

"So, how do you manage to sell twenty pounds a week? He asked.

I had to pull something out of my ass so I said, "I sell quarter pounds and half pounds to a lot of people in midtown Manhattan. Most of my clients are successful people who just want to buy a lot of weed."

"How many customers would you say you have?"

"I have no idea. I don't keep track."

"Seems like something you should know."

"Irrelevant to me."

L Señor got really serious for a moment. He took a rag and wiped the blood off of his hands, which only smeared it around and made the white cloth look stained in blood. "What are you doing?"

"Nothing, what do you mean?"

"How are you moving these products?"

"I seriously don't think it's any of your concern. Especially, when you already have my money for them. Every week when I come get more." *You sound like an idiot.*

"Do these packages find their way going around the country?"

This question had me concerned. I immediately had the thought in my head that L Señor was part of the Rainbow, or any one of the other websites, and he was seeing if I was just pretty much selling it back to them. In that moment, my heart sank and I could myself being buried under dirt.

"Packages," I said, not wanting to clear my throat, "I don't have the man power for that. Should we be looking into that?"

L Señor backed off a little. I had fooled him for the moment. "No, too dangerous. We've tried everything, driving it, mailing it… Nothing works over state borders." He said counting the last stack.

"Yeah I rather keep things in the city I know."

"I agree…" he said and became docile, looked at me and continued, "I hope your telling me the truth with everything. If I find out anything other than what you told me today, it will not be good for you. Your team I will spare, but you will get the full wrath of what I have. Do you understand?"

"Yes." I said, contemplating packing my bags and going to Mexico. He couldn't get away with saying that. There was a debate ensuing my mind if I should say something to him. My temper got the best of me so I said, "Did being a bully always get you what you wanted? Or did it make you such an asshole that you don't know what it's like to be just a regular person?"

He didn't move but his eyes looked at me. Putting the stack down he calmly breathed in and said, "I would watch your tone. You are in my house. You treat me with respect, even if I don't show you the same. I think you think this is a game. This is no game. The dealing environment is fragile. Keep your mouth shut from now on and get the fuck out of here." He said motioning his hand for me to go out of the door,

I left the storage place wheeling my red Marlboro bag to my car and was processing everything that was going on.

I can't believe he said that.

Don't say anything like that next time.

The whole ride home I spent looking in the rear-view mirror because there was the feeling they were going to follow me home. The *paranoia* had settled into my psyche and I was fully engulfed in it.

I wasn't paranoid about the cops, but of L Señor.

Welcome to the point of no return.

Sadie and I were having dinner. A nice homemade dinner we had cooked together. The whole day we were discussing or relationship and decided that it was worth saving and that we had to get more in touch with each other again. The thought of taking a break had crossed our minds but it was not something we wanted. We had been together for years and this dinner was going very well. We were talking, laughing and planning the rest of our lives.

I poured us each a glass of wine and just when we were about to take out sips my cell phone rang.

We paused and let the phone ring a couple of times, but it had to be answered. I could tell it was annoying her. I got up from the table, took the phone out from my pocket and answered it.

"Hello."

"Miklo, they robbed me?"

"Kush? Who robbed you?" I turned around to look at Sadie who was giving me the look when she heard me say that. It was the look of, *I told you so*, it never ends. She drank the whole glass of wine.

"I don't know. These two guys came up to the car, dragged me out of it and…"

"I'll be over there in a minute."

"Yeah, I'm home now."

I hung up the phone and again looked at Sadie who was not amused.

'I'm going to Kush's to see if he's okay."

"What happened?"

"He got robbed."

"Maybe this will help you see that this needs to end." She said leaving the table. The room felt empty.

When I got to his apartment he was sitting at his desk with his head in his hands. I'm surprised he didn't go on a rampage. He did not move at all. He wasn't even shaking his leg. In my mind I could see him smashing everything and taking a bat to his television.

"Miklo, you really fucked me."

"I fucked you?"

"You know who did this right?"

"No who?"

"It has to be L Señor."

That would make sense.

"Did they hurt you?"

"No, they did nothing but point a gun in my face, make me get out of the car and they searched the car, found everything, took it and left."

"How much did they get?"

"No cash, just the QP I had."

"Why would he rob you for the weed, especially something small?"

"I don't know."

"Kush, I don't think its him."

"We can't be certain."

I shouldn't have said what I am about to, "He has been asking me weird questions and being very standoff ish."

"How so? See I told you!"

"He asked if this product goes around the country and if it finds itself in the mail."

"Wow… How long ago was that?"

"Couple days ago, … I got the feeling that he buys from the Rainbow and he thinks I'm just selling it back into the Rainbow."

"Oh, fuck dude, that's probably exactly what happened."

"Did you tell Anthony?"

"No."

"Good, don't. He won't be able to keep a secret."

"Wait, so, we're just going to keep up a charade with L Señor."

"Yupp. We gotta' keep making money."

"I'm down for the money, but no of this will end well if we keep going with L Señor."

"Let's make as much as we can. Sadie has been bothering me to stop selling, so it might come to that."

"I say we keep it up just not with him."

"What the fuck else are we gonna' do? I'm not going back to corners and shit."

Kush just shook his head and said, "It's always what you want."

Like I said before, something good doesn't last too long without something negative happening.

I felt that Anthony had kind of developed this weird 'mob' mentality. There was definitely too much Godfather and Goodfellas on in his childhood that must have embedded itself within him. He began to have this temper but, in my mind, at the time, I felt that at least one of us had to have that kind of feeling. It was better for him because the paranoia didn't affect him, he could care less about the law; but this also made him make stupid little mistakes, or seemingly so at first…

He was waiting for one of his customers at a gas station. He was too stupid to know that maybe that would not be the best place to meet someone for drugs. He was there maybe ten minutes, probably smoked a cigarette or two and all the while the Indian man working at the register inside the station was watching him purely out of boredom. The person pulled up to Anthony and he got out of the car. He made a rookie mistake and gave the product to the man before he got the money and the man gave him a problem along the lines of the fact that he didn't have any money and wanted it on credit.

"Credit?" Anthony asked.

"People do give credit…" The man said.

"Who do you think we are?" Anthony's tone changed and I'm sure the first thing he thought about would be the Louisville Slugger in between his seat and door of his car.

"I'll give you the money tomorrow." The man said.

Anthony didn't want to hear anymore, "No, either give it to me now or I bust your face in."

The man and everyone in his car laughed and I'm sure that infuriated Anthony more because he knew that this dude was acting like that because of the really hot lady in the passenger's seat and his two friends in the backseat. This made Anthony even madder. The man drove up a foot and rolled up his window acting as if he was going to drive away, all he wanted was for Anthony to tell him yes, but that wasn't happening.

Anthony had to put the guy in his place. He went over to his own car and reached through the open window and grabbed the bat he was thinking about. He cocked back and hit the guy's car with all his strength destroying his taillight. Needless to say, that everyone in the car got really pissed and the Indian man who was watching them from inside had already called the piggies. A small brawl broke out and since the Police Department is right down the block, they were there in a matter of a few minutes. Anthony was arrested and so was everyone else there. The cops searched his car and they found nothing, thinking about it now *where the hell did he hide all that stuff?* They found nothing and he really got nothing. The other guy on the other hand had whatever he had gotten from Anthony and that was enough to get him in a lot of trouble because they believed he was the one selling it.

Until then I really hadn't thought about the threat of the police but it was a very real awakening. Nothing had happened to what I was doing but the paranoia just set in that much more. All the 'what if' questions circled my mind. I tried to keep all the negative thoughts in the back of my mind and didn't want to acknowledge them.

I should have been thinking about something else.

At the time, I was unaware of what was going on with Anthony.

When I think about it now that moment is actually really sad, it's when I acknowledged the fact that Anthony was gone, the Anthony I knew at least. He became a different person, somewhat a completely different persona; it was not him. In fact, these words have been the first time since then that I referred to him as Anthony. Over and over again I would think of what he did with the bat and the fight. He earned the nickname I gave him, Spazz. I also blame myself for not addressing this issue. The fact that I gave him a nickname over this and joked about it had been sending him the wrong signals on how to act.

Where was I when this was going on? I was with Sadie playing billiards and having a few drinks. It was one of those perfect nights for us, we barley spoke to each other, just our presence and playing pool was something far more than we ever expected from each other. To just love each other's company is one of the best relationships in the world. We were so inebriated and happy from our night out that when we got home, we made love like dogs. After... we were lying in bed together and I knew she fell asleep. It was when I knew that she was the one I wanted all nights to end with and all my days begin with. That was my dream, forever and ever with her and the rest of the world could just go fuck itself.

My cell phone rang.

I don't know if the ringer woke me up or if I was just up staring at the ceiling but the ringing was annoying. It woke up Sadie to. I jumped out of bed and grabbed the phone, flipping it open to answer the call, "Hello."

I can tell Anthony was frantic and I knew it was him just from his breathing. "I got bagged..."

There are not enough words in the English dictionary to replace the words *oh shit*.

"What happened?" I asked.

"I fucked up, they took me in and I used my phone call on you."

"Why the fuck would you call me? What did you do?"

"I'll explain another time... Can you get me out of here?"

"Anthony, what the fuck did you do? You're calling me from the precinct, not telling me what happened and I'm supposed to get dressed and pick your ass up?"

"I used the slugger on someone's car at the gas station..."

"How many fucking times did I tell you not to meet people at the gas station?"

No words.

"Seriously, Anthony? How many times did I tell you that?"

"A few."

"Yeah, a few. I should let you wait in there to see the judge."

I was so angry at him that I closed the phone and hung up on him. He had to learn. I felt bad for leaving him in bookings for the night but a lesson had to be taught.

I don't think any lesson as learned.

I bailed him out the next morning.

And where was Kush while all of this was going on?

He became sort of a recluse. He only came to hang out with Anthony and I for maybe an hour or two, there was one time he hung out with me when Anthony wasn't there.

He seemed silent as he sat on my couch. Every once in a while, he would take his hand and wave it across the front of his face. At first, I didn't want to ask what was going on, I figured he was just going crazy. After he had waved his hand a couple of more times, I knew something was up.

"What are you on?" I asked expecting him to freak out on me. I thought he would say, 'Oh, so now I'm on drugs.'

But he did the opposite. Actually, he laughed and said, "That's a very acute observation Mr. Miklo. You're the only person so far to notice something off about me... I'm on a low dose of a research chemical that was created by Shura."

"Shura?"

"I'll show you the world of psychedelics one day. They aren't as bad as everyone makes these drugs out to be, much like Marijuana."

"So, what does this stuff do to you?"

"Gives you visuals and maybe, depending on what you take, some hallucinations. I could go on about these for a while..." He paused for a moment; choosing his words carefully. "Can I be honest with you?"

"Of course."

"I'm fucked up dude. Not from the drugs, well maybe some of it is from the drugs, they just opened my mind so much, made me think clearer than ever. Dude, I can't get over this shit. I can't even listen to music or watch television anymore; I can't even listen to good tripping music while on this stuff. Do you know how fucked up the world is?"

"Yeah."

"Everyone is out to get everyone."

"Really man, did these people really fuck you up in the head? They robbed you, get over it, it happened and it can't be changed.

Thinking about it every day doesn't help you get over it either. Dwell on your problems, build a wall and die because that's all you're doing." It probably didn't seem like I was trying to help but I was, I was trying to be a good friend but I've never been good for the pep talks. I saw the problem and tried to get him out of it. I had known about his music thing for a while now and while I was driving on Lodovick Avenue I came up with how to deal with him, that I call the Lodovick Technique which is just to tell the truth to a person and get them back to normal using words and regular conversation. This never seemed to work. Whenever you try helping people, particularly friends, it's always hard and it the words never come out how you intend them to. I've seen friendships end like this.

"I wish it was that easy that simple to forget about it all. Nah man, I rather trip balls at my house all night than come out and see people I don't want to see."

"It's all good, now I know I'm your friend."

We laughed.

"Yeah man… Don't think I'm a drug addict. I'm not on Crystal Meth, maybe some form of Meth. You know I smoke bud, do these substances and still pay my bills."

He did have a point.

"So, are they illegal?" I asked.

"Kind of, two of them are schedule one… Would you like to try some?"

"No thanks, I'm good with weed."

I was dreading having to see the bastard. The entire drive there I tried to talk myself out of going there, but I did not listen to myself. It's funny that money would make people do things they never thought they would. Once again, I was wheeling my red Marlboro bag into the storage place. It started out okay. The flunkies were yet again filling my bag with the usual twenty pounds. There was a vibe, something in the air that needed to be extracted and eradicated.

L Señor seemed like he had something to say to me. He was sitting in the chair staring at me while his flunkies took an inventory of the cannabis in the duffle bags; he was sitting there as if he was a king watching over everything, at first, to me, it wasn't really anything. He got up from the chair and extended his arm to me motioning for me to come over to him. I didn't move, *I'm not an animal that comes by the motion of a hand.*

"Miklo, come, let's talk for a minute." He said to me.

I followed L Señor into the next room where he waited for me to come in before he shut the door. It was the second time the two of us were alone and there were literally a million things I thought would happen.

"So, L Señor, what's going on?"

"I heard one of your guys was picked up in between the time of our last meeting and today."

I hadn't told anyone, not even Kush knew so how did *he* know.

"Nothing... No thoughts?" He said in a menacing tone.

"Yes, one of my guys was picked up."

"Ah, there you go! Taking responsibility for your people, I like that."

"Is there a reason we're talking about this?"

"Of course, ... I hope that that person is no longer on your team."

"It's really of no concern who's on my team or not, part of our agreement was the complete lack of knowledge of who's on the other man's team."

"A person from your side gets arrested for Disorderly Conduct, Aggravated Assault, Disturbing the Peace and Intent to Sell. You do realize that having that person working in a situation like ours isn't a good idea. People going around swinging baseball bats and destroying tail lights aren't to be trusted in this business."

"Are you checking up on us?"

"Of course, I am. I have to protect my stock."

"Protect your stock? Isn't this part of the 'your team, my team' thing?" All the pieces had fallen together and I knew he was having me followed and I was even more sure he was the one who had Kush robbed.

I'm in deep shit.

"Is there anything else you want to tell me now?"

I wasn't going to tell him anything, "Nope."

"Are you sure about that?"

"Yes."

"I don't believe you."

"That's okay, I don't need you to believe me, I know what I believe is right and you have the right to believe whatever you want to."

L Señor looked deep into my eyes.

"A man who can quote the Quran has some sort of sophistication that other men don't…" He was thinking as he was looking at me. It made me uncomfortable. "You work for me now. You're coming with us." He said to me with dark intensions.

"No." I said to him, "Our agreement never mentioned anything about this."

"The agreement is gone, once your piece of shit friend got arrested for that stupid shit. You are now working for me. You do what I want and do as I say. I needed an extra man for this anyway, so this all works out for me." He said and came closer to me, so close that I could see all the pours on his nose and said, "Now you are going to prove to me if you are a trustworthy person to work with."

The four flunkies didn't say a word but I could tell they had all heard this before. I could feel my heart beating and *I couldn't believe I was one of his flunkies, how do I get out of this?* There was no indication of being able to leave. I could smell L Señor's breath and I knew I was in some deep shit.

I heard the warehouse door open and out of the corner of my eye a man walked in. L Señor and the three flunkies faces had the look of surprise on them. The man was wearing a grey sweatshirt and jogging pants. L Señor turned away from me and looked at him, the flunkies also looked at him.

L Señor looked as if he was thinking of what to say, and just before I was able to speculate what he would say he said, "Rico, Rico, Rico… Welcome back my friend. If you are in fact coming back."

"My feelings haven't changed." Rico said to L Señor.

"Then what is the reason you're here?"

"I had a feeling about you guys and I had to just come and see you?"

"A feeling?" L Señor said condescendingly.

"A feeling that you would do something you would regret."

I did not know what to do, I felt as if a fight would break out between the two and that someone was going to get hurt. I stood there, breathing and not moving.

L Señor made a face that I cannot describe, not sure if it was good or bad, and said, "So you are coming back? But my feeling is that your only back until the feeling goes away. Is this a right assumption?"

"I see you haven't changed and I see you already replaced me."

I did not think my reaction through, before I knew it the words, "Um, no I'm not replacing you", flew out of my mouth.

L Señor turned to me and came back to my face and said, "Yes, you are the replacement."

"No, I am not."

Staring into L Señor's eyes I knew if I said anything else it would have led to something physical. I was not ready for anything like that.

He motioned his hand to me, pointed his index finger and touched me with it and said, "You were Rico's replacement." With his finger still on me he looked at Rico and said, "Now that you are here, do you want to do a job with the five of us?"

I didn't know it then but Rico only said, "Sure", because he was looking out for me, he knew I wasn't a flunky and I could tell Rico didn't want to be one again but we became L Señor and the five flunkies.

L Señor finally took his finger off of me, looked around at everyone and said, "Load up the van, it's going to be a good day. A good day indeed."

The three flunkies began doing their work to load up the truck and I stood there, my first intention was not to do anything but be forced into the truck. I could sense that they all knew this and left me there. L Señor went over to Rico and for the next couple of minutes they had a private conversation that I could not hear. I could only see the hand gestures. It may have been an argument but Rico kept looking at me and when L Señor went to give him a handshake Rico pulled away and said kind of loudly, "We shake when I see it." L Señor pulled back and said, "okay Rico, if that's how it has to be."

That did not sound good.

"Truck is ready." One of the flunkies said but I did not see who said it, I was still fixed on L Señor and Rico, but when L Señor heard those words he turned around and said, "Let's go."

I had no idea where we were going. L Señor passed me and said, "Your sitting in the front seat."

After he passed, Rico came and stood in front of me, without anyone looking, "This is not going to be good." After he said that to me, he got into the van and L Señor yelled at me, "Miklo! Get your ass in the truck!"

I composed myself and got in the passenger's seat of the van.

L Señor got into the seat behind me and said to me, "You and Rico are not allowed to talk to each other."

"Too bad you and I don't have an agreement like that." I said feeling his hand slap me in the back of the head.

"Too bad." He said, "Miguel, drive."

So, I guess Miguel got into the driver's seat, looked at me with this look of anger as he started to drive.

I'm not going to survive this day.

After fifteen minutes of silence and only hearing the noises of the road and van, Rico decided to break the silence since he was not in the loop of what was going on, I wasn't either but had to listen to know what I'm getting into.

"Where are we off to?" Rico asked.

I could not see L Señor's face but I pictured him holding a gun to my head with a weird smirk on his face, but he probably was not and had just a regular serious L Señor face. "To teach the competition a lesson."

A clear jab at me.

Teach a lesson to the competition.

To teach the competition a lesson.

This phrase kept repeating in my head the whole rest of the ride. Every single time I repeated it I got more and more angry with Anthony. I can't believe what he did and how it put me into this situation. He spazzed out. Next time I see him I won't call him Anthony; I'm going to call him Spazz. *Kush was right, you should have been doing this by yourself, not have contacted L Señor.*

The rest of the ride we were all silent.

Impending doom was lurking.

I didn't even know where we were going. I spent that time thinking about who this Rico guy was and why he wasn't there and why he came back, all things that would be answered to me in time. In the moment they were burning questions. *And why was L Señor okay with him coming with us if he had this 'feeling'?*

123

We were driving down Bruckner Boulevard and I could feel the tension within the van so that was first indication that we were getting close. We pulled up to a street named Quincy. As soon as we began to pull over, I knew this was the place. I almost started to cry because I was so nervous. I was shaking as if I was freezing.

The van came to a complete stop. L Señor had not waited for the van to stop moving to open his door and jump out. As everyone was leaving the van I stayed in the seat. L Señor saw this and said, "When we get out, you get out, when we stay in you stay in, we are out so that means you are out."

I took a deep breath and opened my door and slowly made my way out.

The flunkies were taking their positions.

L Señor went over to Rico and again they had a private conversation; and after it was over L Señor walked away from him but Rico stood where he was and just looked at me and he gave me a hand signal, he pointed his index finger down which confused me at first but I took it as WAIT. *Wait for what?*

"I go in last, that means Miklo you are in front of me, then Rico, then Carlos, then Jose and first is Miguel. You all but Miklo know the drill."

Know the drill, what the fuck is about to happen?

We were approaching this greyish white house but we did not go up the stairs, we were heading to the ground floor door. Along with my heart feeling like it was going to beat right out of my chest I was also having some heart palpitations on my right side.

Miguel knocked on the door. *He knocked on the fucking door, this poor person has no idea what's going to happen. Fuck, I don't even know what's going to happen.*

It may have been happening in real time but I heard and saw everything in slow motion. I heard the hand on the inside touch the top lock of the door, turn the bottom lock and turn the knob. Before he could even open the door fully Miguel and the rest of the flunkies were already ramming the door with their body weight and ran into the home. I heard the man scream and we heard a woman scream.

They went right for the people, they tied up the man and put him face down on the floor, he was the easy one. From the bedroom we could hear the screams of a women, she had shut door and put a chair under the door knob. That was smart. When L Señor got to the door he touched it and looked back at us. *Wow, I just said us, I grouped myself in with the flunkies.*

"Get the door buster." He said to Miguel.

Miguel didn't even flinch, he turned around and went out of the apartment to the van.

"Women," L Señor said in this low untrustworthy voice, "Come outside and everything will be okay."

We heard the buttons pressing on a telephone through the door, L Señor asked Jose, "Did you cut the phone?"

"Yes sir."

And with that we heard the phone drop.

L Señor knocked on the door, "Come out."

The man they tied up had a bandanna shoved in his mouth and he was lying on his stomach trying to scream as loud as he could but his voice was muffled, no one would hear him scream. The women on the other hand was screaming and I can tell L Señor was getting mad.

Miguel came in hot with the door buster. I had only seen these on television and had no idea they had one in the van. He was running and as soon as he made contact with the door the door broke into two pieces and they swarmed the room, Rico staying back with me. He looked me dead in the eye and just when he was about to say something to me L Señor was directly in front of us.

He held up his index finger and said, "I told you two no talking… Rico, I don't know what you were about to say but I definitely want to know now."

"I was… going to tell him that this all gets easier."

"It certainly does." L Señor said with a fake smile.

The three other flunkies were tying the women upon the bed.

One can never forget the fear in her eyes and when they propped her up to the headboard, she made eye contact with me and it killed me that I was part of this, she doesn't know that and I felt like shit.

"You know Rico and Miklo, you are the two I don't know if I can trust, you two wait over there." He said as he was pointing to the opposite side of the room. We both went to the other side and stood there as the other three were bringing in the man who was now squirming for his life trying to break free from the rope in which he was bound. They put him propped up against the headboard also and the image of both of them tied up staring into my eyes will be an image that will forever be burned into my head. I remember hearing both of them breathing through the cloths in their mouths; the sweat dripping from their heads.

I have spent many nights doing drugs trying to forget all of this; *there is no forgetting this.*

The man locked eyes with me and I couldn't believe it. It was the Preacher. He kept staring at me and I didn't know what to do. I held back tears but I couldn't stop my eyes from getting watery. The thought of this eats at my soul.

"You're a pot dealer, right?" L Señor asked the Preacher.

The Preacher nodded a Yes.

"Do you know whose hood this is?"

The Preacher nodded No.

"Do you know who I am?"

The Preacher nodded No."

"I am L Señor. I am the dealer of the Bronx and you stole from one of my guys. Tell me where my pot and where my money is and you guys live."

No answer.

"This conversation isn't getting through to you?"

The Preacher had this crazed look in his eyes, I know what he was thinking, he wanted to kill all of us, especially this man who took charge, the bastard. The way he was looking at me, he probably wanted to kill me just after the bastard.

"At least tell me where and when you stole it."

No answer.

"Okay," L Señor said in a very angry tone as he yanked the cloth out of the man's mouth, "now that you can talk, where and when did you steal my stuff?"

"You," that man said catching his last breaths of air, "I know who you are now. You come here from the west and think it's all yours. I have heard of you L Señor, people talk about you and it's never good. You and the Weightlifter both deserve to be dead."

The Preacher looked at me and I thought he was about to rat me out. Nothing happened. L Señor had noticed but did not mention anything about it.

That struck a nerve with L Señor and his demeanor changed, he was now angry. I looked over at Rico for his reaction and he was already turning to look at me and nodded his head Yes.

"The hard way it is. Just to let you know this is the easy way out for me, not for you."

L Señor took out a handgun from his back and unloaded the clip, taking out every bullet from it and the bullet in the chamber also. He then loaded the empty clip back into the gun. He looked at me and I knew he was going to hand it to me and make me do something. He came over to me and handed me the gun.

I did not take it.

L Señor handed me the gun and said, "Smack him with it."

I didn't say anything or even reach for the gun.

He walked over, grabbed my hand, opened my palm and put the gun in my palm, closing my hand.

"No."

"No?"

"Yes... No, I am not doing this."

"Miklo, you know, you're really pissing me off. You work for me right now and you will do as your told."

"No, you're a fucking psychopath. I will not step to your level and torture these people anymore. You should let them go and…"

I couldn't get the last half of sentence out, L Señor had grabbed my mouth and said, "You speak one more word for the rest of time we are here and I won't kill them, I'll kill you and leave you on the bed with them bleeding all over. So, chose to be alive or to hit them… Your choice."

No words were spoken by me for the rest of the time. I was holding the gun in my hands and every time I wanted to say something my mind was like, *'who should die? Them or you? I rather have them die'.* Of course, my other was saying, *'there must be something you can do to stop all of this…'* *'No there isn't. What a shame this all is.'*

"Time's ticking." The bastard said to me. "The woman gets hit first."

The tied-up Preacher began to go crazy. I could not make out what he as saying but I know he was pleading with L Señor but he wasn't budging, this was going to happen.

I really wanted to tell the Preacher that I didn't want to do this and that I didn't tell them who he was. I wanted to explain that they had found him and that it was all a coincidence, but I could not.

Then out came the revolver from L Señor's pocket and as he pointed it to my face, he was cocking it. I was not ready to die. I knew what I had to do, and I would never forgive myself.

I walked over to the bed and looked at the female. My education in Darwinism was coming back to be and it all came down to the fact that it was survival of the fittest; also, I didn't want to be dead on the bed with these people.

Thinking about it now I wasn't completely silent, as I was looking at the women, who was scared out of her mind, I took the arm that the gun was in and got ready to hit her, just before I did, I said to her and the man, "I'm so sorry guys." And with that I swung and hit her in the head with the butt of the gun. The Preacher was now screaming but his voice still muffled by the cloth they shoved into his mouth. I walked to the other side of the bed to do it to the Preacher and as I was walking over, I kept saying to myself, *'That's it, you're a goddamn FLUNKY. You are part of this and just as bad as them.'* The Preacher was screaming at me, I could tell as I was standing in front of him. He was saying something to me, all I made of from the muffled voice was something along the lines of, Why? I felt the tears flowing from my eyes and could feel them streaming down my face. I looked at L Señor and the bastard looked happy. He taught me a lesson alright, a lesson that he has to die. Again, I put my arm back and with all my might I cocked my arm back, swung my arm back and hit him in the head with the gun. They both went unconscious which was my goal. I didn't want them to suffer anymore.

L Señor looked at Miguel and said, "Tear the place up, find the money and find the drugs."

Miguel nodded and he and the other flunkies began to do the very thing they do the best. They ravaged the apartment. After all, they found maybe a pound of cannabis and a thousand dollars.

Rico went over to L Señor and said, "All of this to get the competition off of the street?"

L Señor pointed at me and said, "No, this was to show him what I can do." He saw Rico's face and added, "If you're not up to this anymore why did you come back?"

"To try and save you."

L Señor walked away from him and stormed out of the apartment, not before ordering the flunkies, "Let's go, load up…"

They dropped everything they were doing and took the cannabis and cash.

We all got back into the truck.

I felt L Señor get into the seat behind me and he reached over my shoulder with a glove on his hand and said, "Miklo, give me the gun back."

I gave it to him and I heard him take out the empty clip and put two bullets into it. He loaded the clip and put a black ski mask on his face, cocked the gun and he was out of the van. This son of a bitch was going to leave my prints and frame for this. We were silent in the van, no one said a word, we were just listening to everyone breathing. I looked over to the driver's seat and saw Miguel and he was just staring at me.

Shot. Shot.

The shots rang out.

I looked towards the apartment and saw the bastard calmly walking out of the apartment. I could see people looking at him and us in the van from the windows and one person had their phone to their face, I'm sure the cops would be here at any moment.

He got in the car, closed the door and we were speeding away. In the distance we could hear the police sirens, they were too late, they were dead and we were gone.

If I could change anything in my life, it would be to never have gotten involved with this man. Kush had warned me and I did not listen to him because I thought he had the 'paranoia'. Turns out he was right.

After twenty minutes of driving I could tell that we weren't going back to the warehouse, we were going somewhere else.

The day gradually faded into the night and I realized we had driven around most of Queens. They were probably looking for the right hotel to stay in for the night, or whatever the fuck they were doing. I've never felt more clueless in life until this moment.

When we pulled up to the hotel, I got the sense that not all of us were okay with what just happened. My best guess is that it was just one other person besides myself that thought how bad we all were.

I was lying on the bed in the room in total darkness thinking about everything. I wanted to turn my mind off but that was impossible.

What am I doing here? How did I get to this point?

The next day we were back in the van.

The next thing I remember after that was being home.

It would be a while before seeing L Señor again.

∞

I had received a text from a strange number, when opened it revealed a message from Panzer which said, 'The Rainbow is down. Do not log on site.'.

I continued my day to day operations as normal. Like most of us on the site, we didn't know how serious this was until a day later when it was all over the news.

Sadie and I were glued to the television. Those sons of a bitches had taken down the Rainbow and I was watching the DEA take out boxes and boxes of evidence on live TV. I could feel my heart drop. Box after box and with each new one I got more nervous. My hands were cold, my legs shaking, my mind racing.

"Are you okay?" Sadie asked me.

"What? I'm fine."

"You're breathing hard and sweating."

I could not take my eyes off of the television. The world as I knew it was crashing hard.

"What?"

"Are you okay?"

The computer, I have to destroy the computer.

I ran out of the room and into the bedroom to get my laptop and the baseball bat from out of my closet. I threw the laptop on the floor and beat it to pieces with my bat. I wouldn't stop, I could feel Sadie grab me to get me to stop but with the amount of rage I had I wouldn't have been able to.

"What are you doing!" Sadie yelled. "Stop! Stop!"

I stopped, but to pick up the pieces of the laptop, holding them to my body like a child I ran to the bathroom and threw the pieces into the bathtub and ran the water on it. For a moment, I felt relieved and fell to the floor trying to catch my breath. Flashes of the news were in my mind and I thought everything was going to be okay. I had taken all the precautions to encrypt my laptop. I felt okay… Then I thought about my cell phone, took it out of my pocket, broke it in my hands and threw it into the water. Now I felt okay…

I saw Sadie standing in the doorway of the bathroom with her arms crossed and staring at me. I did not want to look at her. I was too ashamed because I had let her down.

"What's going on?" She asked me.

I was still trying to catch my breath so I did not answer.

"Michael, what the fuck is going on?"

She never uses my real name.

"Did you have something to do with what's on the news?"

I looked up at her and into her eyes… "Yes."

She put her arms down and I knew what was coming.

"You lied to me." She said with a tear coming down from her eye. "You promised me you would never sell drugs again."

"I did it for us…"

"For us!"

"Sadie, what were we going to do?"

"Again! You promised me Michael, you promised that part of your life was over! I knew it! All these late nights, all this money you're getting, I knew it!"

I got up from the floor, "Sadie, I did this for us, you might not see it like that but it's what I had to do. We had rent and bills. This is my job."

She was now crying and I didn't know what to do. "This was your job years ago. You and your friends smoking and selling pot. Come on, don't give me that job shit. You said you were looking for a real job, I knew you were lying because I followed you and you met the guy with the tunnels in his ears and I knew it. You are a liar!"

She just said that you met the guy with the tunnels. When had she seen L Señor? I wonder if he knows about her?

"I'm sorry." I said to her as I went to give her a hug but she backed away.

"Don't touch me! What have you done! What did you drag me into?"

"Nothing, nothing is going to happen, this… what I just did wasn't necessary but it was just an extra protection. No one knows I'm in this, no one will find out."

"Goodbye Michael." She said walking away from the door.

"Sadie, where are you going?"

I followed her to the bedroom, she took her luggage and franticly began packing. She was so upset she was just grabbing random clothes and throwing them into the luggage. I knew she was leaving.

"Sadie please don't leave me, I love you."

"Don't say those words because if you really did you wouldn't have lied to me."

"Sadie, I want to be with you, I want to marry you, I want to have kids with you. You are the love of my life."

"And you are the hate of mine. I hate you. All of this, this house, these cars, all based on your selfish lies."

"Please don't leave me, I'm begging you." I grabbed her hand and took away the clothes she was holding and brought her closer to me. "I love you and I need you." She couldn't even look at me, was crying and looking away from me.

She zipped up the luggage and ran out of the house and I watched as she drove away from the house. The tears I could no longer hold back.

She's not coming back. I lost her.

Sadness had fully engulfed me and there was nothing I could do.

That was the last time I would ever see her.

∞

I know L Señor had been calling me for a few days and had broken my phone off as soon as the news broke. I could feel the negativity in the air and knew he would eventually come around. In preparation of the rest of my life and with all the sadness I was feeling for Sadie, I needed to move away from the city and get into the forests of upstate as fast as I could.

I spent one whole day on the internet locating two properties; one about three hours away from the city and one deep into the state of New York. I sent payment to the sellers using Bitcoin and within one day the two properties were mine.

I could not just go and leave.

I had some business to finish. I was not going to leave Kush and Spazz here, they would have to shut down and come with me. It was time for us to move past this shitty life I had created for everyone, it was time to grow up…

The both of them did not share my feelings.

When I told Kush that I was leaving the city to go upstate he said to me, "You're running from the life you made because of decisions you made. That will not help you. You will be trapped within your own mind."

"Do you really believe I'm running?"

"Your judgement is clouded."

"You're saying this to me just because I told you I want to get away from the city."

"I'm fine here, the Bronx is for me, to move upstate and uproot my life wouldn't be what I would want, it's not what I want."

Spazz also did not want to come with me. He did not have an explanation for it, he just said, "If you go up there, the terrorist [L Señor] has won." A statement I whole hardily disagreed with.

Maybe he was right.

I ordered a Pod shipping container and moved all of my belongings in it. I stuffed my Jeep Liberty with all of my personal things. I was moving away from this apartment that reminded me of Sadie, it's our apartment and I could not be there without her. The company picked up my container and it was on the way to the property in the Catskills. I made Spazz drive my Jeep up there. When I told him to do that and handed him the keys, he asked me, "You're not going up?"

"No."

His demeanor changed, "Then what are you doing?"

"Not only do I not want you to know, I don't want you or Kush involved."

Silence, just a blank stare from him.

"I'm ending it…"

"I don't think this is something you can end."

"Well I guess I'm going to have to try."

Walking around the empty apartment felt weird.

A sense of relief, sure.

A tremendous sense of guilt, sure.

I had to face the beast so I bought a new cell phone and just kept letting it ring.

One day, I amassed the courage to talk to L Señor who had already called four times in the day and on the fifth I knew I had to answer."

"Hello." I said, I really wanted to say 'hello asshole'.

"Miklo, you have been avoiding me, and that's no good."

"Well I've lost my taste for a lot of things."

"We have things to discuss. Be at Pelham Bay Station in a half hour. It's forty-five now, be there at fifteen."

The line went dead.

It was confusing that he chose a public transportation hub like that. That's what made me think he wasn't going to kill me.

Tell him the truth if he asks, nothing to lose now.

I made sure to bring the gun that Kush had given me and thought about it the entire time I was waiting in front of the Mini Mart across from the station. There was a lot of life going on around me and it was a weird feeling to think that no one had any idea why I was there. No one would even give a shit about anything that was not concerning them. I was watching the homeless guy buying coffee in the mart. I had seen him many times, a heavy-set white man that was always begging for money. I'd seen him for at least twenty years. Seeing him gave me a new perspective, it gave me a different direction to look at and thanked the universe that I was not that guy and that I had a home and people who had loved me and cared for me.

I had fucked it up.

I saw their truck pull up down the block. They all got out like a gang.

I felt like I was in a movie and that this wasn't really happening.

L Señor and the flunkies were walking towards me.

I found myself thinking of Sadie. I was having this weird fantasy of her naked, lying on top of the bed swimming in rose pedals that were falling from the ceiling. I felt loved and aroused but was brought back to reality. I was glorifying her in my mind. Yet, I realized, that I wasn't thinking of her but was only thinking of her body. This made me feel disgusted with myself.

I kept day dreaming and eventually snapped out of it when L Señor had gotten too close to worry about it.

"Let's go under the el and talk." He said to me with the four flunkies behind him.

The group of us walked under the station.

People were going up and down the escalators completely oblivious of our presence. I couldn't believe this is where he wanted to meet. We were definitely being looked at.

"Where were you the past few days?" L Señor asked with this weird look.

"I was busy."

"Shouldn't you just say what's on your mind?"

"Okay, why would I want to talk to you? After what you did to those people? I'm shocked you have anybody to talk to."

"Thanks for showing me your balls, but now you're in deep shit?"

"Why, why am I in deep shit? Enlighten me."

"How were you guys selling your cannabis?"

"None of your concern. What does this have to do with anything?"

"I have a feeling you were selling it in a certain way."

"So, what?"

"Would you like to know what I think happened?"

"By all means."

"I think you and your associates were selling what you had bought from me on the black market."

"Am I in the twilight zone? Isn't that what drug dealing entails? What is this? What the fuck is going on?"

I was frustrated.

"I find it curious that I haven't heard from you."

I didn't say anything."

He had gotten the message and said, "Four days ago, I got a text from a contact I have with someone from the Rainbow. I was not the only one to get one of these. I just thought it was strange that we have our weekly meetings and this is the first time you had missed a planned meeting. There is only one reason that you should ever miss a planned re-up and that is death. Since you are not dead, I can only assume that you were laying low for a few days."

Oh shit, what the fuck did he just say?

"And what makes you think this?"

"Did you think we weren't going to follow you?

This was a nightmare.

I was trying to think of something to say but I was baffled. When I did gain some mental composer, I tried to level with him. There is no leveling with a bulldozer. "What does it matter? Didn't we make money?"

"It matters because you never said anything. I asked you if you had other methods of selling product and you said no. You are a liar and that's all that matters. I think you have forgotten that you work for me."

"I don't work for you. I work for myself. This delusion is toxic."

"You work for me."

"What is this? Slave labor? In what world do you think I would do anything like that again?"

"You did it once."

"Because you forced me to asshole. Is that what you did to these guys?"

The flunky, known as Miguel, came up to me and punch me in the stomach. I went down hard. Trying to catch my breath I wanted to run but there was no way my body could do that after that hit. A few pedestrian heads turned for some rubbernecking but no one would stop and help. I wouldn't either.

"No one takes me as a fool." L Señor said.

"We had an agreement." I said, catching my breath.

"And now we have to make some amendments."

Jose, one of the other flunkies, was listening to something in his ear, he had some sort of earpiece in and when I looked at him, he was holding that ear, intently listening to whatever it was. He tapped L Señor on the shoulder and whispered something in his ear.

The atmosphere became tense.

Miguel hit me two more times in the stomach and again I went down, just after I had gotten my breath.

Next thing I know I was being picked up by two guys and thrown into the back of their car. They seemed like cops and figured that they had to be, if they weren't than I probably would have already been dead.

∞

They drove me somewhere close to Orchard Beach, a marsh area just past the road secluded in the trees by the water.

Now what are these cops doing to me?

"What is your business with L Señor?" this guy asked me.

"Who are you guys?" I asked, not wanting to talk about anything incriminating with myself.

"Answer the question." He said.

The other guy was just standing next to him, observing everything.

"What is it to you though? What are we doing here?"

They both stood there.

"I buy pot from him and sell it."

"Do you work for him?"

"No, as much as he thinks I do, but I would never work for that guy."

"So, what was this about?"

"He wanted me to work for him and be one of flunkies. He forced me to go with them one day, something bad happened and I tried to never see him again but he's a disease."

"Flunkies?"

"That's what I call his guys."

Tillman was processing that. "What does he want with you?"

"I don't know. Do you think he wants something from me?"

"He's been following you. Seems like he's keeping you on a short leash. I get the idea that he doesn't trust you. You do not fit in the L Señor picture. We've been following him for a while now and he's never done anything like he did to you. Usually, his victims are found on the sides of roads or buried in marshes. He keeps you like a dog on a retractable chain."

"Usually?"

"Yeah, L Señor is no good."

There was a moment of silence before Tillman asked the next question. "Was L Señor selling drugs in the Rainbow?"

Never had information I had just learned helped me so fast. "Yeah he was."

"You bought it… to do what?"

Now I was going to lie to cover my ass, "Sell around here."

Tillman shook his head in agreement, but agreeing to what I don't know.

"Who are you guys?"

"I'm Tillman, DEA. This is my Partner. Can you deliver L Señor to us?"

"I really don't want to be around this guy anymore. I'm trying to get out of this but he keeps trying to pull me back in. I'm ready to move away from here. I'm done with all of this."

"You're in a lot of shit. You know that?"

"Yes."

"Can you deliver L Señor to us?"

"My answer won't change. There's no amount of protection you can offer me to do it."

"I wasn't going to offer any protection. Just reduction in jail time. No matter what your answer is. I still say you're in a lot of shit."

"I didn't want any of this. I want to leave this."

"We've seen you going into the warehouse numerous times. We have you witnessed you sending and receiving packages at the post office and observed you with them at the house off the highway."

"House off the highway?" It took me a minute but then I knew what they were talking about. "That's what happened. He forced me to go with them. I don't know what he wanted to do to me but that day changed me. I'm fucked from that. Do you know how hard it is for someone to want to leave everything that they only know?"

He must have gotten a sense that I was telling the truth.

"I believe him." The Partner said.

"I do too… What is your plan after this?"

"I don't know, but this isn't the life for me anymore."

He thought for a moment when he began to talk, I had seen a different side of Tillman. "If you help us get him, I will put any charges on you. If you leave the city in the next 24 hours, we'll act like this conversation never happened. I will find you if you start the shit again. Agreed?"

"So, if I go away, nothing will happen to me? Agreed." I said.

He handed me his card and said, "If you change your mind about helping us, here's my card."

I took the card from him with no intention of ever calling him again.

They got in the car and left me there.

What is going on?

A Dab from the Rig

Everything starts out with curiosity.

I had acquired a somewhat large supply of psychedelic drugs which I had no interest in doing prior to this moment. They were all precisely labeled and in their own vile within a black waterproof 1250 Pelican Case, which we dubbed *'the box of goodies'*. Upon opening the case one would find white dots with letters on them containing that vile. I had asked myself why I wanted to have a head stash of all of these but could not come up with a good answer. I barely knew about them and could not make a decision. In my search for information on a certain group of drugs, called Phenethyamines, I stumbled upon a book called *Pihkal – A Chemical Love Story by Alexander & Ann Shulgin*. I spent what was now a great thirty dollars on this book and read it from cover to cover; it's not a small book either. I enjoyed the first half of the book which was more of their back-stories but when I got to *The Chemical Story* my mind was immediately flooded with information about the Phenethyamines. A major part of that second half were a group of drugs called the *2c's (2c-* E, B, C, D, H, I, P, T-7); some apparently did nothing when ingested and each very unique in their trips, in their dosages, their durations, but only a few excelled in visuals and thoughts. Then there were the *'feel gooders'* which are MDMA, MDA, MDE, BOB, DOC and DOM to name a few. Most of these you could never find, the only one that was in abundance was MDMA, even if I had to choose just one of these things to have, it's definitely that. It must have taken me a couple of weeks to finish Pihkal. I wanted to explore new horizons and open my mind to new experiences.

'Shura is god!' This had been what I was seeing on some of these drug forum websites. I do not believe that the man who made and

researched these drugs is a god, but a man who opens up the minds of generations of people should be honored for his contribution to society, whether it is bad or good because most of the time it does good for people but you do not see that.

It was time for a change in thought and a random memory popped into my head… About two years prior to this moment, I was at a pool party with Spazz and Kush; by the middle of the night the three of us were split off with our girls. I was hanging around a group of them when one of them said, "Anyone want some LSD?"

I was the first one to answer, so young, so quick and so stupid, "Nah, I'm good." I wasn't willing to take anything like that yet.

"Didn't you say you're a *Beatles* fan? You should be doing this! Lucy in the Sky with Diamonds!" She yelled.

I laughed and took it as a joke and had forgotten about it. Now when I'm thinking of it, I see it as a missed opportunity and wish I had taken it.

Kush invited me to his friends' house saying that they were going to trip. I was curious about it and actually wanted to do it with Kush the first time.

He handed me a capsule and said, "This is thirty-five Milligrams of 2c-E. Pihkal recommends ten to twenty-five… It's a good dose. But it can last between eight and twelve hours… It's a commitment."

I took the capsule from him along with a swig of water and swallowed the capsule. In hindsight it probably wasn't the best psychedelic to take for the first time, Shrooms would have been a better first-time choice. Maybe even LSD.

Then Kush did something weird. He looked at me and even his friend was looking over like he was also thinking what the hell is happening. Kush looked into my eyes and said,

"Cars are real,
Cliffs are real,
Cops are real.
You can't fly,
It's never a good time to die,
And you will come out of it."

When someone first says this to you it takes you for a quick emotional ride. This is a stern warning and guide. Since first hearing this I have probably said it to myself at least a hundred times.

I didn't ask about it, I had filled my mind with Pihkal and felt ready for it...

Forty-five minutes after I had ingested thirty-five milligrams of 2c-E I knew something was off. Clearly, I was about to trip serious balls for the first time and was not prepared for what was about to come. Adrenaline, the only way I could explain the feeling coursing through my veins and radiating thro ought my body; nervously cautious about what was going on. It was a slow transition, especially when you don't know what to expect and when to expect it. I could feel my heart beating and that made me wonder if I had made a good choice. I felt weird and sick as if my brain was in a jar filled with water floating around within it. At the bottom of my throat I could feel myself fighting the urge to vomit. Some psychedelics give you the feeling that you're on a roller coaster.

An hour after I took it...

...There was a weird ominous feeling within me and I could feel my body moving on the inside. The room darkened and tones of orange and purple filled my vision. One of the first things I noticed were my hands. Holding them out in front of me I looked at them, they are the same hands I've had all my life and yet now, they felt and looked weird. At this particular moment they could have been anyone's hands. My breathing was getting heavy and I could feel my lungs filling and deflating with every breath, something I had never really experienced before. All of my life I have been breathing but I never took a second to actually think about what my body was doing. Again, I was focusing on my hands which were still extend out before me, when I lowered my hands it was the first time I had seen vapor trails but it was also when I noticed the wallpaper. Gold lines in the form of a flower moving and swaying in the wind. They weren't really flower's but I was seeing them and they began to spin like gears in a complex machine. I was somewhere else and fell into a deep thought staring into the wall.

I didn't want to keep staring at this wall as I began to feel uncomfortable. Moving my eyes around the room to see what everyone else was doing; also, to see how everything else looked to me, I saw Kush sprawled out under the glass coffee table on the floor.

Probably just judging by my body language he said to me, "I know you're feeling it," and laughed hysterically with that deep loud laugh he had.

I could only manage to smile and nod my head. That's when I waved my hand in front of my face and again saw the flowing set of trails after it. *Wow, this is truly amazing.* I said.

"Yeah man." I heard Kush say from under the table.

Did I say that aloud? I'm pretty sure I didn't. Whatever, I don't care.

Then the other part of these research chemicals happened to me, the dreaded feeling of vomiting. This was inevitable. In a moment of what seemed to be a calm storm of sobriety I looked around... I was not in my comfort zone. I was at Kush's friend's house, that much I knew. They were all cool and we were all tripping really hard.

I looked at his friend and asked, "Dude, where's your bathroom, I gotta' vomit."

"Go for it, out the room to the right." He said.

Slowly I got up and made my way to the bathroom. Everything I looked at left a trail and I caught a glimpse of whatever was on the television but it sucked, or it was too much to look at, and no one was paying any attention to it. The real party was happening in the choice of music his friend decided to play. I hadn't realized it before but the music was weird, even in the state I was in I could tell how weird the music was. It was glorious and had to ask, "What the fuck are we listening to?"

They all laughed.

"*Shpongle.*" Kush said, "Why? You don't like it?"

"Actually, right now I'm enjoying it."

Vomit, yes, I still had to do that.

I turned on the light in the bathroom and the pattern of the pink tiles on the wall and floor grabbed me. I lifted the toilet seat up and vomited. I felt better almost instantly.

After dry heaving for a minute I was done and when I looked at the door, white door, the lights dimmed, they didn't really but I saw it happen, I was tripping balls. All of the vapor trails were more elaborate now. I could not understand how to get out of there but I did anyway and made my way back to the living room, more particularly the couch. Kush had moved from under the table to the spot next to me on the couch and I sat down next to him.

The ceiling fan was on and it was moving, all the blades were moving to the music and the lights were fucking around.

"Are the lights bothering anyone else?" Kush's friend asked.

"Yeah, too much right now." Kush said.

The friend turned the lights off. From the glow of the television I could still see the fan spinning, yet I could not tell if my eyes were open or closed. I was seeing this fan none the less. The blades were moving, independently; stretching down to where I was and they were handing me blobs of colors as if it were an octopus.

I came out of that trance and looked around the room. They both also looked as if they were in another world. I could not help but get sucked back into mine. The music was taking me on a journey I had never been on. Never has music sounded like this, everything, nothing ever looked like this. Was I asleep dreaming?

No, I was up and conscience, well sort of. I was there, I know I was and definitely not asleep. I felt I was, my body along with my mind had no fucking clue what to do. So, I got the feeling that I was melting into the couch. So comfortable that I wasn't; my back was killing me but was too out there to move.

Kush tapped me on the shoulder and asked, "Want to hear a joke?"

"Sure Kush." I said, not really knowing how I was speaking and/or making sentences.

"It's only Eleven Thirty."

The three of us busted out laughing, that in fact was a great joke considering we took this stuff around Eight and felt like we had been tripping for an eternity. How was this possible? *Fuck those made up numbers of time.* I joined them in laughter.

Chaotic. This is the best way to describe everything that was going on. Since it was my first time on any psychedelic, I wanted to make sure I basked in all of its glory. I wanted to take the most from this experience because I wasn't sure I would do it again. Comprehending anything is a task in itself.

That's when I noticed the walls breathing. I could see them take each breath and exhale. After a while of that it changed to vibrating patterns like bad reception on an old tube television. Mind melting; quality time with your eyes and inner thoughts.

Chills went down my spine. That damn ghost had gotten me and my body didn't know if it was hot, warm or cold. I was everything.

Couldn't sit still and my eyes couldn't focus. I needed air and a cigarette. From my pocket I took out my pack of Marlboro Twenty Sevens and took out a cigarette and asked Kush if he wanted to come outside and smoke one with me.

It was hard for us to unlock the doors and sit on the porch, everything seemed so foreign.

We finally got outside and sat on the chairs looking out at the other houses and the streets. The streetlights and sidewalks. I saw peoples lights on and I thought, *how many other people are doing what we're doing right now?* That number is probably more than you think.

I held the lighter up to the cigarette and lit it. The flame stayed in my eyes for a moment and to entertain myself I just kept lighting the lighter. I was amazed by the fire, especially the way it looked, it was already wavy but it was now pulsating.

Kush lit his cigarette and asked me, "how are you feeling?"

"Awesome, I don't know what's going on but I'm going."

"Nice," he said, puffing his cigarette.

I got up and walked to the edge of the porch and looked up at the sky, it was different, it was more orange than ever before because of not only the light pollution but the state I was in. The clouds were even more orange tonight. The few stars I could see over the lights of the city were sublime. Wherever I looked everything left a trail for it. A car passing by left the best trail of head and back lights. In the distance I could hear a motorcycle, though it was not close to me I heard it in glorious stereo and for that moment I was with them, riding on an open highway with the wind going through my hair.

About eight hours after I took it…

The next thing I knew the sun was peaking over the houses behind us and everything was brighter and clearer with a blue haze. Everything seemed dead like a ghost town and had not seen a person walk by the house since we got outside. There was silence, just with birds and cars in the distance with the faint smell of breakfast cooking somewhere. Kush and I had been outside for what were apparently hours. He had fallen asleep in the chair; I was wide awake the whole time and, in that moment, he woke up.

"Dude," he said all fucked up and tired, "I was tripping balls last night."

"I think I'm still tripping now; we were out here the whole night."

Miklo Inaamla

Any one particular solid memory from the night was not up and running at all. I tried to piece together psychedelic pictures from my head to make a timeline but that turned out to be more difficult than I thought. It was impossible. I had done so much but had really done nothing at all. This stillness I had not felt in years.

His friend came outside to smoke, went to light his cigarette, looked over and saw us and said, "holy shit, you guys have been out here this whole time, I thought you left."

"Nope," Kush said laughing, "sitting here."

"How are *you* feeling?" His friend asked me.

"I'm chilln' man."

"Cool," he said taking a puff of the cigarette.

My mind began racing thoughts and all I could think was; *no urge to move, none for drugs. All I know is that nothing bad happened.*

And that was my first-time tripping, a real-life changer.

Later in the morning everything felt weird, it was weird. I was no longer on the same planet I was in last night. Now people were waking up, doing whatever they would do, and I… I was ending my night of a hallucinogenic drug. I felt different in the sense that I didn't want to deal with any of my bullshit. Everything was different; there was also an appreciation for everything.

There is also a saying: *Don't do too much too quick.*

That next week was a party.

Randy, or that's just what I'll call him since I forgot his name, was the friend of Kush whose home I was tripping in. He was this really weird jittery guy and worried about everything, literally would worry about every aspect of his life, I don't know how Kush could sit there and listen to it, I would block out his voice after a few minutes. Even with the fact that there was a small part of me that couldn't stand the guy I could not pass up an offer to go to his house and take drugs for a week. Just from the fact that he told me that he had gotten a wide variety of substances for the week I knew it was going to be a shit show. Kush even told me how much Randy said he liked me; which made the invitation so much better.

When the time came to take the drugs, Kush handed me a pill and for some reason I felt that I was not ready for whatever was in this pill which turned out to be a combination of 2c-E and MDMA.

He handed me the pill and said, "This is a sparkle-flip."

"A sparkle-flip? Sounds gay."

145

"So then call it cheesing, but this will fuck us up."

I took the pill and downed it with a glass of water.

It was time to play the dreaded waiting game.

Onsets of weird and paranoia.

The come up was something I hadn't ever experienced. I could feel the MDMA coursing through my veins and I was going through a wide range of emotions. When I asked Kush about how I was feeling all he did was tell me that, "Molly at first sends you through all of our emotions, it will pass and it will get better."

Things were going on around me but nothing was happening.

I am not feeling sick. I'm not sick. I will not vomit, no sickness. This is all in your head. I could feel it in my throat. I could not sit nor stand. I was not comfortable in any position. I had no idea what I wanted to do; so, I paced around the apartment.

I threw up in the toilet; on my knees before I was plunging my head into it. Everything shifted down, the lights dimmed and the color haze was there. My hands were also feeling weird, one of the signs that it's taking effect on you.

Slowly I made my way back to the couch.

Kush and Randy were laying on the floor with their eyes closed.

I looked up not knowing if my eyes were open but yet I could see, so I held them shut and yet I was still seeing color. Not only was there color but I could see geometric shapes, things flying at me or flying by. It was a very fluid trip.

The radio in my head was tuning in and out of music. I needed to hear music! I unraveled my earphones and plugged them into my ears. I was determined and I definitely was not feeling whatever music they were listening to; actually, I don't think there was any music on.

I carefully chose a song I wanted to listen to; I decided that the best choice was to put on Dark Side of the Moon by *Pink* Floyd and they were taking me somewhere I had never been before.

By the time Money came on…

…I was in the passenger seat of a military jeep driving towards these Middle Eastern looking castles in the distance of the desert. They looked like a small cluster of Taj Mahals from a far. We were going to towards them while they were shooting at us. The desert, that's where I was; looking to the left I saw a helicopter zooming in on the situation. Two other Jeeps next to us going to fight just like I was. I had no idea what I was shooting at but something was there. One of the helicopters was hit with something big and it fell from the sky like a firework exploding on the ground in all of its gloriousness. Troops on their feet running to the target as we passed them. The gunshots piercing my ear, bombs going off with all hell breaking loose. I did not question any of this, it was all happening to me, it was real. I was letting my own mind take me somewhere I never thought I would go. We pulled up behind two tanks where one of our leaders was talking. I jumped off the Jeep and went over to the conversation. "Those goddamn sand niggers want to kill us, let's kill them first." The big man said to the rest of us, yelling over the warfare in front of us. He then pointed at me and said, "you and your men take the left, we'll take the right." I nodded in agreement and went back into my Jeep and the driver took off. I was screaming in anger and I began shooting at things with my rifle. That's when I saw a rocket coming straight for us...

...When it got to the guitar solo: The Jeep itself exploded in an all glorious way. The explosion revealed to me that I was in a spaceship launching into space. The image of the engines blasting into space became a kaleidoscope as if I was the one blasting into orbit. Multiple rockets in one field of vision. Colors began ensuing my vison, green, orange, red, brown...

That's when my mind fell and I was back on Earth only to open my eyes to discover that I was still on the couch... *What a trip. What the fuck?* My eyes opened rather quick and I couldn't believe that I was still on the couch and had not moved. I could swear that everything happened, I was in that Jeep, it did explode. This is when I realized I was tripping better than before.

The vibrations I was feeling, the general sense of the thing we all call the 'fuckedupness'. The rooms' colors were popping out at me and everything became pastel and some tones of purple; the dimmer switch was back and everything was darkening, someone in my mind was playing with that switch and every time I thought I was back to normal the switch would move, at first it was very nauseating but after a while I got used to the sick feeling these drugs were giving me.

I may have accepted the sickness but I could not control the urge to throw up.

"Why do these things make you vomit a lot?" I asked.

Randy was also trying to piece some words together as he was also tripping, probably harder than I was because he had taken more.

He said to me, "These research chemicals in the beginning make you sick, the vomiting is good, it helps develop the trip."

There I was again in the bathroom with my head in the toilet vomiting because this idiot had told me that it was good. In the end it wasn't good and after a while I got over the sickness in general but not this night.

Don't fight it. I said to myself. I washed my face in the sink and when I looked up, I saw the white walls, the white tiles. It felt good to get my white balance on after seeing many different colors for hours. That's when I saw my reflection in the mirror. It was the first time on psychedelic drugs I had looked at myself and I'll never forget it. My face was moving like fluids but yet I was still. My hands became cold and I could feel everything in my body and in that moment, I accepted myself for who I was, not for who I pretended to be. From that moment on I decided not to put any kind of façade on, I would be myself. Twenty-Four years on this Earth and it took drugs to accept myself, it takes people their whole lives to do what I just did. Everything was vivid to me and I must have stared at myself in that mirror for fifteen minutes.

There was a knock on the door that startled me, it was Kush.

"Hey bro, are you okay in there?"

"Yeah man I'm good, I'll be out in a few..." I said, still staring into the mirror.

Eventually I made my way back to the couch and must have been there for hours.

The night gradually faded into the day.

Another trip in the books.

Although I had moved out of the apartment and upstate, I had gotten an apartment close to Kush for a temporary time. I didn't want to drive a couple hours just to hang out. I'm glad for this because after that week I could barely function, it was nice to be in the city with everything close and open all the time.

One particular day I remember vividly. The sun was rising and my alarm went off. It did not wake me because I was already awake, lying in bed with my eyes open. The drug had worn off a while ago but I still laid there staring at the ceiling. Slowly my hand made its way to turn off the alarm.

I was wandering around my apartment aimlessly, pacing back and forth trying to comprehend my thoughts and memories of the previous night. I was thinking and my mind was more open than it ever was. I felt different and saw the world differently and after every question I asked myself I would ask a simple one, WHY?

That's when my cell phone rang. Looking back at this moment I keep thinking how weird the universe is, I had just had this major life changing experience and now the phone was ringing with a private number, that had not happened often to me.

I flipped open the phone, "Hello." I said, very cautiously.

I could hear some breathing for a moment of the other end but within a second, I heard a voice say, "Miklo?"

I had only used that name with people I know and the bastard and his flunkies so it could have only been one man, "Panzer?" I asked.

"Yeah," he said "the pot of gold wasn't at the end of the rainbow."

That's when I started hearing the news reports play in my head about the fall of the Rainbow and reality came back to me in the form of a man, I had never meet but wrote e-mails to. "Is the leprechaun lost?"

"He is no longer in Ireland."

"You sound like you need a drink. Where are you?"

"I made my way to your area."

"Do you know the area, where can we meet?"

"I know Jimmy Ryan's Bar."

"I can meet you there in an hour."

Twenty minutes passed and I thought he wasn't going to come. I was sitting at one of the tables facing the door so I could asses everyone who came in. Since I had never seen Panzer before I had to look at everyone and determine who he was. I already had two Jack and Coke's; needless to say, I was somewhat buzzed with some 2c's coursing through my veins. On the back burner of my mind I thought of what Panzer could want. This was something out of the ordinary and the fact that I hadn't heard from him for a while suggested to me that everything that went down after the Rainbow wasn't good. Then, with the overshadowing thoughts of paranoia I thought he was a cop. I began to tremble in the seat and suddenly felt hot and started to sweat. My heart was pounding and I thought at any moment the cops were going to come in, swarm and arrest me. *Why did you come here? Why did you agree to this?*

The other half of my brain was saying things like, *your knife is in your pocket and if shit goes down, you got this and You have nothing to worry about.* I then finished my third drink and ordered two more.

The door opened and I knew this was Panzer. This guy looked a little concerned; his face just looked like someone had pulled a chair from under him. He then looked at me and I knew it was him. Walking over to me he said, "the leprechaun found his way."

"Nice to meet you Panzer."

"Miklo."

We shook hands and he sat down across from me at this two-person table.

"Want a drink?" I asked.

"What is it?"

"Jack and Coke."

"Yeah."

I slide one over to him and he took it and huge gulp of it. "I'm sure you know by now; the Rainbow is down."

"Yeah, it was all over the news. Is that why you're here?"

"The Rainbow was my work, my job. I can't just give it up and let it die because of pointless overseeing losers inciting criminal exploitation. You are one of the few who didn't go down."

"There's a good handful of guys who didn't get arrested, to me they're the most important ones."

"I want to start a new site."

"Why?"

"People need these and we need to send it out."

"No, people don't need these. I'm willing to do something profitable with you, right here, right now, but not if you say that people need these things."

"I need you to do the connections and everything else you're already doing."

"Why me? I'm sure there are better people for this than me."

"I trust you; I know that we barely know each other from a hole in the wall, but I know the ins and outs of everything from Rainbow. The day it went down, I was in one of the mansions we used to fill the orders. I was just starting to love it, I had risen to where I wanted to be, I was important. While weighing out some doses of LSD, I heard some commotion downstairs. Someone, whose voice was unfamiliar said, 'down on the ground!' I knew it was a raid. That's when I got a text, it said 'run'. All around everyone was being taken down. I grabbed a gun and the vile was still in my hand... I ran... I could hear all the cops running up the stairs and the cars in the driveway. All the screaming. I tried running out the back door but the cops were all over; they saw me. I went into the first room I could and jumped out the window. It wasn't open. They shot at me from the window, but I just kept running... Into the woods... A gun in my hand and LSD in my pocket. And here I am now."

"That's a nice story and all... I'm still not sure what you want to do. It's over..."

"There can still be something there."

"Nah man, the Rainbow is over. All we have now is to go back to the old shitty way of dealing."

"You really don't think we can get this up and running?"

"The problem is that too many talk and forums and especially Reddit. There is no way we can keep that a secret, especially for a long period of time."

"Miklo... I got this... I've learned from the past mistakes. We got this. This is why I helped create the Rainbow. I'm a lawyer, I know the loop holes, no one will know what we're doing. I can promise you that."

"It just goes back to why Me?"

"You were the most reliable person on the Rainbow."

"How? I wasn't on there that long?"

"A lasting impact was made."

"A lasting impact?"

We stared at each other for moment and it was awkward.

Do it. What else are you doing? Why are you pushing this away?

"Leprechauns and rainbows." I said, sticking out my hand for him to shake.

"There is a pot of gold at the end of this one." He said, shaking my hand.

Just like that, is how things get done. He took out from his pocket the vile of LSD he had been talking about and he handed it to me.

"Take this, I don't want it anymore."

That was probably the best acid I ever had in my life. Panzer said it came from the Dead Family. I'm not a Grateful Dead fan but they sure know how to make some good Lucy.

I went around after that, thinking this was good thing. Kush and Spazz did not think so and they were upset with me when I told them why Panzer had contacted me and what we talked about.

"So, you and him are going to make another website?" Kush asked with a tone of anger.

"No, I have no intention of that."

"Then why did you basically agree to that?"

"I agreed to make money with him. Whatever he wants to do he can do."

"Why do you do things without thinking? Why do you act retarded?"

"What the fuck dude?"

Anthony tried to be in the conversation but he was tripping out on something on the couch. Every so often we would hear a grunt or him breathing.

"You just don't think of things sometimes and it bothers me."

"Well," I said trying to be as diplomatic as possible, "I want to make money and do less work. Maybe one more person would help us."

"I don't know Miklo. Can we trust this guy?"

"He trusted me."

"Are you sure about this guy?"

"That is just the same question in a different way."

"I just want to make sure we don't end like those sites. Don't you think the cops know who this guy is?"

This is usually where I would be straight up and tell Kush the truth, that Tillman and the Partner had in fact found me and knew about L Señor. I could not tell him; he would have left and never came back and none of them would ever trust me again.

Spazz and I also had a conversation like this but all he had to say to me was, "I hope you know what you're doing."

Once Panzer came into the group, I could feel the shift in the dynamic.

Things don't last too long without something happening.

∞

Two months went by,
A flash in my mind,
Why should I mind?

Apparently, months went by…

It was the end of October when I thought it was the middle of September. Actually, I cannot give a time frame for this. Now it all seems like a giant blur.

I was binging on the 2c's, cannabis and alcohol with a little bit of MDMA sprinkled in; this was all when I was selling everything, I'd meet people places and be out of it, driving around unknown neighborhoods and sketchy places. Sometimes it was hard to think but I would just have to center myself and would do this by saying the whole 'Cars are Real, Cliffs are Real…' as a mantra.

I would meet someone for something and I would try and tell them about something else. Mostly it was the Molly (MDMA) and I would try saying things like, 'hey have you tried this?' No one ever knew what the Phenethyamines were. Then I would explain how Molly is one of them and they would give me the look I used to have in Calculous class. I loved having to take Pihkal and condense it into an average Joe language; I would try to summarize it in its entirety. Maybe this was just me liking the fact that for a few minutes I seemed smart to other people. This all turned out to be good because most of the time they would wind up buying some. I'm a good salesman with a nice seller's edge. I would make them want these drugs or at least curious enough to try it.

While I was creating a market for those, most people who weren't interested in Molly were all interested in Crystal Meth, Cocaine, Ketamine and Heroine. I refused to argue with my morals so I bought the cheapest of the cheap of those and sold them to everyone for double the price. I figured if they were going to spend money on it why should I not get a great profit off of it. I did not want to sell any of those but over the months my views on Cocaine and Ketamine changed while the other two remained the same. Any drug I could sell was fair game.

When I talk of these drugs with my friends when they are curious about them, I tell them to keep within their limits and we all made a pact that is any one of us developed a problem with any drug it would be straight to rehab. The three of us had a problem together. Although we were close, we all felt very isolated. We each developed our own habits that were no good. I did not give a fuck where I would smoke Cannabis, I would walk up and down the street, crossing to the other side of the street when I saw kids, smoking either a joint or a bowl, I would even do it in my car. I also developed a serious lack of respect for the police and disregarded them completely. Kush had developed this angry attitude to the point where we went to the deli on Williamsbridge Road and Kush flipped out on the guy making sandwiches because the guy had put mayo on a chicken parmigiana hero, how Kush tasted that is beyond me. Spazz, on the other hand, developed a bad drug problem that Kush and I didn't know how to confront. We would try and tell him but he wouldn't listen to it. Spazz was our fault and it sucks to know that now. We needed someone to discipline us and there was not anyone. Panzer did not help any of this, he aided us in all of our actions.

It was at this point I began thinking of the world outside of us and what I would do for the rest of my life. I knew I couldn't sell drugs forever but it sure did not feel like that. After careful thought, I came to the conclusion that my life was destined to be a drug dealer. I was brought up my whole life to be something, to do something, to inspire people, to improve things, make people feel, to be something... My mother always told me to do something good, be whatever I wanted to be. Maybe, not in her words, she was implying it was ok to be that. She did not like that I was doing that but I felt my parents gave me the attitude to be. Maybe it is better than a life of sitting behind a desk getting coffee for all the bosses you have that come and go. The nine to fivers go to work, stress themselves out and for what? Minimum wage. That does not sound like me.

Spazz was out of control with MDMA, he was addicted. I told him if he was going to take it regularly that he couldn't do more than four doses a day and only once every three weeks. He obviously did not listen to that. He then began taking MDMA's lesbian cousin, M1 (Methylone). M1 you could do a whole gram in a night and maybe do it once a week, if you don't care about yourself. Spazz began mixing them and I couldn't take it anymore. One night when we were at the property upstate, we gave him an intervention and refused to give him anymore or even allow him to transport or sell it. We sat him down, Panzer included, and we just talked. We also had aided him with drugs because we all had decided to take Molly, this would be the last time I gave Spazz any, the words came out honestly and without thought. Spazz was better after the talk. Even though we had this serious conversation it was one of the few times we were all on Molly together and we had a great night, we worked everything out and we were all cool with each other.

No.

It wasn't all that simple. I had been watching everyone and even in myself I saw a change. I had developed a daily cocaine habit and I wish someone would have given me an intervention. For me, I had to wake up one day and tell myself to never take it again and that I didn't need that. That would not be for about a year.

Kush was also having a hard time. He was more into the Ketamine than anything else. The cannabis brought him back down but it may have been too much for him.

Sometimes I couldn't understand what Kush or Spazz were saying to me because they were so out of it. I know I was out of it also but I was better off than they were.

It's hard to talk to your friends about addiction. It's much easier when people are gone. And that sucks.

I had been paranoid about Panzer, not that he could not handle himself or that he didn't know what he was doing. I was nervous about L Señor. With Panzer here I felt like he was target and that we should have been protecting him. I would dismiss this as stupid and try not to think about it. It popped in my head from time to time. I figured that if I had not heard from him in this amount of time that he was through with me. Everything was over.

Panzer was weighing out capsules on the living room table to meet someone. He looked alright. I wanted to ask him how he was doing but something told me not to. I just watched him, not because I felt he would screw me but because the feeling, now I see, was there that it could be the last time I saw him. I didn't want to say anything though. Why did I have to drag him into all this? What should I do now? Maybe I should stop now.

He filled one of the capsules and lifted it up, "Isn't it awesome?" He asked.

"The drug?"

"Yeah... MDMA... 3, 4-Methylenedioxy. It really is something different... One day I fear, it will be to mainstream. It's magic, lost."

"Sometimes that's how I feel, and I'm the reason for that."

"Why do you feel like that?"

"Because no one knew about it 'till I started selling it."

"You're bringing it to people who want it, who want to open their mind, who want to experience life."

I stayed silent. I didn't want to hear someone preach about drugs.

"Don't stop."

"How'd you know that's what I was thinking?"

"You, me, Anthony and Kush, right now, were on the same level."

"That we are." He was becoming annoying to me. I began to see what Kush was trying to get me to understand. Maybe I couldn't trust this guy.

"Someone's gotta' do it. You're just the man to do it."

He put down the capsule. Looked at me and said, "Wait. Maybe you should stop. If your mind is telling you to you have to listen to your mind."

"I just don't know what tomorrow brings."

"Tomorrow never knows." He said, filling up another capsule. "Sometimes I wish I never contacted you after Rainbow went down."

"Why?"

"Because I brought this world to you. This empty market. Is it good? Is it bad? I mean don't you just wish we didn't have to worry about anything. I was part of that world and it fell beneath me, why did I rebuild it?"

I could feel his sadness, it ran through me, but I had to ask, "Why did you come to me? And what rebuild? We're not doing anything?"

I think he wasn't all there.

"What do you mean?"

"Do you really not hear yourself talk?"

It was at this point that I realized he was just disillusioned. I'm sure the drugs didn't help that. I fed into this as well, but I certainly never believed it.

He looked at me and his answer would stay with me even until today, "I have no one else. Rainbow was my thing, the world I understood. I couldn't just go back home because I never had a home. I was an orphan. All my life I was alone until in college I met Zeus, the man that made Rainbow, you could say Rainbow was his Mount Olympus. He showed me who Shura was and I may have read Pihkal a hundred times. We had a vision, a website where someone like us could buy their drugs in peace and have it delivered discreetly. A cyber drug superstore. It was the reason I went on to become a lawyer. I spent all law school doing the 2c's and studying. I passed the bar and here I am standing before you today."

"Why not be a lawyer? It's a stable job."

He gave me the looked as if I had just fucked up, "You know why, and I know why."

I did know why.

"After everything," I chose my words carefully, "why keep doing it?"

"That day Rainbow got raided, the text that told me to run was from Zeus. I was his last hope, and you mine. You see, there will always be someone selling this stuff, it's just what happens. Someone needs to keep doing it, or else this stuff will disappear. You see, I don't just believe that everything happened because it happened, it happened because it had to happen, for us to meet. It's not just a coincidence, its life unraveling before us."

"So, in a way, I was always the last hope." I said, really trying to understand everything.

"Miklo," he said, crushing up some MDMA, "we are the last. Whatever happens after this," he rolled up a bill and snorted the MDMA off the table, "has happened because it will."

I don't think he even knew he was making any sense. He sat there; the Molly was now running thru ought his system. He was radiating it and I felt like I was on it.

"If I died today," he said snorting the rest of the Molly, "my life would mean something."

Life would mean something.

Life is something.

He crushed up some more molly and handed me the rolled-up bill. "I know you like Methylone better than this but you should have some with me."

I took the bill, put it in my nose and snorted away.

The colors were changing, at least for me. The sense of security was gone.

The day was the best/worst time to do hallucinogenic drugs. It does however make you appreciate the day even more. A bird flying in front your face, man walking leaves trails of photos of him passing me, even if he is walking normally. What was dreaming, was I dreaming? Slowly my eyes made its way to the concrete where I saw a jungle of birds. Flying, when it suddenly became an optical illusion. A squirrel ran in front of me and that's where all my attention went as I followed him up the tree only to see a face in three, within all the trees. Things were going on in the bushes and the leaves were dancing in the wind. That's when I took the jay from my pack of cigarettes and started to smoke. That was at one of the parks in the Bronx. I had one of the best experiences of my life upstate in my backyard one day. I went for a hike for about an hour and found a spot with a clearing. It was one of those days with a crisp breeze and blue sky with the occasional cloud. I laid on the ground looked up through the hole in the clearing of the tops of the trees and watched as clouds go by listening to the song *Imagine by John Lennon*. Then I watched as chipmunks ran by me and birds flew past me.

While I was incapacitated during one of those trips, Panzer was in need of help.

Two ounces of Molly and a sheet of LSD he had on him, waiting to sell it to the person who called him.

I now know what happened.

He was in his car and the person called him and said they were on the way. Panzer was rolling hard, probably blasting his music. Really into the song. Smoking cigarettes. When his door flew open and was pulled out by the man I so despise. L Señor dragged him out of the car. Threw him onto the floor as his flunkies raided the car.

Where this happened, I am unsure.

They picked apart and searched every crevice of the car.

"Only this was in the car." One of them said to L Señor handing him the huge bag of Molly.

L Señor carefully inspected the bag, opened it, touched the substance, and closed the bag.

"MDMA. That is what this is isn't it?" L Señor asked Panzer.

Panzer stayed silent on the floor while he tried to piece together who he was seeing.

"You, I know you." Panzer said.

"Do you, well in order for you to keep knowing and living, you need to tell me who you get this from."

"No."

"No?"

"Yeah, No."

"We worked together for so long, but now you don't want to talk to me?"

"L Señor, you know what happened. What did you forget about the desert and the Bodybuilder?"

"I know what happened. What happened to you and Zeus? I heard you guys were careless and that it was really easy for the DEA to get you."

"Yeah, what happened to the Bodybuilder. You two are real fucks you know that!"

"Panzer, are you working with Miklo?"

"What's it to you?"

"I'm just upset that you didn't come to me. I see what you guys are doing, why couldn't we have been in the loop?"

"You know Miklo?"

"Oh yeah. Threw you off by asking where you get your stuff from. Look boys," he said looking to his flunkies, "we have a pseudo-celebrity here, the co-creator of the Rainbow graces us with his presence today."

"Why do you do what you do?"

"Why did you? You sent those guys out to kill us. Zeus wasn't all innocent either, was he?"

"I think we can leave Zeus out of this."

"He can't be treated any differently just because he's dead… Okay… I am being too harsh here. I just want you to know that I know you are working with Miklo. I know where Miklo has his hideouts and all I want is to just hear you say it."

Panzer wouldn't talk.

"Panzer, you're really bothering me now."

"How do you know who I am?"

"Is that like an existential question? Not a good time to be asking one."

That's when one of them turned to Panzer. "You better hope I die," Panzer said, looking deep into the man's eye, "'cuz when were done here, I'm going to come for you." And then he turned to L Señor, "And you, you will die as well."

L Señor took out a knife from his pocket, got down on one knee, and stuck the knife to Panzers throat.

"You won't die if you tell me who you got this from. I know it's Miklo, just say it."

"Die, I've already died once, so kill me, make me meet the maker."

With the knife to him L Señor said, "No, your wish will not come true. Now, where did you get this MDMA from?"

"CVS, they sell acetone as well, it makes for a good drink."

L Señor punched him in the face. Breaking Panzers nose. "Okay…" He said to Panzer with a crazy look in his eye, "I've been calm with you until this point. Do you really think I don't know that you work for Miklo? Do you not know that I know him? Or are you just being intentionally thick?"

"You're L Señor," Panzer said with a mouth full of blood, "you are the biggest piece of shit on the planet and most people in the community blame you for Rainbow going down. You and Pablo are both scum pieces of shit."

"Don't group me in with that bastard."

"You've become that *Bastard*."

"So, since you are well informed, I don't have to keep explaining then… Give your boss Miklo a message, tell him I would like to speak with him at the warehouse at his earliest convenience."

"He doesn't want to do any business with you."

"Are you him? I'm not telling you to ask him just hear an answer not from his mouth. You can either do what I say or we can just take care you now."

"Then you might as well kill me now."

"Sure, because the choice is yours… Take him," L Señor said to one of his flunkies. Before the bag went over Panzers head, L Señor looked him dead in the eye.

"You like killing," Panzer said just as the bag was going over his head, "You are enjoying this. I could have said everything you wanted but you would kill me anyway. You are a sick individual and you motherfuckers are just as bad for being with him. I hope you all rot in whatever hell you believe in."

Then the bag went over his head.

When I woke up the next morning sadness is all I felt. I didn't even know what had happened I just knew that the world wasn't right anymore. The sun wasn't even up yet but I was. All of the windows were open and I could smell the fresh air from the forest creeping into the home. The sky was gloomy blue, one of its best shades of color. I opened up my front door just out of curiosity for the weather. As I was making coffee, I decided to turn on the television.

Panzers face was all over the television. No one knew what had really happened to him. They said he was killed by Orchard Beach and that cops had found him outside of his vehicle while it was still running and just on the fumes of whatever gas was left inside it. No cameras. No witnesses. No information. It was on the news and for someone who didn't know him it would have been easy to dismiss it like anything else.

Every day I saw his face and there was nothing I could do. I knew that Panzer had not given me up, but there was no way I was mad at him, because this man is now dead. In my mind, everything played out and I knew everything. When I first heard about it, I didn't really have a reaction to it. I was upset with myself that I was so cold towards this situation. It wasn't until Kush called me really concerned.

I told him, "Nothing… nothing is going to happen."

"Do you think L Señor had something to do with this?"

"Yeah I do."

"We have to stop, at least for a while."

"Stop what?"

"You know… Just for a while… I thought you didn't want to be doing this anymore?"

"I don't, but we haven't gotten the amount of money I would be comfortable stopping with."

"Yeah? And how much would that be?"

"When I feel it."

"Yeah," he said in a tone, "when you feel it."

Where the Grass Grows Greener

When I got off the phone with him, that's when I got mad. I knew it was L Señor. I wanted to send him a message and I also was starting to realize what Kush was saying. It was time to end it. My phone was still in my hand as I was debating what I was going to do next.

I called Kush back.

"You're right. Stop everything. Pack it up. Come upstate if you want."

"Okay, I'll see you there."

"Yeah, I'll be back tonight."

"Back tonight? Where you going?"

"I gotta' run some errands."

"Errands?"

"Errands."

"Be careful with those errands."

"Always."

While I was pondering, Tillman was only finding out about Panzer, he didn't really know who Panzer was. But during his morning donut and coffee as Tillman was watching the television there was Panzers face. Taking a sip of his coffee Tillman slowly put down the cup on the table but that's not where it landed, it fell to the floor and splattered all over the rug. He had seen this man before, he saw him at the mansion. He was the one chasing after Panzer and it finally clicked.

I remember this day being a Monday and through the course of my relationship with L Señor I noticed this day of the week was the most important one for them. It was payday; when their dealers came to pay L Señor for their services. I always wondered what services they provided; thought it was something out of *The Godfather*. The most important part of that day was the early morning drive to a house on City Island. I never cared and never asked a question but I wanted to know what was going on.

I drove down the night before and after three hours of I had made it back to the Bronx.

I wanted to find L Señor before he found me. This was proving to be difficult because he wasn't at any of their usual haunts. They would frequent the Morris Park / Throggs Neck sections, so I drove around for almost an hour. I was driving normally, following all the traffic laws so I would not attract any pigs.

162

I was distracted by the gun I had stashed in a bag in the trunk. *You should have loaded it already. Do not actually use it.*

As I was driving down one of the desolate blocks, I saw one of the flunkies, Carlos, sitting in a black late nineties Lincoln Mercury, a rare sight in the year two thousand fourteen.

One of the flunkies was double parked in front of a hydrant.

That's when I say my prey.

I had passed him but was not noticed. So, I drove around the block and pulled over halfway down so he wouldn't notice me. Knowing that I had a gun in the car did not help me make the decision but thought that killing would not solve anything and a more powerful message could be conveyed without some sort of bloodshed. I could feel my heart beating and almost ripping out of my chest. *What am I going to do?* My plan was then to just use the gun as a scare tactic. All the different scenarios of this were playing out in my head and I didn't know which of them was better. They all seemed pretty bad. Then began the playing of the consequences which did not help anything in my mind.

Once again, I thought there was a way to reason with L Señor. This scenario seemed like the best and most likely the one that would turn out okay for everyone. I was sadly mistaken.

I parked the car where it stood and frantically went into the trunk to get the gun ready. I decided to carry the bullets in my pocket and keep the gun empty. I knew that if I pointed it at someone's face, they would know it wasn't loaded. I wanted to do this as cleanly as possible, in my mind this was proving to be difficult. I didn't think I could be intimidating enough and that he wouldn't take me seriously.

I could feel the cool crisp air around my aura and yet I felt calm from the goosebumps I was getting and was trying to figure out which flunky was in the car. *What are they doing here?*

That's when I saw L Señor coming out of the house followed by Rico, Jose and Carlos. So, that means Miguel was in the car. Something was odd. From the distance I could hear L Señor say, "Back to the warehouse."

I could feel my heart beating faster as I got closer to the truck. I wanted to get inside of it and hold Miguel for some sort of social ransom. Instead I did this…

"L Señor." I yelled from maybe twenty feet away.

"Well, well… Look who it is boys."

"Yeah, boys, look who it is!" I yelled.

They were all confused by me.

It seemed like no one else was going to say anything so I had to, "Why can't you just leave me alone?"

"That's what you say to me? Not anything about killing your friend."

He knew what would shut me up.

"You come here," he said in an angry tone coming closer to me with his flunkies following behind, "two days after I kill one of your friends and you say that I can't leave *you* alone? You didn't give a shit about Panzer, did you?"

"You know, that's really none of your fucking business. You killed him to get to me. He told me about you and what you did. So really, it had nothing to do with me."

"He told you everything? Everything?"

"Pretty much."

"So, what is this?"

"What is it going to take to leave me alone?"

"Pretty sure I did leave you alone up to this moment. This was something you just brought upon yourself."

At that moment I was brought back to reality and realized that nothing had happened yet, I was still in my car and had scared myself to the point that I decided to do nothing.

L Señor did in fact come out of that house with his flunkies and they drove away. It was when they were about to drive away that I noticed a car across the street in between where they were and me. I had the feeling it was Tillman and the Partner. It was the same car they had picked me up in. L Señor drove away and they followed.

It was very reliving that I had done nothing and seeing Tillman and the Partner gave me a sense of reality. Between all the conversation I had with Panzer about L Señor and the ones I had with Kush, and the fact that Tillman wanted me to give them L Señor I realized that there was something bigger than me going on. Something else that I am missing from this story was playing out. I drove home immediately. With this new sense of freedom, I couldn't wait to get up the property and hang out with Kush and Spazz.

I'll probably never see L Senor again.

I need to lay off the drugs.

∞

I had just gotten a new batch of 2c's fresh out of the lab and a blotter of some high-quality Dead-Family LSD. I was worried that the 2c-P order was missing from the shipment. I figured that it would come in another package. It was the last big order that I ever planned to do. This was it. It was all for us. When I was holding the package before opening it, I knew that we had to stop doing what we were.

Panzer was still in my mind. I hadn't forgotten about him. I thought about him every day, yet my feeling toward him still did not improve and I was mad at myself for that. I could not find a single ounce of me that actually missed him. I ran a few of the stories he told me in my mind constantly because they wouldn't leave my mind.

My repetitive nature had found the best of me. I found myself listening to the same songs over and over again, the same thirty seconds playing over and over. Waking up in the middle of the night with them in my head and in the morning in the shower I was hearing them. It bothered me but not that much to care. Always thought about Panzer. Then about what I thought about him. Should I have done more or less? Probably more…

Anyway, I called Kush to see if he wanted to join me but he didn't answer. I got some E, B and T-7. I was supposed to get some 2c-P but that package never came and I didn't think about it. I just thought the DEA or someone like that had confiscated it. So that, was just one loss to me.

Awe.

The only word that my mind could fathom.

I felt as if I wasn't there but my body was, the sights were moving like the sea, the walls, the floor, and the Monet I had hanging. There was a lot in that painting. I was swaying but I wasn't. My vision became water and everything was moving. With all these pleasant visuals came the feeling of sickness. I felt like I had to vomit but I didn't want to. I held it all back. But that feeling wasn't leaving anytime soon. I needed to get out of the house. I looked at Spazz and said, "take a walk with me".

"Are you sure you want to go out there?" He asked.

"Yeah." I said.

165

The world was so different. Quiet, it was. We were walking down the block, that's when I attempted to take out the joint from my pocket. It was so hard to light a jay tripping balls. The flame of the lighter was so intense that I felt the little heat it was giving off on my skin which warmed me up. I took a hit but also took another one before I exhaled. Hello vomit. I could feel it crawling up my throat. Handing the joint to him I knew I couldn't hold it in anymore and ran into the ally way we were about to pass. I threw up all over the place, nothing got on me. I had passed this place numerous times a day and never gave it a second though, I maybe never even thought about it until this moment. I looked up at the brick walls, although it was nighttime and the bricks were red, they were flashing purple. Purple lights going on and off illuminating the ally as is some star-studded event was taking place. The visuals were intense.

What am I doing?

The rest of the walk was interesting. The street lights were giving off an orange haze and upon further inspection of the sky I realized that we were in the Bronx because of the sky. The New York City sky is a subtle orange color from the light pollution. Nothing seemed the colors they were supposed to be. After the jay I just wanted to back home. I was so messed up that I didn't know where we were, I could have sworn we were upstate. That's one of the big problems I find with certain psychedelics, the feeling of your internal compass turning off.

During the comedown I was rambling to myself. Every time I caught myself, I tried to stop.

How could we, I still be doing these things?

Poor Panzer, what have I done?

Worst time to be thinking about that. There was another problem with these substances, they make your mind think about things you probably shouldn't when you're on them. Sometimes it helps to do this but most of the time you don't get any answers and it just kills your mood and begin to think about it more than the experience of tripping which is the real sad part.

I focused on something else, the trippy curtains I gotten specifically for this purpose. I watched the fractals morph into faces and scenes that I cannot even begin to describe. I closed my eyes and was bombarded by more faces. Clowns turning into dogs, dogs turning into chameleons. I put my headphones on and listened to *I Want You*

(She's So Heavy) by The Beatles and I was transported into some animal evolution and morphing into each other. It began to feel really heavy and by the time the storm in the song began to happen I felt the world pressing down upon my chest and my raced like never before. I even had the thought that I might have had a stroke, but I didn't not want to freak myself more than I was already. The song itself abruptly ends and I suspended in animation. My eyes were still closed as I enjoyed the silence which lasts only three seconds. When the guitar of *Here Comes the Sun* began, I opened my eyes to reveal that I was in my chair, on my property in the middle of the woods.

I was sprawled out on my seat, the one-seater chair that reclined. I leaned back all the way and starred at the sky for what may have been hours until I drifted off to sleep.

It was a very pleasant experience watching the clouds go by against a blue sky in the window of the trees that were blocking some of my view. In the opening of those clouds I put my iPod on shuffle and the song that came on was *Imagine by John Lennon*. That was magical and cannot be explained in words.

All things must pass.

I woke up in the same position in the chair I had fallen asleep in.

I made my way back to the house. It was time to get cleaned up and be sober for at least the next twenty-four hours.

I had this gut feeling that day, but didn't know what to think of it. Something in your body tells you that something is off. Not anything in you, but that the universe is sending out signals, weird vibes all over.

The phone vibrated on the table.

Just the sound of it made me what to physically harm somebody. It could only be one man, only one man's phone call could cause me such anger before I even answered it. It had been a week since what I did, or a month. To be honest, I have no idea the time frame of any of these events, it's all one blur for me.

So, I wondered... on the backburner of my mind was the fact that my 2c-P order didn't come in the mail. That made me even angrier. But for the most part I was thinking of Panzer and what I had done to him, what he had done to me, and what I did for him.

'Fuck, what did this man want?' I heard Panzer say over and over again that someone has to do what I'm doing and it's me.

The phone vibrated again.

The rage built inside me.

Just by looking at the number I knew it was L Señor.

There is a burning hatred inside of me of this name.

I answered, why not.

"What the fuck do you want?" I asked.

"Is that how you answer the phone?" He said.

"What do you want now? Leave me alone."

"I want to talk. I'm starting to think you're a pussy."

This man will die by my hands.

"I'm tired of this shit, why are you bothering me you fucking cunt."

"Let's talk somewhere and deal with this like men. Have a good conversation about what we're doing."

"What we're doing? We're not doing anything! I'm doing my thing and you do yours. We, there is no we."

"I like your attitude more and more but save it for when we meet. Let's sit down and talk just you and me."

"Just you and me? No one else?"

"No one."

"None of your flunkies or your delinquent friends?"

"Just me and you Miklo. You know your name is known around here. Miklo, but we both know that's not your real name."

"Enough, when and where?"

"Whenever, wherever you want."

"I'll call you when I figure it out." I said, hanging up the phone.

What kind of trap was I going to walk into?

Really? Am I that good at what I do that someone wants to take it all over? What kind of monster had I created? Where can I meet this guy, what is he going to do to me? I would be stupid to meet this guy. What a world I was in. So dark for me, even the day could not let me see the colors.

∞

There are other moments in our lives that we reflect upon years later only to fully understand and process everything.

At this particular moment in my life all I could think about was drugs. I needed a drug. I wanted them. I can clearly remember sitting on my couch debating what should be done. Psychedelics, no not in the mood, Molly or M Weezy? No, did them a couple days ago. The only other things I had were Crystal Meth, which I would never touch, still haven't, and Cocaine and Ketamine. So, I did some Coke. Then I did some Ketamine. After some online reading I found out that it was called the Calvin Klein. Anyway, so now I was doing these other two things just because, now I sound like a drug addict but I wasn't an addict.

Looking back on this now, I was addicted but somehow was able to turn it off at some point.

What bothered me about all of this was the fact that we had a conversation with Spazz about his behavior and drug addiction. It did not seem to help because he was still doing it and dismissed us, this was apparent to us after the fact because we were all on MDMA, it could be thrown away as just people talking on drugs, it was the substances talking. It sucked that we couldn't actually say what wanted to each other unless we were having those drug induced 'bro' moments. I could see Spazz saying something like this to himself which is probably he did not take us seriously. Since Kush and I told him how it affected us we did not see the need to say anything again. Our feeling was mutual, if he really wanted to change, he would have listened to us. We dismissed him and it really wasn't fair. Things he was doing should have been a warning bell for us but it was hard to tell with him. Most of the time we attributed his behavior to him being normal, sometimes he was a lot to be around and with the drugs he was just more stimulated. It sounds horrible but I began to not care for him. I was sad about Anthony. It got to the point of being with him that I had to fidget with whatever was in my pocket because I couldn't stand him when he talked. He was fried and became a fiend. The cherry on top of this was that I had a feeling he was having people buy from me for him. Sad. In the end, Kush and I are at fault for him, just for the reason that we did not address it again, under the rug it went with all the other dust.

This was when the three of us started to drift apart.

Kush, on the other hand, was not doing so well himself. He seemed distant even in his own mind. I noticed him more since Spazz wasn't around. I would have to repeat myself to him about three times and sometimes he wouldn't understand what I was talking about. He wasn't like Spazz doing the Calvin Klein, he was doing just straight ketamine all day.

If you don't know about ketamine, maybe I should explain something about it now. It's an animal tranquilizer that I believe is used on horses. The handful of times I did it, I found that it was not enjoyable. The first time I had taken a bump of it we were watching a New York Rangers game, sure it made the game more interesting but it felt like someone took my brain out of my head and I was trying to comprehend everything that was going on , only to realize that nothing was going on. It was so chaotic that twenty minutes later when it began to wear off, I thought, *this shit sucks*. The other times I had done it, it was more social when they were all doing it. After a while there was no reason to do it.

There are two things I never want to experience, those are *K-Holes* and *Ego Death*. From what Kush was telling me about his experiences on ketamine, I know he must have K-Holed a few times.

For Kush, mundane tasks became obstacles and music became pain. He expressed to me that doing anything was taking a lot out of him, that he was tired but couldn't sleep and that he couldn't collect a single thought.

"You got a problem." I said to him.

He was shocked and looked at me, "What do you mean?"

"You've been staring at your black laptop screen for five minutes saying words that are in no way a sentence."

He was still looking at me, back at his screen, and then back to me. "Yeah, I do have a problem."

"I can't be around you anymore. I'm sorry man, I can't see you like this. You gotta stop."

"How?"

"Flush everything you have at home."

"No."

"Dude," I said in frustration but also trying not to yell, "You're a smart guy and I'm watching throw everything away."

"Yeah, what the fuck am I throwing away?"

"Your mind."

"What the fuck you talking' like that for?"

"I'm happy you're able to form these sentences."

"What the fuck does that mean?"

I was confused, "have you not been a part of this conversation?"

"Then what's my problem?"

"Since you've been here, you've done four bumps of K in the span of an hour. I've watched you just forget you did and was about to do another one."

He looked down at his hands, semi covered in powder.

"I have a problem?" He asked.

I could not figure out his tone so the question kind of scared me. "Yes, you have a problem and I think you need to stop the K. You can't listen to any sort of music anymore with words because it makes your brain wonder and think bad thoughts too much. You consistently have to told the same thing a few times to understand it… I think your worse than Anthony right now."

"You compare me to Anthony?"

"Yeah, our friend that we had to tell he had a problem. Now I'm your friend, a brother to me, and I want to be able to hang out with you in ten years. I don't want you to die because of these drugs."

"Would you say that to Anthony?"

"No. He is too far gone. You aren't gone, but you're going."

"Alright, I'll try and stop."

"Nah, you will fucking stop. I'll even take you to rehab if it comes down to that. And yes, if Anthony wanted to go to rehab, I would drive him to."

That's where the conversation ended.

The next morning, I woke up to find that he had left me a note on the living room table.

> Went home. Thanks for the
> talk, I will clean up.
> I need some time alone.

Reading that made me feel better inside. I was glad that I had gotten through to him.

It was the first time I was truly alone in my house upstate.

I called Spazz to talk to him, but he didn't answer. I wasn't sure if the morning was too early or too late to call him.

As I sat on the couch I came to another realization, I also had a drug problem but no one was around to tell me that. I cried that day because no one would tell me that. Telling myself that made me sadder. I thought about cocaine on a constant basis and because of the molly I had been grinding my teeth more than I ever did. I began associating songs with certain drugs and would get high just from hearing them. I was smoking a pack of cigarettes a day and going through at least a joint an hour with vaping ang bong rips in between. Even after I had told myself I had a problem I was still doing cocaine. It took me two days before I had the courage to put down the drugs. I didn't want to throw them out, I still wanted to be able to do them, but I had to get off them for a while.

One of the thoughts I used to hate was thinking about Sadie. If she had seen me, she would have been upset. If she never left me, I wonder how I would have been. It was all probably for the best, I guess.

When they found him, they said he had been dead for a couple of hours.

His music still playing through his speakers, *The Massed Gadgets of Auxemities (The Man & The Journey)*, that's what was repeating on the computer. I know that because once I heard that they had found him with the music blasting I wanted to know what he was listening to and what he had been; his parents had given me his computer. I never heard that album, never will. I was glad there was nothing I knew or else I wouldn't be able to listen to it ever again. How ironic that he was listening to The Man & The Journey by *Pink Floyd*.

Men and their journeys.

They had come to the conclusion that it was a robbery attempt. Yet, nothing was taken, just a life, a life that wanted to be bothered by no one no more. Kush was someone who gave up on everything and wanted to be alone, live out his days. He hated everyone equally including white people, rednecks, Nazis, spics, niggers, kikes, gooks. Everyone was equally worthless to him.

That's the problem with most of these cannabis dealers, maybe dealers in general through ought the Bronx at that time, but not all. Usually they began selling drugs in high school and that's all they know how to do. They get stuck in their own age bubbles and are forever who they are. Some were even brought up to hate different races and as they grew, it never changed, products of their environments.

Back to Kush, someone once said to him that he is the most racist person they'd ever met; his response was I hate everyone equally and everyone deserves to be an asshole when the situation calls for it. Now I share that philosophy. Everyone can go fuck themselves and take their bibles or gods and shove it up their asses. I'd rather listen to *Ghost* and hail Satan all day.

In my mind this is how it all happened.

Kush was tripping. I know that because he had hit me up, asking if I would be down to trip with him. I was in no state of mind to do anything like that. I had just come off a month long phenethyamine binge.

Would things have turned out differently if I were there? Would we both have been killed? Would it even have happened?

It also bothered me that here I was telling him he had a problem and I was debating going to take drugs with him. What a terrible fucking friend I was.

He was in his room, surrounded by the music of the Floyd. Someone broke into his home, found where the music was coming from. The person got to his door and kicked it open. Kush, in the state of mind he was in, did not know what was happening, or I'd like to think he was smart enough to know. He probably didn't. The person shot him, in the head.

The cops said the front door was busted in; his room door same and that it seemed like there was something used to do it.

I called Kush the next day to find out how his trip went, only to speak to his mother who answered the phone.

In tears the women said to me, "he's dead. They shot him in the head." That's all I could make out in between the crying and the hysterical yelling.

Kush was dead.

My friend, best friend was dead. I sat down on the floor, putting my head between my hands. I cried. A feeling I had never felt before engulfed me.

Absolutely devastated.

The worst part was that I could only blame one person. Myself.

His funeral was a nice ceremony. His mother cried the whole time. They could not have an open casket. At one point she tried opening the lid herself, her family restrained her. "My baby!" She screamed.

I hated to be that guy, but as this was happening, I was thinking, wow, his parents treated him like shit his whole life and now he's dead they're both really sad. We need to start learning to appreciate things while we can.

How long could Anthony and I sit there and not show an emotion. I was coming down hard from a week long 2c – E binge. My mind was not there at all.

No emotion we showed. A small shred of emotion and I could have broken down.

Everyone was looking at us, suddenly it was clear that this is somewhere we shouldn't be. We wanted to come here; our friend has died. Pay our respects to him, but his family only had questions for us and we were in no state to give any answers. My heart, I could feel the whole time, only time I really thought I was going to have a heart attack.

Don't cry, I said to myself, *don't do anything, you're going to fall apart if you do.*

The diamond shaped designs in the rug were moving. I didn't want to be tripping anymore. This had been the worst trip. For some reason time did not add up to me. Was this the same trip? I had heard Kush had died, yesterday? Why was I still tripping now? This is what I was thinking when his father sat down in front of me. The pattern of black lines on his grey suit. Don't look at his suit. Oh man but don't look at his face, don't look at anything. Anthony couldn't take it anymore; he just left; made me feel even more awkward. But if I was him, I probably would have done the same thing. One person had to stay and 'defend' the honor of our friendship with Kush. I could always tell when I knew my father was upset. I just saw it in his face. This man had the same face. I could have no idea how he felt, I'm not a father. His son had died and I now was the only friend left. I could already think of the answers of the questions he might ask me.

"How long did you know my son?" He asked.

"Uh," I tried to find my words, "since grammar school."

"Was he a good friend?"

"A better friend than most, he's like a brother to me."

"Why did you guys did you guys do what you did. You were all smart and threw it away."

"I – I am sorry for what happened to him. I loved him like a brother."

"What did all those drugs get you? Was it worth it?"

"No, no it wasn't."

"Are you happy now?"

I did not want to say anything; to keep my composure I began to cry on the inside and just thought about being in my truck crying alone on the way home. Whatever words that were going to come out of my mouth were going to make me cry.

He began to tear up and something in me snapped. I had flashes of my parents and what I did to them and how I was not speaking to them and I began to cry. I don't think he knew what to do with me. I decided to tell him the truth. Within that moment I also decided to not tell the truth for it could hurt more than a lie.

A tear streamed down his face.

"The sight of you and your friend have made my wife cry. You should leave. We don't want you here."

I was shocked at what I heard.

Like I said though, I snapped and said, "you and that bitch you call your wife treated Kush like pure garbage for his entire life and no all of a sudden its 'oh my son'. He told me what you guys used to do to him and it isn't a wonder he took drugs sooner. You fucking people put on a mask and parade yourself like your shit don't stink. He told me how you used to pad lock his bedroom door so he couldn't leave. How you threw him out of the house when you caught him smoking weed for the first time. He told me that you had found out he was being abused by his teacher and you let it happen. You treated his whore of a sister better and it shows. I hope the sight of me bothers you for the rest of my time here because I'm not leaving until I see my brother being laid to rest. I loved him more than you and the cunt ever will. And, if you don't get out of my face and act like nothing happened between us here, I won't hurt you. Remember, the Academy Awards are only for movies."

He was stunned and so was I.

Can you believe you just said that?

He stared at me and wanted to say something. I had so much more to say if he did, but he causally got up and walked away.

I, along with five other people who did not know Kush, carried his coffin from the hearse to the hole the grave. I stayed to the end, even after his parents had left and watched as they lowered him in and buried him.

My father used to yell at me all the time and say, "Who's going to be there for you in the end? No one, just yourself." That statement I never thought would be true.

In a way, this was probably the best thing for me. I stopped doing drugs but my mind still was not good.

I was missing some sort of closure.

It was three twelve in the morning; I know that because I was looking at my phone while smoking a cigarette on a rock in the middle of the woods. I had walked there from home and I wasn't sure if this was part of my property or not, I had walked for hours. A chilly night as I sat there looking up at the stars. Trying to plan out my life but could only plan so much until I realized I couldn't plan anything at all. What would tomorrow bring? A madman could come up to me now, kill me and I'd be dead, no good for anyone and maybe no one would ever know. Calmer I felt after every hit of a cigarette, but I smoked almost a whole pack that night for no reason, no logic behind the smoking of a cigarette. Felt like I was the only one who smoked Marlboro 27's, whenever I'd go to the gas station, they'd always be filled with it, but Newport's or Marlboro reds, gone in a couple days. I guess I was thinking all this because I thought there was a chance that when I met L Señor that I'd be dead. I didn't know when I was going to meet him but it was going to happen. I was trying to make peace with my life so if anything, I'd be ready. But you're never really ready, *are you?* I wonder what death is like. Ceasing to not exist anymore. Mind boggling stuff. Not something to be thinking about all the time. I can see why some people go crazy when they do.

In the white room again. My recurring dream that had been a plague for a long time. White everywhere. Blinding, even for me. Was it empty or was it blank? Was it foggy or just the dream? Why was I having this dream? What was it trying to tell me? Maybe I have nothing planned; maybe my life isn't destined to be what I think it is. Can a dream really be this profound? What did it all mean? There was nothing in there. Green and orange, green and orange I would chase but never caught it. In the distance I could see a green haze. I wasn't sure if the green was the floor or I was above what it was. It was like looking at something without your glasses, there was a breeze and I could see the green blob moving with the wind. Wondering around aimlessly in this white room felt like I was in a funhouse. The room started to flash, flashing like a strobe light. Faster and faster until…

I woke up, comfortable in my bed, on the nightstand next to me was the mirror I was using to cut up the Coke and Ketamine along with their empty bags. The razor blade was covered in the white powders. Maybe this was my last week and that's why my bed feels awesome. I had to face the music at some point. But not now, now I just want to be me, and enjoy what I have. Then it would hit me that I had nothing.

Clearly, that cloud of sobriety didn't last too long.

I did miss my family. I haven't spoken to them since I moved out those many measurements of time ago. I can't talk to them now, not after everything, what do I say to them?

I guess in the end all you have is yourself and really no one else.

I had to confront my problem. I needed an end.

I had to meet with L Señor even though every nerve in my body told me not to. It was a stupid decision on my part, I could have met him and he could have killed me. I was procrastinating. Found anything else to do but call him. I thought if I called him, I'd be killed and if I didn't call him, he'd just find me and kill me. So, either way I was dead.

I sat on my porch smoking. Watching the world, looking at the beautiful blue sky. Breathing in the air between every toke. Slowly I got high, very high. I wanted to cry but I was now a man with real problems and crying is not something a real man does. And I am not weak. I cannot cry for myself because that would just mean I'm weak and can't handle my problems. After the joint was done and I was high I sat there soaking in the highness. I didn't like it, maybe because I was under so much stress that I didn't enjoy it and actually regretted smoking it. The feeling was different now, not a relaxing thing, it made think about everything more. The thoughts in my mind were racing. That's when I came to the conclusion that I can't smoke unless my life is in order and I feel happy inside, and I had to finish with L Señor. That boycott only lasted about an hour.

I had nothing to lose, so I got the courage to call the bastard. I needed to know it was him and hear it from his own mouth.

"Hello Miklo. I see you got my message." He said with weird happiness.

"You killed Kush, didn't you?"

"That would be the message."

"I am going to kill you."

"I don't believe you."

"Pelham Bay Station, two hours. Keep your flunkies at bay, if you know what's good for you." An empty threat I knew he wouldn't take seriously. I wanted him thinking I had a plan but I knew he wasn't going to think that anyway.

I don't know what I wanted to get out of this.

The next thing I knew I was again waiting in my car, but this time I was waiting underneath the El across the street from the supermarket which gave me a direct line of sight to the station at the end of the tracks.

Something wasn't right.

I was watching everything and had this feeling that they were watching me already. Something I noticed was that the more you look at anybody the more suspect they become. Looking out of all my mirrors I noticed a biker with a blue hoodie riding in my direction on the driver's side. I sat there and watched him ride closer. Something else grabbed my attention and by the time I looked back at the biker, he was passing by me and threw a two-way radio to me which fell on my lap. I got so nervous I could feel every part of my body and thought I was having a heart attack. The biker made a left down the next street and was gone.

"I know you have the radio by now, so just respond to this as normal." L Señor said through it.

"Why the theatrics?"

"Why hang up on someone before they tell you what they want?"

"Why'd you do it? What do you want from me?"

"You want to talk and have it all explained to you?"

"Yes, I do actually. I want to see your face covered in blood."

"So, my question to you now is, what do you want from me?"

"I want to kill you. I want you to suffer for what you did."

"Do you think I would let you anywhere near me?"

"Cowards usually don't. I want to go one on one with you right now."

"You think you can take me?"

"You're nothing without your flunkies as back up. You are nothing."

For what felt like a long time, he did not respond.

"And you want to do this here, at Pelham Bay Station?"

"I figured, the real winner is the person to get arrested and snitch on the other. Makes for a good competition huh?"

After a long pause he said, "No weapons."

"No flunkies."

Another pause, this time a short one, "This will draw too much attention."

"You bitch ass nigga', I don't give a fuck, I've got nothing to lose. I want to break your fucking nose and stomp your face out."

"Alright. Hope you're better with your hand than your words."

That was it, he didn't say anything else.

I looked around quickly but I didn't see them.

That's when Miguel, wearing a blue hoodie, was standing at my door with a gun to me.

"Unlock your doors." He said.

I did as was told.

The three flunkies got into the car, one in the passenger's seat and Miguel and the other one in the back.

"L Señor will not fight you here. Drive."

"Drive where?"

"Just fucking drive!" one yelled from the backseat.

I began driving and was feeling very uneasy.

"Why are you guys doing this?"

"Shut your mouth." Miguel said.

"Seriously, why is this happening?" I asked, almost pleading. They were as stone and didn't even look at me. "Why do you follow L Señor? Why are you guys going along with this?"

A voice from the passengers' seat said, "L Señor was there when no one else was."

"What the fuck does that mean?"

Miguel was getting agitated and yelled, "Shut up, the both of you!"

"Nah, fuck you, my fucking car. Why? Just answer me why?"

"If you don't shut up and keep driving, I'm going to kill you before you even to get to L Señor." Miguel said pressing the gun against the back of my head.

"What are you guys going to do to me?"

These fuckers said nothing.

"What happened to the other guy?" I asked this but it also made the atmosphere tense.

"Worry about yourself." The one next to me said.

I was getting frustrated, "At least tell me where were going."

Again, no one said a thing.

179

"How would you feel if you guys were in my situation?" I asked, sort of trying to appeal to whatever humanity they may still have in them.

The one next to me looked over and said, "You knew what you were getting yourself into L Señor. You don't know us, so don't even try to understand us. We've been through shit that your pussy bitch mind cannot even begin to think. He knew what you were doing and you lied to him. Now you're going to lie in the grave you've dug for yourself."

"And is that how you became one of L Señor's flunkies?"

Miguel had almost busted my skull open when he hit me with the butt of the gun which almost knocked me out. I don't remember actually feeling the hit although the pain after was felt.

I was in the white room.

I awoke in my dream, or what I knew was my dream. I opened my eyes and there was white, white all over the place. The white fog, white just because everything else was white, which dissipated in a short amount of time. The only words I could mutter to myself in my mind were; *what the fuck?* I got up and could not believe my eyes. The green haze was becoming something, a field of cannabis plants; tall, green, beautiful and majestic. So green, they almost looked fake. The smell of it put me in another plane of the euphoria. It seemed like an endless field of them, as far as I could see, there were plants. That, my friends, is where the grass grows greener.

I looked down next to me and there was the *Stoner Pineapple*. This guy, I had not thought of in years. It was looking glorious. It just looked at me with its blank stare as it turned around to look out into the field.

A joint appeared in my hand and of course I took a hit out of it.

Then. a stage appeared in front of me and from the floors emerged a band; a drummer, a guitarist, a bassist and a keyboardist. They began playing a familiar song and behind them rose a huge white wall with massive bricks. At first, I could not make out the faces but soon enough I saw that the four of them were me.

I was playing to myself.

It all felt so real.

The bassist was singing and he sang, "If I had my way, I'd have all of you shot." He pointed at me and I took another hit from that joint…

That hit sobered me up and awoke back in reality.

I wasn't all there yet. The car was stopped but I couldn't open my eyes yet. I could make out everything they were saying but I didn't have the strength to open my eyes.

"What the fuck Miguel!"

"Why Would you hit him!"

"He wouldn't shut the fuck up!"

"We're lucky I pulled the emergency brake or we would have crashed into that car!"

"What happened?" I heard L Señor ask through the radio.

"We hit a bit of a snag."

"I see that."

I see that, the fucker said, *he has to be around.*

I got enough strength to open my eyes and there he was. The bastard was walking towards me. I had to get up, I had to kill him. Slowly, I regained my consciousness and jumped out of the car. The flunkies were stumbling after me.

As I ran to him, he clenched his fists and he was bracing for my impact. The closer I got to him the angrier I got. Just thinking about how he looked pisses me off.

He was able to hit me first but I hit him really good and the fucker went down as soon as I made contact with him, I beat the shit out of him. I got on top of him in the gayest way possible to beat the shit out of him. My hand was covered in his blood after a couple of good hits to the head. I could feel his breathing slow.

I was taken off by his flunkies who wrestled me to the ground.

They were on top of me like savage cannibals. I took a few decent hits to the face and my head was numb. They carried me off into the car where they threw me in. My own car I was being thrown into, by the way. This was a feeling I never thought I'd feel. I had failed what I wanted to do.

I woke up some time later, tied to a chair with my hands handcuffed behind my back. I found myself staring at a swinging light bulb hanging from the ceiling. I remember exactly how the room smelled, stagnant air and cement particles. I must have been there for a while because my hands were numb. There is still a question in my mind as to how long I was there. How long was I knocked out? How long before L Señor came in?

181

The door opened and L Señor calmly walked in.

All I could think about was making a fist which I couldn't do. Immediately, the feeling of rage built within me and all I wanted to do was kill him. Stab him in the face and watch him die.

He grabbed the steel chair from the other side of the room and dragged it towards me. The steel sliding against the concrete floor isn't the best sound in the world to hear. He violently placed the chair on the ground and slowly sat in it.

Never have I accepted death so quick.

I was face to face with the man.

I have to kill this bastard.

His flunkies left the room, shutting the door behind them.

It was just he and I.

"Miklo," he said, just him saying my name mad me furious, "why are you still fighting?"

I was breathing loudly and could not control my facial expressions. I was angry.

"Not going to talk to me?"

My head started to twitch and I could feel different parts of my body having spasms.

You are now the Preacher.

"Panzer and I went way back." He said trying to evaluate if I would respond. After a pause he continued, "Before we were who we are today, we were much like you. Maybe even more naïve. Panzer and his friend, Zeus, they made a living hell for us. Well, they really didn't do it, but they indirectly made our lives a living hell. Because of those two, I had to do business with an uptight Mexican asshole. But, one night in the desert out in California, the destiny changed. You, were part of this destiny. But one thing I hate, is lying." He said all of this and at the end held up his index finger and pointed it to me.

"You and I could have done so much together, but you wanted to lie to me." His took his finger away from my face.

I was ready to speak. "So, someone treated you guys, like how you treated me and instead of growing from it, you kill my best friend… to prove a point to me? Why'd you kill Kush? Panzer, sure, fuck him, but why Kush?"

"You, have not suffered like the rest of us in this industry. You see this black market as all to yourself. You must have thought you were so cool, being on this website. Panzer and I had a mutual agreement that if anything happened to the website, he and I would start a new one. He broke that promise for you. You carry around with you this air of confidence that is just a charade. You on the inside, are nothing more than fear and loneliness, and that is what I want you to think about."

I put my head down because I no longer wanted to see them.

He grabbed my head and made me look at him.

"You will suffer. We are no longer good people. Good people don't survive in this world."

He spit on the floor by my feet.

"Bring it in!" he yelled and a flunky came in with a bag of white substance.

He handed it to L Señor and the flunky stood next to him.

"Do you know what this is?" He asked me.

"I'm guessing its some sort of drug. Maybe MDMA?"

"It is a drug and it is yours. Right now, you should wish it was MDMA. This substance I have here was confiscated from your PO Box and believe it was something you expected."

The 2c – P I ordered that I never got.

My fucking luck.

"I had this for a while and I've come to find out its something called 2c – P. A low dose hallucinogen lasting up to about seventeen hours. I have taken it and it isn't fun if you're not ready for it. According to Pihkal you only need about ten milligrams."

"You are not worth reading Pihkal, someone like you should never read that book."

He punched me in the face and my jaw went numb and the taste of blood filled my mouth and was also pouring out of my mouth.

"Who are you to tell me what I can and cannot read?"

I spit some blood out of my mouth and said, "These drugs aren't meant to be sold or fought over, they're meant to be given out and taken. But you will never understand that, you would be the reason these things are given bad names. You said you have taken it but you have not understood it."

He got up from his chair and took off his jacket. Rolled up his sleeves. The flunky cracked his knuckles and stared at me.

L Señor moved the chair he was sitting in away from me. He squatted in front of me and got to my eye level.

"Miklo, this is it, the last time. You can come be one of my guys, or you can choose your own path."

"I would never join you fucks. I wouldn't even waste my piss on your corpses."

L Señor motioned to the flunky and the flunky hit me in the face a couple times, stuck his hands in my mouth, my blood pouring all over me. L Señor took the bag of the P and put some in his hand. I couldn't move, the flunky had a good hold on me. L Señor was closer to me and poured the P into my mouth, it stung like a mother fucker.

The flunky closed my mouth and had no choice but to swallow the drug, trying to spit out as much as I could but nothing would come out. L Señor put a piece of duct tape over my mouth.

I felt the substance go into my bloodstream.

Once more he got eye level to me.

"You have a week. One week to make a decision and I will come for you; I know where you live upstate, so don't bother trying to find or contact me. If your anything like I am than the P should really fuck you up, I was fucked up for almost a day, hopefully it'll make you change your mind. But for now, we wait. Until you start feeling it, you're gonna be in that chair so make it a good trip."

I could barely breath with the duct tape of my mouth. The flunky left the room and it was just me and L Señor again.

He took his hand and put it to my throat, wrapping his hand around it and could feel him chocking me.

"I can kill you right now. Miklo, we can change everything, we can make a new Rainbow, and we can make these drugs awesome. I can't take all the credit for everything though; you introduced the Bronx to the pure MDMA and I know what you did to EDC. So, join me and the empire will be ours."

I don't know how long I was there but his face started morphing into other things.

He kept looking at his watch and eventually said, "It's been 45 minutes."

His face became that of Satan and horns came out of his head.

He unlocked the handcuffs and removed the duct tape. I was coughing up blood for a few moments. The world, to me, was shaking, the colors changing. The swinging light became a swinging sword.

L Señor and his flunky dragged me out of the room.

I was carried through all these corridors, monsters in cages, and L Señor became a monster and his flunky a demon. Suddenly I found myself tripping really hard and the more I thought the more it fucked me up. I was thinking about shrooms then I felt I was on them. Thought of acid and suddenly I was on it. The P is a very fluid substance and can change with your mind. They threw me in a car and the next thing in my journey I knew was that they had dropped me off at Kush's apartment; I tried to chase after them but their car quickly turned into other things.

It was weird being in his apartment. Now it was empty and seemed like a crypt. It was sad to be looking around the apartment and I went through most of it. I didn't want to take anything but just wanted to see what was going, get some last-minute clues as to what his last days seemed like. His laptop told me the most and saw his last played log and found out what he may have been listening to. One of his dresser drawers opened to reveal his drug stash, which was way more impressive than mine but the quantity of the substances that were there was unnecessary and dangerous.

Among his belongings was hidden and hard cover black notebook which intrigued me from the very sight of it. Kush had been using this notebook to write about his thoughts and reflect on his life. I read the whole book and it was a mind opening experience. There were things in there that were hard to read because he spoke of Spazz and I, some good and some bad. It seemed like he was using writing as a medication, a sounding board for his problems to get them off his chest.

In this time of reflection, I called Anthony and not shockingly enough, he did not pick up.

I needed to get out of this world. I can to the realization that I was alive and Kush wasn't. I can't be sad for the rest of my life. I decided to do some of his drugs and broke one of my amendment rules, *don't do too much in too little time.*

And of course, I had done, *too much in too little time…*

Looking back on this day of my life, it was all the drugs… I was taking something different a day, taking MDMA and its crazy cousin Methylone and now the feeling was different, I was cracked out on all this shit. It changes your perception and persona; the drugs were making life something different. I found myself places at times I never thought in a million years I'd be. Soo many sleepless nights, smoking

185

a pack of cigarettes sitting on the benches in the park all hours of the night.

I was also combining things that probably should not go together. One of those things I called a *Fuck My Face*. This consisted of some of the following, 2c –E, 2c – B, MDMA, and a pinch of Methylone. The reason I gave it that name is because you will get fucked, everything will be anything and anything is everything. It was the first time I had taken a combination like that and at first, I was in a panic. I seriously thought I was going to die. It felt like someone was twisting something inside of me and I was brought to the squatting position a few times and took a while for me to be able to stand back up. An hour after I took it, I fell on the floor and was unable to move. All I could do was stare at the ceiling. The more I stared at it, the more fucked up I felt. They started melting, like candle wax to a flame. I thought I'd be stuck there forever. The rug on the floor vibrated and each piece of fabric danced in the breeze. I was stuck within my mind, an infinite loop of the same information passing my brain. I was in hell and there was no way out. I could only imagine a wonderful world.

I had a flash of my life before my eyes. I saw my mother and I felt like a child I saw my father and brother. *Where are they? Why am I not with them?* These were the questions I was asking myself while I was repeating what my father used to say to me, *In the end, no one is there for you but yourself.* I missed them at that moment and felt that I had truly fucked up my life.

I was fighting back. I was not going to accept that my life was fucked up.

Reality set in real quick and I was tripping balls screaming at the top of my lungs for help. No one would come save me; I had to save myself…

My life was now feeling brief, everything happened but I don't remember anything. What had everything come to? What am I doing? It was the first time I had yelled for help. No one was there to save me, no one heard my screams and I realized something I should have a long time ago, I was alone and would be for the rest of my life.

I was repeating things in my mind and was trying not to do that. It was hard, some of these stimulants come with this effect though, so you must accept it and deal with it. I found myself thinking of Kushs' words…

Cars are Real,
Cliffs are Real,
Cops are Real,
You Can't Fly,
It's Never a good time to Die…
I Will Get Out of It…

I was still lying on the floor.

Nothing I could do.

Every color I saw fell in a glorious puddle and mixed to create lights of glowing liquid. I was able to get up and made my way to the front door and opened it. There was the world. I had to leave this house, it was making me trip bad and I thought maybe I was able to move all along and that my mind wanted me to have the epiphany.

I don't know how long I was walking around but the world was different.

The next thing I knew I was…

Rotting my brain on the train.

Six, eight, or midnight, what time it was I don't know. Weird feeling being on the train when no one's on it. Empty, I could do whatever I wanted. The pack of 27's in my pocket were tempting. Fuck it. I just light the cigarette. Moving with the motions of the train gave me the feeling of a good trip. Swaying left and right, the sounds of the rails went right thru me, I could feel them send their sounds waves and it radiating throughout my body. The lights would kick off sometimes and it would snap me out of the trance.

Hi reality.

I must ride the whole way, I kept thinking to myself and had no idea why I was. Turns out I was on the five train and took it to the Brooklyn Bridge. One of the MTA workers told me I had to get off. It was the last train.

I wound up waiting for a couple of hours at the station.

In silence by myself.

This was during the come down of the *Fuck My Face*.

I was just sitting there, looking out at the empty platform and tracks.

Someone could go crazy like this. I, especially, felt like I was going insane and thought about tripping more. Much like bacteria, it engulfed me in the feeling. I wanted to trip harder, get higher.

Why was I subjecting myself to silence? You have an iPod, use it!

It's a mad mad world.

That's when I decided to take two hundred fifty grams of MDMA and 20 milligrams of 2c-E. A Sparkle Flip. I had made the pill before I left. If it was a good idea or not, I wouldn't care. Looking back on it now it wasn't a good idea at all considering I was still feeling the after effects of the FMF.

I had nothing to do but wait for it to kick in. I must have been there for an hour, sitting all alone and hating myself. The slight change in mood and perception meant that the drugs were kicking in. I was gonna have an experience of a lifetime. I could see the lights dim out.

The train was just there, not doing anything. The trains lights turned on and the doors opened. The amusement park was open for business. The train had been there the whole time and I didn't notice. I walked onto the magical train. Sat down wherever I wanted, across from a big window. The train spoke to me, the next stop is, I don't care, three words that I loved at the moment.

I don't care.

I don't care.

There must be a problem with me. I felt pathetic. Who would torture themselves by isolating themselves from everyone? I had a life, I think, why was I keeping myself from it? Kush was dead, Spazz was binging somewhere. So, I guess I really had no life waiting for me.

The train pulled away at a speed that felt really fast.

There I was on the train, all alone. The lights went out for what seemed like a long moment. When they came back on, I was almost blinded by them. I had taken the train so many times in my life and I don't think I ever noticed that before.

There I was, all alone on the train.

The lights went off.

Not sure if my eyes were open or not as I was looking around the train. The sound of a lighter took me by surprise. I was just staring into the darkness, and when the lights came on, I saw myself lighting a cigarette. I was seeing myself, sitting across from me. I may as well be looking into a mirror; I couldn't tell a difference. A nice deep breath he took as he put the lighter back into his pocket. It was me. The only difference was that he was wearing sunglasses. A surge of adrenaline I could feel moving thorough ought my body.

I sat there looking at myself.

I had gone mad.

But I was always mad.

One of us had to initiate the conversation. You don't just see yourself and not talk.

"What's up." I said, not really sure if I was expecting an answer back.

He pulled the cigarette from his lips, *Sup*, he said.

"Am I crazy?"

Are you?

"Why are you here?"

I don't know, why are you on the train.

"Touché."

A moment of eerie silence.

"So, uh, what should I do?"

That's what you should be asking. What is there left to do, you've already ruined your life, what else is there? I already know what you're gonna' say.

"So, what am I gonna' say?"

He gave me the look, the look that knows it all.

"Sadie."

Fuck Sadie. You don't want her; you want the idea of her. I know you. You would not have lied to her and would have actually listened to her if you loved her. If you wanted her in your life you would have done everything in your power to get her back. You didn't even try. You wanted a future of you, alone, but not really alone. You wanted to have a big house, live with your friends, the ones you call brothers. Hanging out with them, taking drugs. You wanna' fuck bitches, have money. But that can't happen now, Kush is dead, Spazz became a tweeker and this is all because of you.

"Wow, thanks, you're a great help. Fuckin' lunatic talking to yourself."

I'm helping you more than you think I am.

"What do you want? What the fuck do you want?"

To be happy.

"Happy?" I just wanted to be happy. "How do I do that anymore?"

He smiled as he smoked.

What makes you happy? What will make you happy?

189

"I don't know."

You do know what you need to do to try and be happy.

The lights turned off and when they came back on the cigarette was in my right hand.

I was still on the train and when it broke into the morning atmosphere of the elevated track, I noticed the horizon and saw the purple red dawn and knew I had to go home. At some point I had to face the music and go back to my life.

For days I had been thinking about my hallucination of myself and realized I needed to figure out how to get back at L Señor; I wanted him to suffer. That is where my happiness could start to begin.

At first, I thought I would just go to the warehouse and kill them in cold blood, but I realized that would not happen as I thought. I did, however, have another thought and wanted to take him and the flunkies by surprise. There was also a suspicion I had that they were following me around, more of a feeling that I was never able to prove. After countless hours of debating, I knew what I would do.

The plan came together in my head and knew who I needed to contact. It took a while to find the right phone number but eventually I found the number for the DEA and they transferred me to Tillman after much explaining why I needed to speak to him.

I would have never thought I would be doing this.

"Tillman." He said over the phone.

"Do you still want me to help you get L Señor?"

"Miklo?"

"Yeah."

"It's been a while; thought you were trying to get out this."

"I told you before, it's not easy. I can help you get him."

"Why now do you want to help me?"

"L Señor is a horrible person, he has done things to me that I don't even want to speak about. I'm going to get my revenge on him but it definitely can't happen by myself, I need you guys."

"Where and when?" Tillman asked.

"Just like that? No talk of me going to jail?"

"If you're sincere with this, you don't have to worry. I'm sure you'll get the help that you need. Where and when?"

"Every Monday they take Pelham Parkway to City Island. It is in fact, every single Monday, it is a ritual. If we can stop them at the U

Turn before the draw bridge going east, you guys will be able to nab him."

"What do you want us to do?"

"You should be at the draw bridge, watching and waiting."

"What do you want us to do for you?"

"I want him to myself for a few minutes before you guys come out of the shadows."

I hung up the phone and knew Tillman would not miss this.

Little did I know that after Tillman had gotten off the phone with me, he stood up from his desk and said to his partner, "Monday…" Later on, Tillman would talk to me about the whole investigation on us.

I had half a plan and needed to figure out the rest of it.

I took at least ten thousand dollars with me to a car dealership and was going to buy a car to do this with. The salesman definitely thought I was crazy. I saw an old teal green and white Ford Bronco and thought, *that's it, that's the truck I'll use.*

"I'll take that car."

He seemed confused, "That truck isn't for sale but we do have these…" He pointed to the newer trucks.

I interrupted him by saying, "Why isn't it for sale? Does it run?"

"Yes, but it's been in this lot since it opened in the late eighties."

"Is there an emotional attachment from the owner of this place to that truck."

"Not that I'm aware of."

"Then why can't I buy it."

I could tell he was confused, "The only thing I know about that Bronco is that the transmission is on its way out."

"How much?"

With that he sold me the truck for one thousand dollars, a thousand more than it was worth.

I was now ready.

Monday…

Mondays are always good for L Señor and his flunkies. That's the day the dealers working under him come to pay him. One by one they go to the warehouse and give him his money. It was also the day they made their rounds, basically the day they would drive to City Island so he can meet with someone, never found out who. I knew the road they would take. I knew they would be in the truck. L Señor never sat in the passenger's seat so I knew he would be in the back seat. They always drove down Pelham Parkway passing the cut through lane, the lane that cuts across the parkway to go west. That's where I will get him. I'll smash my car so hard into them that I hope we all burn in a blast of fire.

Just remember to keep the gun on you, don't forget the gun.

Half of my mind kept telling me not to do it, that it was not worth it. The other half of my mind kept replaying a car crash and a feeling of euphoria. It was almost like having the feeling I was getting when having this dream but it was happening when I was awake, playing with my emotions.

Monday came and the sun was rising over Pelham Bay Park. I sat on the hood of this Bronco looking at the water. I was loving the feeling of the wind run through my hair and caress my face. I had been there for hours and when I looked at my watch, said to myself, *they'll be driving down the parkway in about a half hour*.

I drove to the parkway and parked the truck in this inlet facing the street. I wouldn't have much time from seeing them coming to actually hitting them.

About two minutes they'll be here.

Maybe another minute.

I turned the key in the ignition to get it started. It had problems starting and I wanted it to be ready.

The goddamn truck wouldn't start. I began to panic; I had fucked up. I tried to start it three times and on the fourth time, by some miracle, it turned on. The engine sounded rough, like a giant industrial size fan.

I could feel them coming and there they appeared to the left of me. I went to put the truck into Drive and when I pressed the gas pedal it wouldn't move. They were going to pass me and I was going to miss my shot.

With some luck and fiddling with the gears in this chaotic nightmare I was just unwrapping for myself, I put it back into park and thrust the shift knob into drive causing the truck to speed ahead. I was flying across the parkway and even cut off a few people, the only way I know that is because I heard horns and the sounds of brakes with tires against the road.

L Señor turned and saw me coming for them. I didn't know what he said but it seemed like his lips said, "Oh shit," then went on to say things I could not figure out.

The steering wheel was shaking. This was because the truck had not had an alignment for at least twenty years. I could barely keep it straight. Even with my hands were clenched in the ten and two o'clock positions.

That's when I noticed something different about his flunkies Today of all days, they weren't his regular flunkies. The bastard had thrown me a curve ball.

Impact.

I thought I died. I know you can't think when you are dead but for only a moment I woke in my dream, the white place. But this did not last for long as I was sucked right back out of it. It was as if it was loading but aborted, or maybe my mind couldn't process what was going on.

When I came to, I saw that my airbag had deployed, there was blood coming down my face and had white dust all over me. The smell of the coolant burning was burning my nose and the engine was suck in drive which made this terrible screeching noise. I couldn't lift my head off the wheel and felt paralyzed.

When I finally did lift my head up and saw that they were all ok, my survival instinct kicked in. *Get out of the truck.*

This was not good.

They were all stumbling.

I had hit them hard, their airbags also deployed.

L Señor was looking at me, while he was trying to balance.

I tried to reach the door handle but I couldn't find it because I was frantic, my heart was pounding.

"Miklo!" L Señor yelled, "get out here now!" He pointed his finger at me and then pointed to the ground in front of him. It is a long way down.

I was shaking. Taking the gun out of my pocket I came to the conclusion that something bad was going to happen. I didn't want to hold it up, it would ruin the surprise.

"You know," L Señor said, "I'm really fucking tired of you. We have less than ten minutes before the boys come."

From his pocket he took out a two-way radio and said into it, "Miguel, drive faster. We got into an accident."

Oh fuck.

L Señor began to walk over to me. I was not going to let the same thing happen to me again. I held the gun up to him and yelled, "This is it asshole. Don't come closer."

My left hand was still trying to open the door and finally got it to open. Slowly I got out of the car and there in front of me was L Señor and three flunkies I had never seen before. I held the gun firmly in my hand and just when I was about to pull the trigger, I heard the screeching of car brakes. When I looked to the left and saw the real truck barreling towards me, I knew, *this was not going to go as planned.*

It was just a ploy, Miguel wasn't going to actually hit me, he just wanted me to do what I did, I dove out of the way. He swerved and blocked L Señor from the oncoming police officers.

That's when Tillman and a handful of NYPD cars came screaming from the draw bridge.

I had dived out of the way of the truck and was on the floor. I had to do something so I unloaded all six rounds of the revolver and began to hear shots ringing out from all directions. I had hit the truck three times but only managed to break a window.

I was now out of bullets.

Tillman and the police were trying to surround L Señor and the flunkies.

L Señor jumped into the truck with Miguel and they left the other ones there, they were the sacrifice.

This did not go as planned.

I got up and ran. Out of the corner of my eye I had seen Tillman looking at me, so I stopped. I thought, *if this is the end, then so be it.* Tillman took his hand and shooed me away, he gave me an out. Tillman and the cops went back into their cars and began chasing L Señor down the wrong way of the parkway.

I knew they weren't going to catch him.

I knew it wasn't over.

For the last time that day I heard more screeching of brakes grinding down to their metal.

A black Honda Civic pulled up in front of me and inside was Rico.

"Get in."

Why isn't he with L Señor?

"Get in," He said to me again.

"No. Tell L Señor, if he wants me, you're going to have to take me dead."

"I'm not with L Señor, get in."

Against my better judgement I got into the passenger's seat of the car. He sped down the street, it seemed like we were heading to the Self-Storage place.

"Why did you pick me up?" I asked.

"I'm a rat."

"You're a rat?"

"Yeah. I've been working with the DEA for a while now."

"Wait... You're and informant?"

"Yeah. Don't talk to me until we get back to the warehouse."

"I don't want to go to the warehouse..."

"L Señor won't go back there. He wouldn't send anyone back."

He looked over at me for a second and quickly back at the road, "I need to collect my thoughts, all your questions I'll answer when we get there.

Again, we found ourselves in the lair of the beast.

Rico had just sat down and light a cigarette. He handed me his pack and I took one also.

"What do you want to know?" He asked me.

"Why?"

"Why for which part? Why did I pick you up and what are we doing here? or, why did I rat out L Señor?"

"Why me?"

"L Señor didn't trust you from the beginning. I noticed Miguel following you and I knew something had to be done. As for why I just got you now... I am going to give you some weapons you can use against L Señor and I want them to be his weapons used against him."

He was taking another hit of the cigarette and I had to ask, "Why did you turn on L Señor?"

"L Señor turned on us... Sort of."

It may have been hard for him to tell me this, but I could feel him trying to piece it together for himself.

"Okay, you want to know what happened?" He said, taking yet another hit. "Two guys we killed in the desert. It wasn't a great situation but L Señor got us through it. He got us work and kept money in our pockets. Our zeal for fortune made us turn a blind eye to L Señor and for the most part we were absorbed into his mentality. After this, it was different. We we're sort of like you, well how you and L Señor are. He turned us into a bunch of bodyguards and we started doing things we never thought we would have. At the time, we were working for some asshole in California, things went sour there and we split up for a while. I just didn't go back. The DEA had found me and told me everything about Rainbow and the Silk Road. I agreed to help so I started feeding them small pieces of information. If I gave any more information, L Señor would have known something was up and would have looked internally. Here we are today."

He also told me everything else, but you already heard it all.

It took me a moment to replay what he was saying in my mind.

"I'm sorry to say this but, that really didn't answer my question."

"I know, you should be happy I shared anything with you. I became a rat, more like a pig, because now I'm rolling in my own shit."

He took another hit and threw the cigarette on the floor. He got and went into the other room. I could hear a zipper and things being put into a bag. I went over to the door and peeped in.

"I don't need your weapons."

He paused and look at me.

"You must be somewhat delusional after the accident you were just in."

"I have a gun that's all I need."

He stood up and almost got in my face, "He will come for you within the next forty-eight hours. He will kill you."

"Yeah, so what? Death seems to follow him like body odor. I have a gun."

"He will come for you."

"Yeah, so you keep saying. He wants to kill me, he's gotta come to me first."

Rico stood there in confusion.

"Why don't you come with me? We can get this fucker together."

"No, I've been done with this for a while and I don't want to go back to doing what we were doing before. As satisfying as it would be to see him dead, I can't handle any more of this kind of shit."

He stuck his hand out for me to shake.

I shook his hand.

"Good luck. I'm sending you positive vibes. Burn it down if you have to." Rico said.

I did listen to Rico's warning and did somewhat mentally prepare for L Señor's appearance.

That day the air was clean and crisp. The trees leaves were all multi colored and I was in awe of the different shades of yellow and orange swinging in the wind. Any other moment I would have felt that the day was peaceful but I was not at peace.

I woke up with the thought of L Señor killing me and was completely prepared to die. I thought about everything I had ever experienced or felt, every emotion, every feeling. I knew where my gun was and constantly thought about it, it would flash in my mind and I would mentally count the bullets in it without seeing it. Every minute I thought about it. My gun was the last thing that could potentially make happy by ending everything I knew he was coming.

With that thought I found myself back to when L Señor had me tied to the chair. My new problem was thinking too much, maybe even overthinking.

I just want the thoughts to stop. I want to stop thinking about everything.

I could sense L Señor coming, making his way to my home. I unfortunately became in tune with his wavelength and could feel him sitting in the truck on the way up here. The storm was collecting its energy waiting to explode. He and his flunkies were driving in that old beat-up cream-colored pick-up truck they had. This was going to be the end. No matter what I was ending it a today.

I waited in my room for maybe three hours, holding my gun in my hand. I had a firm grasp on the gun, my fingers hadn't moved in a while and when I moved them slightly, I could feel the cold metal and immediately would move my finger back to the warmth. My thumb also began to cramp but I wasn't going to let go of my grip.

There was a certain doubt that he would never come.

In the silence I could hear the truck in the distance and my heart began to race, I knew the feeling and through the force felt we connected for the last time.

I had already accepted my death. Now the thoughts I was having were about being shot and what the feeling of that might be and began to have visions of myself bleeding out, dying on my floor with L Señor looking into my eyes telling me, 'You lost, you fuck'. *You did lose you fuck.*

The truck was coming closer and I could feel the negative vibrations. For the first time in hours I checked my clip, full of bullets, cocked the gun and it was loaded. I was ready to kill.

This feeling engulfed me once before and it was not something good to be feeling. This constant nervous feeling and disappointed mindset would drive anyone crazy.

I was still lying on my bed, naked, rubbing my sheets in sexual ways and kept thinking that I was rolling but had not taken anything in a couple of days. I was taking too much drugs, especially MDMA, and had ruined my mind for it. I *was* rolling for no reason. The coldness of the bed felt awesome and I was sexually charged by it.

This euphoria was short lived when I was sent back to reality. Life could be good but when you really think about it you realize just how shitty this existence is. For the next hour I thought about this and it certainly didn't help mood or thoughts. Slowly I felt the hairs on me stand and chills went down my spine. This is when I got out of bed. I put underwear on, shorts and a t-shirt; tightened my belt and looked at myself in the mirror. I've never looked at myself in the mirror and thought, '*wow, you might never get to see yourself again.*'

I could feel the truck stop a few hundred yards away. They were on the back road that leads to my home. I left my room and opened all of the doors, going back into my room I shut the door and went into the other room, not before changing my mind and going back into my room. I did this on purpose, my room was down the hallway to the left, the only door that would be closed, I knew they would come in and start destroying everything they got their hands on, L Señor would lead the charge and would get to my room first, maybe there is some talking to him. That's when I remembered the flash bang grenade, for a frantic moment I pulled out my bottom dresser drawer and went through everything and when I felt the can I grabbed it and that didn't leave my other hand. That's another weird feeling, not being in a war but yet I'm holding these weapons and I'm about to fight a battle.

When the truck actually stopped, I felt the disturbance within the force and knew something was coming out of its cage. It may have been a two headed lion but it was just L Señor and his flunkies.

I heard the truck move, more like hearing the dull roar of the engine. It was no surprise to me what was in there. They pulled up to my home and the flunkies quickly got out of the truck and crept to my door as they were trying to find a weak point but I had taken some precautions and nailed some 2x4's to the door to make it just a little harder for them. They assessed the situation.

L Señor got out of the truck and surveyed the house. I was looking through the blinds, just enough to not be seen.

"Good thing we brought a gift." One of the flunkies said.

"Good thing I have great ideas like that." L Señor said, staring into his eyes.

The funky knew he had fucked up by saying that.

Out from the trunk the other flunky took out what I called 'the door buster', the things the cops use to break down people's doors. I got nervous just at the thought of it making contact with my door, every door that that thing touches doesn't work too well for the owner of the door at the end.

I remember how my room smelled and was breathing in and out very slowly and quietly because I wanted to hear everything before they heard me. My life was summarizing in my mind and accepted that these would be the last minutes of my life. What I wanted to happen was just to shoot whoever opens my bedroom door, I already know it's not going to be *him* and it's going to be me who is shot. I held the gun firmly in my right hand and my left hand was cramping from holding the flash bang. Two things I have never used. I was more worried about the gun and the consequences of this mechanism. I was growing tired of having to hold thins thing.

L Señor stood in front of the truck, took out his gun and counted the bullets. He only thought he would use one, and it would be for me.

His flunky jumped off the truck with the door buster and made his way to my door. All the Whos down in Whoville came out to see what was happening as he busted down my door. L Señor and the flunkies swarmed my home like water flowing into the Titanic. They ripped apart my living room, tour up my couches, destroyed almost everything, knocked my bar over and made an absolute fucking mess. This was expected, this is what they do.

L Señor was the only one who came upstairs. I heard each step he took. While everything else was going on I focused on the sounds of my creaking stairs and knew exactly which step he was on. When he got to the top the air stagnated and I didn't hear a thing. He was looking at the doors and he saw the only closed one all the way down the hall to the left. He kicked open the closet door, I'm not sure if that was to throw me off his scent but it didn't work. The next door he touched, mine and stood there for a moment. He took a deep breath loud enough for me to hear. I was on the ground with my body against the door and could swear I felt him breathing on me through the door. I stood up and set up my stance.

He kicked the door, but not to break it, just to let me know he knew where I was.

"Miklo," L Señor said, "it's over, just come out and we will all be done of this."

"No, why don't you just leave."

Silence.

I gathered some strength and said, "I have done nothing to you, you did all of this because you're a fucking psycho. Just leave me alone."

"I will leave you alone. You knew what the consequences of all of your actions were. When you signed on to be these 'partners' you knew what I was about. You had this whole idea of it being a joke that's why I had to take you under my wing and show you what this life is really about!" he changed his tone, "Now all you have to do is come out here and accept your fate, you know there's only one bullet I want to fire."

"L Señor, you don't see how mental you are? Do you really not see how you are acting. I'm going to come out, back away from the door."

I heard the step he took back. Slowly and quietly I took the pin out of the flash bang grenade. My hand was reaching for the door knob. I was trembling and thought the flashbang was going to drop and burst on me. I didn't want to fuck this up, *I had to survive.*

For the first few seconds of opening the door I did it slow, when I go it to about 45 degrees, I threw the door open, tossed the grenade and used my body to slam the door shut, it had worked. For a moment I thought the door was going to break but it held together. Two thuds I heard, one was him and one was the gun.

He was now unarmed.

I opened the door and saw him on the ground, and that his gun had been knocked a foot away from his hand. With my foot I dragged the gun and kicked it into my room behind me. He was coming to and saw me pointing my gun to his face.

I heard the flunkies' footsteps coming up the stairs.

"Don't come any closer!" I yelled and they stopped, "I'll blow his fucking brains over my wall and paint the house with him!"

The roles were now reversed.

You are going to survive.

L Señor had the nerve to look into my eyes and ask me, "Can you find happiness in what you are about to do?"

Without a single thought or brain cell given to it I said "Yes" and pulled the trigger. It may have happened in an instant but I saw the bullet enter his head and saw the blood splatter and was able to look into the hole of the wound.

I was disgusted with myself and saddened for what I had to do.

Suddenly I was sexually charged by that. My sick mind actually felt as if I was making love to then gun. The trigger was a women's beautiful clitoris and its barrel a nice huge nipple. I was a few seconds away from masturbating but I knew there were three flunkies in my home, and who knows what they were going to do now. Slowly I made my way down the hallway to the staircase.

What am I going to do to these two flunkies?

I became frantic.

"L Señor!" One of them yelled, I could not tell which one it was.

I became infuriated and yelled, "L Señor is dead! Leave my house now!"

I heard footsteps, whoever it was, was standing on the second step. They were coming upstairs.

The bottle of Knob Creek on my nightstand flashed before me in my mind and the next thing it was in my hand. Luckily, there was a pair of underwear on the floor and grabbed that to. I felt around the inside of my pocket and that's when I felt my lighter.

Rico flashed in my mind, just him saying to me, "Burn it down if you have to."

With my teeth I popped out the cork and spit it out while stuffing half of the underwear in the bottle. I wasn't even sure it was going to work. I was waiting to hear them getting closer.

They got the top of the stairs.

I lit the underwear. A ball of fire I threw at them and it hit the floor just before they got upstairs. The flames engulfed my hallway very quickly. For a moment I was frozen because I had never seen a sight like that, my next thought was *How the fuck am I going to get out of here?* That question answered itself in a few seconds when I looked into my room and saw my window. The first and only time I ever thought of jumping out of a window. And through the window in the wall I went right threw it and landed a story down on the grass with glass all over me. I hadn't realized that I even went through the glass. All my body wanted to do was run, so that's what I did. I ran as fast as I could into the woods. No matter how many times I almost fell I never lost my balance.

I had to stop. My feet were hurting. Leaning against a tree, I turned to look at my home, not knowing if the flunkies had survived but in the small distance, I saw my house engulfed in flames and black smoke rising from the place that was a sanctuary, which it now no longer was. I was out of breath and couldn't move.

What have I done? I just killed three men and didn't think twice about it.

Watching the house burn, looking for any sort of movement, there was nothing. From that small distance I could hear the flames and smell the smoke. I could hear the leaves of the trees rustling and wind hitting my face. My hair and beard waving in it.

Maybe five minutes I was there, suddenly my legs gave out and was brought to my knees leaning against the tree with my back. I cried uncontrollably. The tears were real and my emotions were running ramped. I screamed in mental pain so loud that my throat hurt after that.

When my mind cleared, there was a thought about Tillman. I wanted to let him know what happened and where he could find L Señor so I took out my phone and did something I would never do. I called the Drug Enforcement Agency and when the operator got on the phone all I said was, "Connect me to Tillman, tell him it's Miklo." In less than a minute Tillman was on the phone and he asked, "What do you want?"

I took a deep breath and said, "L Señor and three of his friends are dead. I killed them."

"Where are you?" He asked.

"THEY are at the house in Preston Hollow, New York… The house is on fire, you'll see the smoke…" I hung up.

With my remaining energy I took the phone and smashed it against a rock. The flip phone broke in two pieces. Now all of my energy had to go to my legs to get up and go to the Jeep I had waiting for me. Slowly I got up and took one last look at the house.

The past is gone and dead, the future is waiting.

It took me 20 minutes to walk to the back road where my car was. It was the only time in my life I could say that for the entire duration of the walk I did not think, did not speak, nor did I do anything stupid. I was not me anymore In fact, I had become some sort of different man that I had never met. I thought about my parents and what they would think about me and had to get over wanting to call them but I had grown so much that I could never see them again. If I could I would go back in time and become a nobody and still live in my parents' basement and sell pot from there. Those were the good old days. Before I met Sadie, not saying that she ruined my life because she did not. She tried to save me from this, she knew I wasn't ever really happy.

In the end I have no one.

I got to the Jeep and got into the driver's seat. One more sigh of relief.

I was on my way to my other property. Packed full of my drugs, clothes and personal belongings. I cried for the first hour of that trip and drove in silence.

Once again in my life, my hands were clenched to the wheel of another car as I was driving for a few hours already. I was almost to the property but still had some ways to go. I may have gotten lost because I only went there twice. This property was very far from any towns and buried deep in the forest. I accepted that that was where I would spend the rest of my life. I didn't want to leave New York City but there is nothing left for me there, no friends, and my family probably would not accept me back, although they probably have no idea what's going on.

My own thoughts were making me crazy because I could not stop thinking about everything, mostly the fact that I was worried because I began to think how I wouldn't talk to anyone anymore or meet anyone again. I was ready to get to my property and sit in a chair, rotting away, dying of starvation.

There was even a thought about just taking a handful of drugs and overdosing.

It is a unique feeling when you longer want to live.

A Hit from the Pen

The white room was different now. Instead of this negative feeling vibrating throughout my body it was replaced with a positive cool and calming breeze which was passing over every inch of my body and flowing through my hair. That's not all that was different; the sky was still white but the ground was covered in beautiful grass, not cannabis but actual grass. With every whip of the wind on the grass they would sway and their auras were pulsating this awesome shade of green. That is a place I could have stayed. I have found where the grass grows greener, for myself.

One notable absence from my dream was the weird *Stoner Pineapple* that showed me that field of Cannabis. It had not appeared in the past few dreams, which were just of grass and wind. In this particular dream it had appeared, but not as I had seen it before, it was back to the blurry round orange ball with a dab of green just looking like some eye floaters. When I had realized that the colors were present, they disappeared, never to come back.

For some time now I had been thinking about the past, constantly, while trying to live out my days trying to forget, which was not easy. It has been about five years since it all and can't get over everything I've done. How many times have I said to myself, *'start a new life'* or *'my new life began'* which at the time were both small celebrations but were actually nothing to celebrate. It's disgusting, but again, for the second time in my life I was moving from a place I did not want to leave with my hands clenched to the wheel of another SUV. The strange feeling of butterflies was inaccurate, it felt like bricks flying around the inside of my stomach. I was going somewhere I had only been once and it was with the surveyor who was plotting out the land. I was holding back tears because to even let one tear flow down my face it would cause a waterfall of tears. Two excruciating hours went by and there were some signs I had recognized to know that I was getting closer to the property. This part of the road had seemed familiar, even in total darkness. I wasn't driving fast, there was nothing waiting for me but emptiness, all that was at the property was a house trailer, no one was waiting there for me and I knew no one in the surrounding areas.

Driving alone is a different experience than driving with at least one other person. A long time ago Kush and I had driven out to Colorado, in all it took us thirty-six hours that included two stops at motels for rest. We learned a lot about each other and had some great conversations that brought us closer together. This time, being alone, and driving not even a fraction of the distance, had learned so much about myself. Most people who are about to break down usually start going to a psychiatrist, then take a few years digging into themselves while someone evaluates you. One car ride alone in silence was all that was needed to accept everything and understand the consequences of everything that was done. It was all my fault. The thoughts were swirling within my head which was making me go crazy. My hand kept shaking and it was not because of a tremor, I was purposely doing it, all my energy had to be transferred to a part of my body that could potentially hit something, the radio was the first victim in mind but decided that would not solve anything.

It was this particular memory that made me want to write down everything. Never have I had that thought before and the past few days I have been tirelessly writing everything I can think of from that part of my life. The main reason of writing is to accept all of this within myself and maybe put it past me but even after it is a hard thing to do.

So many memories, so many problems, so many friends no longer with us. All of my dreams have crashed and burned; I used to think of me, Kush and Anthony partying in a huge house in the middle of nowhere when we were older but that will never happen now. My eyes have teared up and thinking about Spazz… Now, I think I should go back to calling him Anthony. I hadn't talked to him since I told him he had a ketamine problem, that killed me. A couple years ago they found him in a drug apartment with other people. Tillman went on television and showed his face to the city. I felt that he was also giving me a message because they claimed that this person was, in fact, working for Miklo, whom hey pictured as L Señor. He gave me an out and I took it. They claimed Anthony had asphyxiated in his sleep due to a heroin overdose. Since I left New York City the opioid problem is worse than ever. I was a horrible friend to him. Once, he was shooting up heroin in my bathroom. I could hear him clear as day say loudly, "Yeah." That's how I knew the needle was in and that he had actually injected himself with that drug. That drug ruins lives. I can't even write this without crying for him. A better friend I should have been to everyone. I could not bring myself to go to his funeral; I did not want to face his parents, a fool would have been made of me. At that point I would not have a filter and hold nothing back.

The last time I saw Spazz was weird. He had this cocaine and ketamine problem that I kept putting under the rug, I should have been a better friend to him and I even tried calling him to see how he was doing but I wasn't able to contact him. I heard he really went hard on Meth and Coke. I really do feel awful for that because that was absolutely one hundred percent my fault. Thinking about it now it was probably the death of Kush that got him upset, I was too, but he probably didn't know how to handle it. I tried not to think about it.

The pain I feel from the deaths of everyone I know is really bad, not a day has gone by that I don't think about it and I am glad Sadie had left me, if she died, I don't think I'd be here writing these words to you. I'm glad she's living, where ever she is, whatever she's doing, I just hope she's happy and hopefully someone is treating her right.

The first month here was a disaster. Every single day I sobbed uncontrollably. It got to the point that I would wake up in the middle of the night and cry. No one should feel how I am feeling. After that first month things seemed to be better. Mentally I had gotten a little tougher and had gotten over the thought of *you should be the one that's dead instead of the rest.*

I began to venture out of the house, walking around the town for hours in search of a bar I could call mine. Before this moment, I used to wonder why there would be lone men drinking in bars all hours of the day and answered my own question; I became one of those guys. When the bartenders would try and talk to me or even just when they were being nice to me, I would say to them, "I just want to drink." I would apologize for my actions sometime later and would just say something like, "I've had a long few years", and they would kind of understand and leave me alone. I would get so drunk that it would take a forty-five-minute ride an hour and a half because I would drive so slowly no matter what time of day or night. Those winding roads can kill you up there.

Now I spend my days trying to keep myself occupied. That has not worked out too well and I feel more isolated every day. Sure, that is my fault.

Some things never change though. The DEA tried tries to stop all of these websites. I even found a new one and ordered some drugs through it, the package never came. I don't know why they think they can stop it. They might as well embrace it.

∞

For the past month I have been working on this book. It has been left on my desk and every so often I would sit down and add something I remembered and change things as I remember them. Then after each time I would print out a copy and leave it on my desk. At one point I felt I was done and it sat there collecting dust. I felt better after writing everything down and came to peace with everything and there was no intention of ever reading it.

One day, as I was smoking a joint watching another Seinfeld episode when there was a knock at the door.

This never happens and I was nervous about who was on the other side.

I took the gun from under the table and went to the door.

When the door opened it was revealed to be Tillman and my heart dropped. He was holding a box; looks like the package I was waiting for.

"I'm here to talk. You can put your nervous feelings away." He said to me.

"Talk?"

"Yeah… may I come in?"

"Sure," I said, gesturing my hand for him to come in, "Make yourself at home. If you're here to talk, I'm going to finish smoking my joint."

"I could smell it, go ahead."

I sat down on the couch and he just paced around the room, looking at things.

"This package," he said, holding it up before throwing it on the table, "was confiscated during transit. It had a name I had not seen in a while. Why did you order this?"

"Personal use."

"I figured as much. You are a hard man to track down."

"Good, this is what I wanted."

He went over to the desk and looked at the book. Picking it up he began to go through the pages. I had gotten nervous and said, "That's private."

"What is this?" He asked.

Be honest with him.

"I had to write down my thoughts and feelings in order to make them pass and feel better. I wrote down everything about this whole mess I call my life. What are you doing here?"

"I'm here to give you this package. I'm also here to ask if you want to be part of the DEA. We don't know how you found this new website, but we can't. We would like for you to come work with us, you would be essential in our team."

"If I pass on this offer, are you going to arrest me?"

"No, Miklo. I'm retiring in a week and they asked me to find you. I could simply say I didn't find you."

"Then the answer is no." I said taking a hit from the joint.

He took off his jacket and put it on the back of the chair across from me that he sat in.

"You wrote down everything you went through?"

"Yes. It helped in getting me over things."

For a moment he was silent as he collected his thoughts.

"Would you like to know my view of this mess?"

"Are you asking me to include you in my writing?"

"Yes."

"Why?"

"Sometimes, it's good to know the story from all sides. If somebody reads it, I want them to have the full story."

"Okay, I'll do this. But first I have a couple of questions, if Rico was the informant, why didn't you say anything?"

"I did not know that until it all went down that day on the parkway. He had done a good job keeping it secret. If I had known I would have told you. We were working on those guys for years."

"Wow..." I said, getting up and walking to my desk to grab a notebook and paper. "My other question is, what happened with them and the two guys in the desert?"

"Yeah, that's a famous story we had heard for a while. It is not clear. We think the two men were other informants and L Señor took them out, but there is also a group of us that believe they were two of Pablo's men that he sent to kill L Señor and his partner, who at the time was someone referred to as The Bodybuilder."

"I tried to get the story out of Rico when he picked me up that day, but he didn't give me an answer either."

"I'm ready to talk whenever you are." He said to me.

I got in position to start writing and for the next couple of hours we talked about everything we had gone through.

This is when I learned some of things he had seen. I got to see things from his point of view, something I never thought would happen.

In the end, Tillman shook my hand when he left and said to me, "You sound like a good guy from what you told me. Do not isolate yourself. Go on with your life."

"I feel like I can't. I feel like I can't talk to people anymore."

"When I was a police officer in the homeless shelter, many people straight from prison would come there and talk just like how you're talking now. They all felt that they could no longer go back into society. I believe you can. You know what I always told them? Start out small, get a part time job in a small store and take it easy. Make friends and go on."

"Do you really think I'm good?"

"Yes, I do. If I didn't, you would have been arrested that time we got you at the station."

That was the last thing he said to me as he left. I watched as he got in the car and drove away.

Over the past five years I've tried to keep myself occupied by building a house and furnishing it with everything I would ever need. After I while, growing bored of being in this no human contact life, I came to the realization that it was not good for me. So, I followed Tillman's advice and got a part time job in a record store. I was happy when I was working but when I got home, every day, I would cry and think about my life. No one ever knows the pain someone else keeps buried inside them. All my dreams of the future were shot down.

Some people might like this, smoking alone, being alone, not me. It all means nothing now. Money can buy a certain happiness, who ever said it couldn't buy any happiness was dead wrong, or just dirt poor. I am somewhat okay now, not happy. The question that runs through the mind now is, do I go on? Live out my days alone? I've been fucked up, my mind messed up. The real world just seems wrong.

I've become a man, full circle, dependent of no one. Or, at least what I think is the definition of being a Man.

Now? What is there for me? A joint in my hand waiting to be smoked. When I look to the left of me, no one's there, to the right, same thing. No one to share anything with, no one to smoke with, no one to talk to or share my experiences; no children, no family around. The drugs had taken them all from me. Not the drugs itself but the laws the drugs were under.

How had it all come to this?

At what point had I had enough? At what point would I get sick of everything I now have, and don't? Tired of rambling, reminiscing the past. Nothing can be changed. Nothing will be improved. Am I set to live out my days? Should I live or should I end it now? Maybe I shouldn't and maybe I should.